I0547446

IN MEMORIAM:
JOSEPH S. PULVER, SR.
(July 5, 1955 – April 24, 2020)

Along the shore, the cloud waves break,
The twin suns sink behind the lake,
The shadows lengthen
In Carcosa.
Strange is the night where black stars rise,
And strange moons circle through the skies,
But stranger still is
Lost Carcosa.
Songs that the Hyades shall sing,
Where flap the tatters of the King,
Must die unheard in
Dim Carcosa.
Song of my soul, my voice is dead,
Die thou, unsung, as tears unshed
Shall dry and die in
Lost Carcosa.

—"Cassilda's Song"
The King in Yellow
Act 1, Scene 2

AN AMERICAN STORY
Darrell Schweitzer

"But *I* can't tell an English club story," I protested. "I'm an American."

The circumstances were extraordinary enough that you might have thought that I could. Here I was, in this day and age, in one of those old-fashioned London gentlemen's clubs of the sort most people think only exist in old books or BBC serials. I had travelled in Great Britain extensively, on both literary and business matters. I had many British friends. I had even made something of a hobby of British regional accents, which I could definitely hear, if not reproduce (nor would I insult my hosts by trying). In Yorkshire they speak in a distinct manner, in the Midlands quite another, in Devon, very differently, and none of these could be mistaken for the speech of London. Once, in Scotland, I had even asked a local about James Doohan's accent on *Star Trek* and was told that 1) he was doing it very badly and 2) if Scotty were an engineer he would be an Edinburgh University man, and the first thing he would do would be lose that accent.

So I think it's safe to say that I was that rare sort of American who understood just enough of British culture and ways to appreciate that the two societies are *not* the same, and that I had, just barely, glimpsed beneath the surface where tourists never see at all. It was enough to make me understand why I couldn't tell a proper English club story. I couldn't tell *this audience* what English life was about, when they knew more about every aspect of it than I did.

"Oh do go on, old chap!" my Brit friends said. They used such expressions as "Smashing!" and "Capital!" and "Jolly good!" which surely do not exist in living memory outside of a P.G. Wodehouse novel, and—here's the important part—every last one of them rendered these phrases in a *perfect imitation of a Hollywood fake English accent*, which is not the same as an American snob's fake English accent, or even an American theatre accent. That was when I realized I was helpless in the presence of ancient and inscrutable subtlety and cultivation, like a round-eyed barbarian surrounded by Chinese mandarins. These fellows could not only cross the divide between cultures, but turn around and look back from the other side.

They had me. I was after all, a guest. I despite my long acquaintance with some of them, I was only allowed in the club on the basis of a letter from my late father, and even then some will doubtless conclude that it

Weirdbook

VOL. 2, NO. 13   ISSUE 43

Features

Short Stories

Poetry

Artwork

Weirdbook #43 is copyright © 2020 by Wildside Press LLC. All rights reserved Published by Wildside Press LLC, 7945 MacArthur Blvd, Suite 215, Cabin John MD 20818 USA. Visit us online at wildsidepress.com and bcmystery.com.

FROM THE EDITOR'S TOWER

Here it is, *Weirdbook* #43. Our 13th regular issue since the relaunch.

I really can't decide on whether calling this our "Baker's Dozen" issue or our "Advent of the Apocalypse" issue. We're not even halfway through 2020 and all of us have had to deal with Covid-19 and massive social unrest. Luckily it seems that the virus isn't going to kill us all. This doesn't do anything for the hundreds of thousands who lost their lives, but it still doesn't seem as though it will reach the predicted/feared levels. I guess a small comfort is better than none. Now I have no idea as to how the global civil unrest will play out, but as far as I'm concerned, *both* sides better sit down and start talking and listening or we are all damned. No one will win if things escalate. 'Nuff said.

On a brighter note, we have a wonderful issue containing 13 stories and a fistful of wonderful poetry. Onboard are Sharon Cullars, Darrell Schweitzer, Ann K. Schwader, Adrian Cole, D.C. Lozar, Nicole Kurtz, Frank Searight, and many esteemed writers (and poets). All of them representing the very best in today's weird fiction, horror, and dark fantasy.

I will close on a sad note though. This issue contains one of Joeseph Pulver, Sr.'s last stories, "Will Home Remember Me?" I say "last" because Joe passed away April 24th. It such an honor to receive the story last year. Joe was a genuine giant of weird fiction and a great man in his own right. He'll be missed by his legions of fans and friends.

I want to believe that he's giving them hell this very minute in not-so-Lost Carcosa and is enjoying himselv immensely while doing so!

Godspeed, Joe.

—Doug Draa,
Editor

Staff

PUBLISHER & EXECUTIVE EDITOR

John Gregory Betancourt

EDITOR

Doug Draa

CONSULTING EDITOR

W. Paul Ganley

WILDSIDE PRESS SUBSCRIPTION SERVICES

Sam Hogan

PRODUCTION TEAM

Sam Hogan
Karl Würf

was only two world wars and the loss of the empire which caused such a lowering of standards. But there I was, and as I sputtered and hesitated somebody pressed a fresh whiskey into my hand.

Right.

Blame the whiskey.

The fire in the fireplace burned low. Everyone leaned toward me attentively.

* * * *

You will have to excuse me for being vague about the geography and other details (I began), because I have this story second-hand at best. It happened to my father, before I was born. Now my late father, James Simpkins, was widely travelled, particularly in the company of his closest English friend, Frederick Darblethwaite—that's not his real name, I hasten to add. *Those two*, I am sure, could have told many fine stories, and indeed my dad told me some of them, including, in confidence, the one I am about to relate now.

It seems that he and Freddy—that's what he called him—were not only close pals—not *mates*, because an Englishman and an American can never really be "mates" in that sense—but colleagues during the Second World War. They engaged in top secret research and carried out certain missions, the nature of which I am not at liberty to divulge even now.

Let us just say that on a certain afternoon some while after the conclusion of the war, my dad was being driven in the pouring rain through what looked to him like very bleak English countryside, green enough to be sure, but grey with rain, a monotony of low, rolling hills, and little clusters of trees which doubtless have a name, a forester, and are recorded in the Domesday Book—one of the perceptions Americans have of England is that there is *no* empty, unused land there, any more than there are any serious distances—but I digress. It must have been weariness or the monotony of the ride which caused him to dose off.

He awoke to a thump, as the car's wheel splashed in and out of a particularly large pothole as they passed through the narrow streets of one of those thatched-roofed villages which you only expect to see on *National Geographic* specials or on quaint postcards. He later learned the name of the place was—call it Nether Cheebleford. Where precisely it was, I suppose you could figure out on a map, but he didn't and I haven't.

Just before he reached the castle he fumbled about, because he had dropped the note he'd been holding in his hands onto the floor of the car. He found it, and glanced at it one more time before he put it in his pocket. It was a calling card which had been left at his hotel. There was a coat of arms on it, and a message scribbled on the reverse read:

Jim—

Come see me at once. I have something quite extraordinary to show you.

—Freddy.

The reason for the coat of arms, not to mention the perfectly maintained, ancient limousine which looked like it belonged in a museum, driven by a button-lipped, uniformed chauffeur who looked like *he* belonged in a museum, plus the castle which had been converted into a country-house sometime in the 18th century ("The best time to do it," it was later explained) was that my father's friend's father had recently died and Freddy had inherited castle, grounds, limousine, chauffeur, coat of arms, and all. He was now *Lord Cheebleford*, and my dad—never mind all his long acquaintance with Englishmen, the safaris, and close cooperation during the war—by being on a first-name basis with an actual lord was definitely moving up in society.

The house was one of those establishments you think only exist on the BBC or in Wodehouse novels. There were servants lined up to greet him, a butler, several footmen, maids, the whole works. Then Freddy came bounding down the front stairs with something less than the customary English reserve, pumped my dad's hand vigorously, and said, "How good of you to come! Splendid! Splendid! You must come see!"

Before my father was even settled in—the servants had made off with his luggage—Freddy, talking a mile a minute in a state of great agitation, conveyed him into the Conservatory, which was an ancient stone structure with a wall knocked out so it could expand out quite a distance onto the lawn into a series of greenhouses. It seemed that Freddy's latest enthusiasm, in which with his newfound title and wealth he was fully able to indulge, was the collecting and raising of rare plants, particularly orchids. Now my father had only a passing interest in botany, and no particular fondness for flowers. In his generation, American men who liked flowers were either swishes or lounge lizards—although of course the English have always had their eccentrics, and that's different. In any case Freddy was hardly the stereotypical orchid collector. You know: about four foot six, stoop-shouldered, ninety pounds, capable of speaking only in the tiniest, squeaky voice, and dominated by terrifying female relatives. Freddy was a tall, broad-shouldered man with a bristling, grey moustache. He had been a major during the war. His credentials as a scientist, of the wealthy, amateur variety, were impressive. He had been on expeditions. He had shot lions. He and my dad had saved each other's lives a dozen times in tight situations. So if Freddy said a plant was worth seeing, if you will pardon the expression, it bloody well had to be.

It was too. At the far end of the greenhouses was a large, cleared area, in which had been placed a clay flowerpot the size of a small swimming pool. It was filled with earth, and there was a shovel handy, but nothing had been planted yet. There was something wrapped in a tarp, on a table nearby.

"I wanted you to see this before I put it in the ground," said Freddy.

He unwrapped the tarp.

"My God!"

It was a bulb, or at least vegetable matter of some sort, about the size of a watermelon, ovoid, and covered with hairy tendrils or roots, which visibly writhed in the air. It may have been his imagination, but perhaps the thing even made a faint *sound*, like a teapot whistling in another room.

"Then you appreciate what this is," said Freddy.

"Yes, I do."

"It's not totally without precedent, you know. There is a certain amount of literature on the subject."

"But—Wells, Collier, Clarke—I thought that was all fiction."

"Not entirely, old boy. Not entirely."

"Where did you *get* it?"

All Freddy would say to this was, "We collectors of such things have connections. It's an old system." No more than that. There are some things the English will not reveal to foreigners, even if they happen to be close friends. It is the famous English reserve, you know.

As Freddy pulled on some quite ordinary gardening gloves and picked the thing up, fondly, gently, as if he were holding an infant—almost as if it were his own child, a thought my dad found decidedly disquieting—its tendrils reached up toward his face, but he pulled back before it could touch him.

My dad found it increasingly repulsive.

"It looks like it's from outer space," he said.

"It quite well could be," said Freddy, and without further ado, he planted it, and then watered it with a watering can.

Some while later dinner was served in the great hall. One did dress for dinner. Freddy's valet had laid out appropriate attire for my dad. They sat beneath rows of stuffed animal heads, many of which Freddy himself had shot; some of the others dated back to the late Middle Ages. There were suits of armor in the corners, shields and pole arms alternating with portraits of ancestors along the walls, and if a couple ghosts had tittered softly up in the dark above the heavy beams overhead, it would only have been appropriate. This was the kind of place where if there isn't a ghost or two, you have the right to ask why not. Sitting there, my father realized, he could well have slipped back in time. This could have been 1900, or 1800, or even 1600, and if gentlemen in Tudor costumes accompanied by Queen

Elizabeth the First had come thundering into the room, Dad might have been at a loss for the proper etiquette, but not wholly surprised.

The dinner was of course superb, and the evening very pleasant. They *were* the closest of friends. They reminisced for a while about their previous adventures. Lord Cheebleford—Freddy—inquired tactfully about my dad's future plans, and when he said he expected to return to America soon and get married, Freddy congratulated him heartily. As for his own plans, Freddy expected to live here at Cheebleford Hall, as the place was called, cultivate plants and tenants (for in this part of England, the old sense of *noblesse oblige* was not a thing of the past) and take his father's place in the House of Lords.

It seemed, my father began to suggest, that their adventuring days were over.

But Freddy's attention was suddenly elsewhere. He was listening to something his guest couldn't hear.

After dinner, they carried their drinks into the Conservatory. Freddy was all too eager to see how his prize plant was doing. My dad thought this a bit obsessive. How much could a plant have grown in just a few hours?

About five feet. When they got there, it had shot up several greenish yellow stalks in all directions, of a rather ghastly, unpleasant color somehow, but Freddy looked on the thing as if it were his darling and his treasure. He was even more interested in the bulbous area in the center, which had swelled into a mass like an artichoke waiting to open, only about three feet high.

Pale, greenish-white tendrils floated on the air, extending out from the artichoke.

My dad should have run screaming into the night at that point, and I am sure no one would have blamed him if he had, but he was no coward, Freddy was his close friend, and in any case Freddy didn't seem the slightest bit alarmed.

Maybe it was just nerves. Delayed combat fatigue or something.

In fact, Freddy *had* become obsessed. In earlier times—1600 or so—they might have said he was bewitched.

By a plant.

In the days that followed, Freddy and my father went through the usual round of activities. They toured the countryside, visiting everything from Neolithic sites and Roman ruins to Norman churches, since my father was interested in that sort of thing. They called on the neighbors, who lived the castle across the valley, and even participated in a traditional fox hunt, for all my dad didn't ride a horse very well and struggled to keep up. ("But I thought all you Americans were cowboys," someone said. He reminded them that he was from Philadelphia. There are no cowboys in Philadelphia.)

But whenever he could, Freddy spent his time in the Conservatory, seated in front of the plant on a folding chair. Soon its bulbous center was over six feet tall. The tendrils could reach almost to the edge of the room. And there was no question that the plant was making noises, first whistling sounds, then something that sounded disturbingly like music, and finally like *speech.*

My dad tried to draw him away. He asked to be shown this or that local sight, and maybe he even came close to wearing out his welcome a couple times, but of course Freddy remained properly polite and accommodating. Sometimes, though, there was no help for it. Freddy was in the Conservatory with the plant, while my dad either wandered the grounds or sat in the library, looking for answers in some of the very curious volumes the lords of Cheebleford had accumulated over the centuries.

By the time he thought to take Blodgers, the butler, into his confidence and express his growing sense of alarm, it was too late.

The two of them discovered the inevitable result one morning, in the Conservatory. They found the folding chair, broken, and Freddy's shoes, and the remains of his trousers, but that was all.

"Oh my God," my father said. "We'll have to call the police, or maybe the army, or MI5."

"I don't think that would be appropriate, Sir," said Blodgers.

Dad looked at the plant with loathing. He reached for the shovel. "Well the least we can destroy the damned thing!" He swung the shovel into the field of waving tendrils, which caught hold of the shovel and yanked it out of his hands with surprising force and tossed it aside. Blodgers wrestled him away, into the corridor, well back among the more conventional greenery.

"Sir," he said firmly. "You are a guest here, so I must ask you to observe certain proprieties. Nothing may be changed, much less destroyed, without the permission of Lord Cheebleford. His Lordship's effects cannot be touched without specific instructions."

"But your master has just been eaten by that goddamn cannibal plant—"

"Not, strictly speaking, 'cannibal,' Sir, I shouldn't think, since it does not devour its own kind."

"And you have time to worry about propriety, or even grammar."

"More the correct vocabulary—"

"But your master has been eaten by the plant!"

"That is, admittedly, a bit awkward, Sir. He was unmarried, you see."

"I know that!"

"That means he had no direct heir."

"I *know* that!"

"Which means the ownership of the estate, and the preservation of Cheebleford Hall itself could be tied up in the courts for quite some time, during which time…where would the servants go?"

My dad stared at him in amazement. "Do you mean to tell me, that after your master has met what was no doubt a hideous fate, and all England, maybe even all the world may be in danger, *you're worried about your job?"*

Very stiffly, he said, "There's more to it than that, Sir. You Americans would not understand."

And before my father could say anything more or do something desperate, *the plant* spoke up behind him.

"Very good, Blodgers. Quite right. You may go."

In the few minutes while my father's back was turned and he confronted Blodgers, the plant had grown perhaps another five or six feet, because now it towered over both of them. Dad turned back around and saw that the artichoke section was now at least ten feet tall and *it was starting to open.* At the top, inside a greenish-yellow, pulpy mass, was what was at least a startlingly realistic replica of the face of the late Frederick Darblethwaite, briefly Lord Cheebleford.

Maybe not so late.

It opened its eyes.

"Jim," it said. "I know how this appears, but things are not quite what you think."

"Really? What makes you say that?"

"If you will just come a bit closer, I will explain."

Dad stepped closer, just a bit. The stalks rattled. The outermost tendrils brushed against his face. Instantly he hurled himself backwards.

"Oh, Jim, old chum, if only you were where I am now, it would be so much clearer. You would understand."

"Well I don't intend to be where you are," he said. "Never." He looked around for the shovel, but Blodgers, before leaving as instructed, had removed it.

That was the beginning of a tug-of-war of sorts, as my dad was before long just as bewitched or obsessed by the plant as his late friend had been. Because he was less and less sure his friend *was* entirely "late." He got another folding chair and sat just outside of the reach of the tendrils, for hours, while the plant-thing tried to lure him closer. Blodgers, as long as the thing spoke with his master's voice, considered it to *be* his master, and therefore took orders, saw to the running of the estate and the direction of the servants, and, to hear him tell it, all was placidly right with the world.

My dad listened endlessly, and spoke with the thing, as they went over old times and their old adventures. It knew all his jokes. It knew things he had confessed in intimate moments when they were such danger together that it seemed unlikely they would ever see another dawn. Even more strangely, it began to look more and more like Freddy. The face became clearer. Then as the artichoke-thing opened wider, the entire head emerged, and then his shoulders and upper body.

It was about that point that my dad had a very close call. He fell asleep in the chair, and while he slept the tendrils had grown even longer, wrapped themselves around the chair, and were ready to yank him into the thing's gaping gullet, when he suddenly awoke and leapt free, and crashed into a table of potted plants, sending them spilling onto the floor. He lay half stunned and only slowly did he realize what the plant-thing that looked and spoke like Freddy was actually saying. It was repeating numbers, formulae, top secret stuff, the very things the two of them had worked on during the war, on which the security of the Free World now depended. So, for all he had yet another perfectly justified excuse to run screaming into the night in the conventional manner, it was his *duty* to stay here, for security reasons, to make sure that those secrets didn't get out.

Shortly thereafter, the artichoke-like section opened all the way, and Freddy stepped free, onto the stone floor.

It wasn't him, of course. It wasn't human. It was green, and dripping, and comprised of fibers and leaves and tendrils, like one of those Renaissance paintings in which the human form is made up from fruits and vegetables, but it spoke with Freddy's voice, and when Blodgers discovered it, he sent for the valet, and the two of them got the thing cleaned up, and touched up with a little makeup, and dressed in the proper clothes, and before long it could more or less pass, at least in a dim light, as Lord Cheebleford.

My dad had dinner with it on several occasions. There was a lot more meat on the menu than there had been previously. Freddy had been somewhat of a vegetarian, a preference he'd picked up in India. But now, it was meat and more meat, served almost raw. But he gradually came to look more human. The tendrils and fibers on his face blended together into something that looked more like skin, particularly if powdered with a bit of talc.

The tenor of the conversation changed. It was no longer about past adventures, or military secrets. Now, quite openly, the thing spoke of the trans-human condition, how, once he'd "passed over" Freddy had come to understand things from an entirely new and broader perspective. It spoke of conditions on other planets, and of vast intelligences which waited for us, out in space, and of the secrets soon to be revealed. It even conversed in alien languages, which no human ear had ever heard before, but which my father, perhaps more telepathically than through intellectual effort, was able to understand. He of all living men actually heard the haunting poetry of the *Yh'ghai*, which dwell on the outer three planets of star so far away it hasn't even a name that you can find in astronomy books. There was much that I could not follow after that, as the tale was told to me, something about a mystical union of all intelligences in the cosmos and the awakening of a second "inner soul," whatever that was, and so much more. I am sure that my dad would have been pulled in eventually, that he would have finally walked hand-in-hand into that Conservatory with the creature that had perhaps once been his friend Freddy, and confronted the plant-thing, and let it have its way with him. He knew his resistance was giving way. He could not escape. It was only a matter of time.

But, miraculously, he was saved, and the instrument of his deliverance was a telegram, from my future mother. It said simply:

WHY HAVEN'T I HEARD FROM YOU stop ARE YOU GOING TO MARRY ME OR NOT stop.

Dad could only show this to his host, who may have been a plant, but was still a gentleman. He said, "You've given her your word, haven't you?"

"Yes, I have."

"Well you *can't* go back on your word. You'll have to leave."

So he left. He returned to America and married my mother, and a few years later produced me, the humble teller of this tale. He never returned to England for the rest of his life, though he told me much about it. He even confided some of the really strange things that he'd heard toward the end, though once he was out of the immediate proximity of Lord Cheebleford he could no longer call to mind a single word of the alien languages, or very much of what had been revealed. Yes, he made inquiries, and passed certain warnings through proper channels, and I when I got older could tell that he was on edge much of the time, and frustrated, very likely because he was not believed, or else there was some kind of conspiracy to cover up the truth. Despite this, we used to get Christmas cards from England, from Lord Cheebleford, and I even got some addressed to me, from "Uncle Freddy," but I was not allowed to answer them, and my parents never answered theirs. Shortly before he died, Dad told me what he could, and I think what haunted him most was that, just before he left the estate, he had seen the plant one last time, and the artichoke section had blackened and collapsed in on itself, while the outer stalks had all quite definitely *gone to seed.*"

* * * *

Somebody started to laugh while sipping his drink and snorted.

There were a few polite murmurs as I finished my tale, and then the Club Skeptic tore into me.

"Now wait a minute," he said. "What *happened?*"

"Apparently very little."

"You would have us believe that sometime in the 1950s England was invaded by intelligent plants from outer space and *nobody noticed?*"

"Well there are certain accounts," said another member. "Wyndham and all."

"But those are fiction," someone said.

"Yes, definitely, they are," I put in. "It wasn't like that at all."

"Well then," said the Skeptic, "*how do you explain* the incongruities between your account and the condition of Great Britain today? How do you account for it?"

Maybe this was where I made my fatal mistake. I paused, then held up my empty glass. The waiter filled it with whiskey. I took, not a sip, but a good stiff gulp. Yes, I think the whiskey was at fault. It clouded my judgment. It caused me to overestimate the value of my wit.

"Maybe there was nothing to explain," I said. "Maybe my father got himself all worked up over nothing. This Freddy Darblethwaite inherited the estate and went through all the conventional motions as lord of the manor and lived out the kind of life expected of a member of his class, and he took his father's seat in Parliament, and maybe one more vegetable in the House of Lords *didn't make any difference.*"

I sat back, waiting to relish applause, but there was dead silence in the room. You could have heard a cliché drop.

And that was when I understood that I had gone too far, crossing some line of propriety that no American can ever cross. That was when I understood that I had been right to protest at the beginning, because I had no business trying to tell an English club story.

The rest of the evening passed with stiff politeness. There were other stories told. One elderly gentleman with white whiskers began, "When I was in In-*jah*, I was shooting tigers, until one of them shot back. Now that was a story," and he told it, but I cannot remember the details, any more than I can recall what followed when another older member with a slightly Irish accent, who had clearly been awaiting his moment, began, "Ghosts? It is not so much a matter of what I believe but what I have seen."

All the while the vast chasm between the condition of being American and that of being British gaped before me.

The whiskey clouded my mind. I fell asleep in the cab on the way back to my hotel.

I have been in the U.K. several times since. I have even spoken at conferences there, in the course of my business and literary career, but I have never had an opportunity to tell—or even hear—another English club story, because, unsurprisingly, they never invited me back.

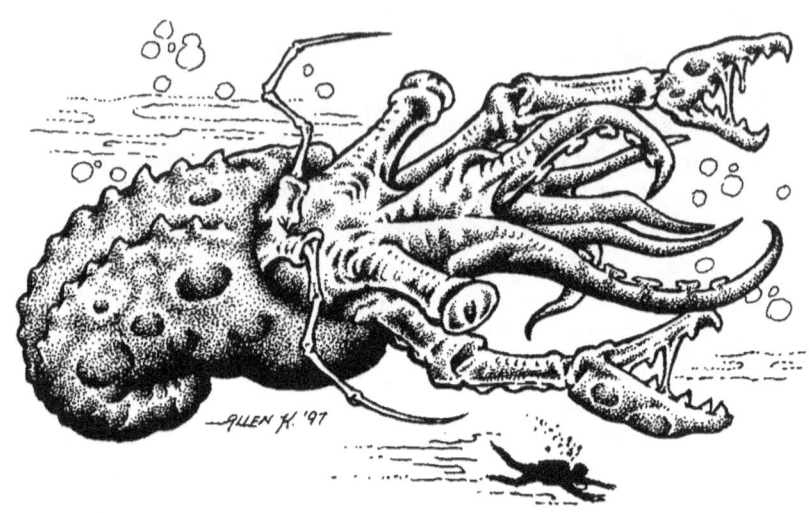

DANSE MACABRE

Jeff Barnes

Every year they bloom in my garden,
rising from the graves of the dead.
Listen to the clicking of dancing bones
and see the smiling skeleton heads!

Every year when the pumpkins are sprouting
and the leaves turning orange and red,
I tend my garden faithfully,
preparing to welcome back the dead.

Don't bury your loved ones in cemeteries.
Bring them to my garden instead,
and celebrate with them every year
from Halloween to the Day of the Dead!

IMPERVIOUS TO REASON, OBLIVIOUS TO FATE
John R. Fultz

It was not Shango's custom to meet with strangers in the dead of night.

Evil spirits of seventeen kinds were known to roam the Forest of Heavenly Streams, but a lone traveler was more likely to meet one of the three bandit tribes who called the forest home. Shango had walked the woodland path without company all day, but he was not alone. The blade of his great-grandfather kept him company, nestled in its scabbard of fine leather at his waist. Sometimes he spoke to the sword, as if to his great-grandfather. He asked it many questions, but so far it had never answered him.

Now the naked blade gleamed silver and orange across his knees as he sat before the campfire. A roasted squirrel simmered on a spit above the tiny flame, but Shango let it burn and blacken. A tree bole guarded his back while his eyes searched the darkness beyond the firelight. Whoever or whatever spied on him from that darkness would see the drawn sword. Perhaps the mere sight of it would frighten away any bandit or spirit who crept near. Shango did not want to kill anyone in this place. To spill blood in the forest was to invite the intervention of its spirits.

A soft wind made the dried leaves rattle as three men emerged from the dark. They wore the robes of swordsmen and masks of painted wood. The masks showed the grinning faces of red demons with golden tusks. Each man carried a sheathed blade similar to Shango's, yet they were forged of newer steel by less expert hands.

Shango grinned to see that they were neither spirits nor bandits.

"Sangzara knows you are coming," said the middle swordsman. "He offers you one chance to turn around and go back to Huan-gao alive. Will you accept his generous offer?"

Shango stood up now, the sword of his great-grandfather steady in his right fist.

"I cannot," he said. "There is a man I must kill in Huan-zuo. I am aware that he serves Sangzara, but this does not concern me."

"It does now," said the middle mask.

The three men drew their blades in a single motion, but Shango was already leaping over the campfire, his steel sweeping wide before him. As his sandals hit the earth and his legs bent low, blood sprayed from three necks. Each man was slashed from ear to ear below the pointed chins of their masks. They clutched at their spewing necks, dropping weapons to lie among the dead leaves. Shango whipped his blade twice to clear it of gore, then slid it back into the scabbard. The twitching bodies of his assailants hit the ground a second later, and soon they grew still inside puddles of red.

Shango carefully removed each dead man's mask. He set the blackened squirrel carcass aside and fed each mask to the campfire's flame until all three were charred to embers. He was about to try and salvage some of the burned squirrel-meat when an unexpected voice startled him.

"Why do that? Why burn their masks?"

The voice spoke in his own language, flawlessly and without accent, not even a trace of the twelve regional dialects. It was almost too perfect, marking the speaker as an outsider who had mastered the formal tongue, probably from books. Shango turned and drew his blade, holding it at arm's length. It pointed directly at the stranger standing at the edge of firelight.

His face was that of a young man, his odd eyes and dress unfamiliar. He could not be from Huan-gao or Huan-zuo. He was an outlander with a ludicrous robe of gaudy colors that flared to points at the shoulders. His dark hair was unbound and longer than most women of Shango's people, windblown and disheveled in a blatant dereliction of style. Yet Shango was entranced by his eyes, which gleamed and swirled in every possible color.

Shango stood with his blade between them and felt compelled to answer the stranger's question. The man seemed in no way dangerous or threatening. He carried no sword or any other visible weapon. Most of all he seemed entirely out of place in the Forest of Heavenly Streams.

"These men are the disciples of Sangzara, the cruel wizard who governs Huan-zuo," Shango said. "They are murderers sworn to evil gods. If their masks aren't burned, their souls return to Sangzara and serve him from beyond the grave."

"You have slain many such men." It was not a question. "Far more than these three."

Shango lowered his sword. "They gave me little choice," he said. "How do you know these things, Vagabond?"

The stranger laughed. "I suppose I must look rather bizarre to you," he said. "I am a long way from home…" He lifted the multi-colored robe from him as if it were a light cloak, and cast it on the ground before the campfire. Now Shango saw that it was a thick-woven rug, not a cloak or robe at all. The stranger, dressed in a simple buckskin tunic, sat down on the rug and motioned for Shango to join him.

"My name is Magtone," said the stranger. "Formerly of Doomed Karakutas…may she rest in peace…."

Shango had never heard either name. Yet custom and manners dictated his response. His head bowed slightly as he introduced himself, and then he sat cross-legged again before his fire. The carpet was soft beneath him. It had been a long time since he had felt anything so soft.

"How is it you speak the language of Huan?" Shango asked.

Magtone produced a flask of wine from somewhere on his person, popped the cork, and offered Shango the first drink. His smile alone convinced the swordsman that it was not poison but hospitality that he was offering. The flask was made of black glass and shaped by clever hands into something resembling a woman's body. On Shango's tongue the vintage was of extreme quality.

"It's a long story," Magtone said. "Language is never a barrier to me. Suffice to say I've been the victim of a few wizards myself. One in particular." His eyes stared at the stars above the treetops, as if looking into the past.

"Did a wizard's spell send you into exile here?" asked Shango. "Is that why you are so far from home?"

Magtone took back his flask and drank deep. He wiped his lip with the back of a lean hand and his magical eyes flared against the firelight.

"Not exactly," Magtone said. "I'm looking for the great and ancient city known as Odaza, where gods walk among men. Do you know it?"

Shango nodded. "Only from legends. Do you seek a legend?" He took another drink from the bottle, which calmed his growling stomach. "Only madmen seek legends as if they were realities."

"Ah, you may call me mad if you wish," Magtone said. "But at least I have a goal. How many madmen can say that?"

Shango drank a last sip of wine and turned the bottle upside down to show his guest that it was all gone. "I don't know," he said. "You are the first madman I've ever met."

Magtone laughed. "I'm a poet actually," he said. "Or at least I was…"

Shango grinned and was about to ask for a poem. A sound from the darkness stopped him. He put a finger to his lips, and Magtone nodded at his request for silence. Something dark and heavy moved among the trees, sniffing at the air, coming toward the dead men in their pools of cooling blood.

A long arm, apish and purple with a black claw on every finger, reached from the shadows and grabbed a swordsman's corpse by the hair. It pulled the body into the dark, where the sound of gnashing teeth and ripping flesh drowned out the crackle of the campfire.

"It's only a forest demon," Shango whispered. "The bodies will appease its bloodlust as well as any sacrifice. Stay near to the flame and we have nothing to fear."

Shango and Magtone watched the arm slink back again, then again, as each corpse was devoured in turn by the skulking beast. Afterwards it slipped off into the moonlight and disappeared. Only pools of red mud and a few bones remained of the cadavers.

"This forest is quite a nasty place," Magtone said. "Yet I hear there are two great settlements at either end of this path. I've been lost in the wilderness for so long that I crave civilization. I know your language as I know all languages, but I do not know your customs. I thought perhaps to travel in your company awhile."

Shango shook his head. "You do not want to travel with me," he said. "There will be only blood and death where I am going."

"You told the masked ones you seek to kill a man."

"Yes," Shango said. "And I can accept no man's help in this endeavor."

"So you will not turn back, you will not accept aid, and you wish no company?"

"You begin to understand me," Shango said. "Perhaps you truly are a poet."

"And perhaps you truly are a killer," Magtone said. "Is this the sum of your ambition?"

Shango turned away from his campfire guest. He did not want to lose his temper and break the bonds of hospitality. He spoke without looking at Magtone.

"The man I seek is named Shira Zo, Master Swordsman of the House of Zo. He leads the masked ones who serve Shangzara, and by their ruthless skill the wizard rules this province. Six times has war come to our lands during my lifetime, six times have the soldiers of Huan-gao and Huan-zuo matched blades in the sorrowfields, and six times sixty men have died. The last of these wars nearly destroyed Huan-gao, which lives now under the subjugation of Sangzara and the Zo swordsmen."

"I see," said Magtone. "You've come to slay the wizard and his champion for the good of your people. You are a hero, Shango of Huan-gao."

"No," Shango said. "That is not why I march toward death."

"Well, if you're not doing it for your people, then you must be doing it for yourself."

"You are unusually perceptive, Poet."

"You wear simple robes, affect a martial demeanor," Magtone examined Shango with shimmering eyes. "You travel in humble style, with no need of comfort. You wear no jewels or golden rings. It is not treasure you seek…so it must be revenge."

Shango said nothing.

"If you wish to travel with me, we leave at dawn's light," he said. "Get some sleep." He rolled into the grass and rested his head on a mossy root, his back toward Magtone. The wine had made him terribly sleepy. He clutched the sheathed sword to his breast like a lover and closed his eyes. He could not speak to the stranger of what he had lost. Not here in the Forest of Heavenly Streams, where spirits often listened to mens' conversations and took the forms of dead loved ones.

Magtone curled up with his back to Shango, wrapping the carpet about himself like a blanket. "I'm told there is a fine library in Huan-zuo," he said.

"There was one in Huan-gao as well," Shango said. "But not anymore."

There had been so many wonderful things in Huan-gao.

So few of them were left now.

Despite his request to travel with Shango, the stranger was nowhere to be found when dawn broke. Shango stamped out the remains of his campfire and followed the forest trail toward Huan-zuo. Singing birds filled the trees, and the wind brought cherry blossoms like tiny fairies dancing through sunbeams.

Shango walked the better part of the morning until he topped a rise and saw the blue stone towers of Huan-zuo Citadel rising beyond the treetops. The ancient fortress crowned a steep hill rising above the town proper, which sat walled and gated, surrounded by miles of working farmlands. Shango walked a few more hours until the forest thinned out, and he followed the river that flowed through the center of town. Huan-zuo looked much as he remembered from previous visits, a collection of peaked roofs and painted temples gathered at the foot of Sangzara's high stronghold. River boats with blue and yellow sails glided east or west, moving produce and livestock to and from the city's crowded wharves.

Shango drank from a public well after he left the forest shadows. He walked in the sun like a man unworried and in no pressing haste. He did not stop to speak with any man or woman, although peasants dropped their baskets as he approached and fled to the side of the road. In the huts of field workers women drove their children inside as he came down the river road, staring out their windows with wide eyes. The men stood their ground with spade and pitchfork, as if they would stand a chance against a swordsman of Shango's experience. He ignored them and entered the city gate, which stood open to evening traffic.

The guards eyed him warily and waved him through, moving aside their long spears.

"Shango of Huan-gao!" One of the spearmen called to him as he passed. "Master Zo awaits you in the Pit of Vipers. Seek him directly and none else shall contest you. That honor is claimed by the master."

Shango gave a slight bow and resumed his walking. The townsfolk wore brighter clothing, but they were just as frightened as the country folk.

They hid behind the doors of shops and hovels, children clinging to their knees and shoulders. Guards on every corner wore the demon-masks of Shangzara's service, yet they made no move to stop Shango as he went deeper into the city. As the sun fell behind the nearby hill, the governor's fortress became a mountain of darkness, a shadow that lay over the entire city. Perhaps the people who lived here no longer felt that shadow because they had grown used to its iron weight.

Shango avoided the blinking eyes of children as he passed by.

The Pit of Vipers was a staging ground for gladiatorial events and ritual combat. Such violent delights were popular in Huan-zuo as they never were in Huan-gao. Many things were allowed here with the wizard in power, things that used to be forbidden and unholy. The smell of rotting meat came to Shango's nostrils as he walked the lanes below the high castle.

A crowd stood gathered into a circle ahead of him, most of them swordsmen wearing demon masks, some of them well-dressed noblemen making bets with one another. All eyes turned to Shango as he entered the plaza and approached the pit. The swordsmen and spectators together must have numbered in the hundreds, and they spread wide before him as he progressed. Finally he stood at the edge of a deep square hole and saw Shira Zo sitting cross-legged on the far edge. Between them lay the open space of the pit, and the mass of crawling, hissing serpents that littered its floor.

Shira's long white hair was tied in a traditional top-knot, something Shango had forsaken years ago. Shango wore his dark hair in a single long braid now, like a southern-born barbarian. A drum began to beat somewhere in the crowded plaza, and someone played melodies on a wooden flute.

Shango sat down on his side of the pit, laying his great-grandfather's sword upon his knees. Directly across from him Shira sat in the same position, naked steel gleaming across his lap. His eyes were closed as Shango approached, but now they opened. Shango hated the deep green of them, eyes so bright and yet so empty. He longed to see the light go out of them as Shira's head rolled across bloody ground.

"You have been given the opportunity to avoid this death," Shira said. He did not move a finger or a muscle, but he caught Shango in the grip of his emerald gaze.

"I have," Shango said. "I refused it."

"I see," Shira said. "You are impervious to reason."

"To seek revenge one must be impervious to reason and oblivious to fate," Shango said.

Shira smiled. "You quote the Book of Elder Wisdom well. Yet your fate is to die here, today, at my hand. Can you be so oblivious to this fact?"

"The spirits of the murdered dead bring me here," Shango said. "The children you hacked to pieces in Huan-gao...the women..."

"Your child..." said Shira. "Your woman. I remember them well..."

Shango winced. "You have no honor, and I have forsaken mine to face you. So I will gladly die to sink this blade deep into your heart. With my dying breath, I will rip out your life and offer it to the Gods of Hell. If that is to be my fate, then I cherish the unfolding of it."

Shira grunted. His head turned sideways a bit.

"Then follow me into the pit," he said, and jumped.

Shango followed him immediately, his sandals crushing the coils of several angry vipers. He swept the blade about his feet and legs, sheering off the heads of the nearest serpents, dodging their swift fangs as he cleared a tiny space for himself amid the slithering mass.

Shira stood calm amid the serpents, his blade poised. The snakes glided about his feet like kittens, raising not a single fang to molest him. Shango had known it would be this way. Pit-viper venom was deadly, but Shira had raised these snakes and weaned himself on their venom. This was his way of ensuring a victory—the murderer of innocents doubted his skill. He feared the kiss of Shango's sword, or he would not have met him here. With a pit duel Shira could preserve his honor while giving himself an unfair advantage.

A viper dug its fangs deep into Shango's heel as he leaped across the pit floor. The two swords clanged and silver sparks flew. Shango guessed the viper's poison would begin to kill him in seconds, so he must take his revenge quickly. There was no time for anything but a killing blow.

The two men danced about the pit while their clanging blades sang a discordant song. The bored noblemen cheered at the lively entertainment, but the demon-faced disciples of Sangzara merely stared. Perhaps they would leap into the pit and finish what the vipers had started if Shango struck down his foe. He did not care. Let them slice him to bits, let the serpents live among his bones. He had come for only one reason: To kill Shira Zo.

Shira's blade sliced Shango's chest. Shango answered the hit with a shallow slice across Shira's abdomen. The Swordmaster of Zo paused his attack to tear off his sliced and bloody robe. Two more serpents dug their fangs into Shango's lower legs as he lunged for a killing stroke. Shira swirled and parried his blade, then scored a deep cut on Shango's left shoulder. If it had been his sword-arm, the fight would have been over in that second.

Shango dodged a swipe that would have taken his head off. He sliced again and again at Shira's defenses but drew little blood. The longer they fought, the more viper venom slowed his blood, made his limbs grow heavy. Death rose up from the earth like a black fog to cloud his vision.

He fought on, dancing through a swarm of blows, the shock of each one shivering his arm bones. Sweat poured from his brow into his eyes.

No longer could he feel his legs at all. He countered a downward stroke but fell backward into the incensed vipers. They latched onto his body with curving fangs, at least a dozen more sending their poison into his blood. Shira stood above him now, grinning, bleeding from a dozen shallow cuts, sweat and blood glimmering on his naked chest.

Shango released all the energy of his dying heart. It flowed into his numb legs and burst like a flame from his eyes. He leaped to his feet trailing a cloak of serpents that would not let go of his flesh. For one brief moment, he saw the fear shining in Shira's eyes. The snake-breeder had hesitated a moment to make his deathblow more dramatic for the crowd. In that moment, Shango's blade flashed through his exposed neck. Shira's head tumbled into the viper's nest, and Shango fell to lay beside it.

Shira's headless body stood for a few seconds, spewing crimson across the masks of the observers about the pit's edge. Then it collapsed into the snakes, hand still wrapped about its useless sword. Shango's limbs had gone completely numb. He bled from twice as many cuts as he had given Shira, and the venom of multiple bites overpowered his blood. He lay in the squirming pit but felt as if he were floating on the surface of a warm pond. The red demon faces staring down at him slowly withdrew. He turned his head and found himself looking into the face of Shira's fallen head. Now the green eyes were truly empty, and the mouth wore a child's expression.

As Shango lay dying in the pit of vipers, the faces of his dead wife and daughter came to him like spirits, floating above him as he faded. He spoke their names, but so softly that no one else could hear him. No one but the viper crawling past his cheek.

Suddenly Magtone was there above the pit, sitting on his carpet that floated like a cloud. It lowered him toward the pit floor, and he peered over its edge at Shango.

Shango coughed blood and blinked cold sweat from his eyes.

"Have you come to watch me die?" he asked.

Magtone shook his head. "That depends," he said. "Are you truly oblivious to fate?"

"I am dying," Shango said. "This is my fate."

"If you wish to die, I cannot stop you," Magtone said. "But I can save you. I have the magic inside me. I know the ancient words that mend the flesh and anchor the spirit."

"I have taken my vengeance," Shango said. "Now let me die."

"Have you?" Magtone asked. "You said Shira Zo served Sangzara. Is that not the same Sangzara who dwells in this hideous castle? Did he not give the orders that sent Shira and the Swordsmen of Zo to Huan-gao?

Your wife and child are avenged, but how many others have died in Sangzara's reign? Will you not defy fate to avenge them too?"

"You..." Shango said, spitting more blood. His eyes grew blind, and he barely heard his own words. "You came for the wizard. You came to face Sangzara..."

"Not at first," Magtone said. "But apparently he has the only library in town. Plus from what I've gathered he's a terrible governor. Take my hand and live. Deny your fate."

Shango laughed. Death seemed terribly humorous all of a sudden.

"I thought you had decided not to follow me after all," he said.

"Oh, I followed you every step of the way," Magtone said. "You simply couldn't see me."

With the last drops of strength in his body, Shango raised his bloody hand to find Magtone's fingers. Magtone spoke a few words in a language Shango did not understand, and Shango erupted from the prison of his dying body. He stared down at his own mangled form lying among the vipers. He floated now beside Magtone, who stood on the floating carpet.

"Am I a ghost?" Shango asked.

"Not yet," Magtone said.

"My body..."

"Too full of poison, I'm afraid," Magtone said. "I'll have to build you another one. But we'll have time for that later."

"You said that I would live," Shango said. His arms and legs were transparent, and he was a weightless thing now. A cloud of living memory. Was he truly alive at all?

"You will, you will!" Magtone said. "Take up your great-grandfather's sword."

"But how?" Shango asked. "I'm only a spirit."

"Trust me," Magtone said. Shango reached down and took the blade from his own dead hand. Somehow his ghostly hand lifted the solid blade. Holding it gave his ghost-form more solidity. He almost felt alive again, weighted down with a modicum of mass and substance.

"Why did you do this to me?" he asked Magtone.

The carpet rose higher and higher into the evening sky, until Shango could no longer see his dead body, the Pit of Vipers, or the plaza of violent entertainments.

"I told you," Magtone said. "I wish to travel in your company awhile. Call me lonely if you must. But first I must gain access to the library of Sangzara."

"Sangzara will never allow such a thing," said Shango. He still wasn't sure if he was a living man or an undead spirit, but he did not want to consider the question too deeply.

"Then Sangzara must die," Magtone said. "Besides, he wasn't about to let your soul escape his kingdom after you killed his best swordsman."

The carpet now floated level with the topmost towers of Citadel Huanzuo. Shango stared down at the benighted world and a great dizziness overcame him. He was falling, hurtling like a meteor through a sparkling void, the howling winds of infinity assaulting his fleshless ears. He held onto the sword of his great-grandfather as if it were his only link to sanity. Suddenly he found himself in a dark hall standing before a black throne.

On the throne sat Sangzara, wrapped in the purple robes of conjury, a crown of black crystal rising from his bald head. His face was incredibly ancient, a mass of wrinkles with red eyes blazing like a devil from Hell. The nails of his fingers were longer than claws, tipped with poison spikes, and his teeth were black. A massive crystal ball sat before him on a pedestal of jade carved into twining dragon-shapes. A thousand naked skulls lined the walls of his sanctum, and a thousand black candles burned to support his dark arts. The statues of multi-armed devil gods stood behind him, their faces matching exactly the masks worn by his disciples.

"This outlander steals your soul, Shango!" Sangzara said. Shango stood before the wizard now in the center of an unholy sigil carved into the chamber floor. "But you are mine not his, as the souls of all who die in Haun-zuo belong to me. Spectre born of mine enemy you may be, but the power of my sorcery demands that you serve me. Kill the one who comes now to kill me! Kill him…"

A flash of light and Shango found himself beside Magtone again, atop the flying carpet. The moonlight flashed along his blade as they rocketed toward a broad window in the highest tower of the citadel. Shango's arm moved of its own accord while the voice of Sangzara boomed in his head. "Kill him!"

Shango thrust the naked blade through Magtone's belly and out his back. Magtone looked at him with a disappointed expression, yet there was no blood spewing from the terrible wound. Shango pulled his sword free and a mass of colored lights erupted from the hole in Magtone's body. At that moment the carpet glided through the open window of Sangzara's tower, crashing into the chamber of skulls with the obsidian throne.

Magtone and Shango tumbled across the marble floor, knocking over braziers and candles, spilling flame among the obscene tapestries and skull-lined shelves. Shango felt his human weight again, but still he was far lighter than he had been. When he leaped toward the black throne, he made it there in a single bound. He was a leaping ghost who somehow wielded a blade of solid metal in his phantom fist. Sangzara no longer sat on the throne, or Shango would have taken his head. The wizard was nowhere to be seen across the gloomy sanctum. Magtone lay on the furled carpet, convulsing and spewing rainbows from his gut-wound. He chanted in a language that confused the ear, and his convulsions grew less and less. Soon he staggered to his feet and closed the open wound with his hand and a final incantation.

"Why did you stab me?" Magtone asked.

Shango stuttered. "He forced my hand..."

"Of course," Magtone said. "Sangzara commands the spirits of the dead."

"Not only their spirits," Shango said. "Their very bones will obey..."

The oaken doors of the chamber burst open, and the stench of the graveyard rushed into the room. A company of rotted mummies and demon-masked skeletons invaded the chamber of skulls. They brandished ancient swords blighted by rust, or battle-axes strung with cobwebs. It seemed the entire population of the citadels' crypts had been called from their resting places and sent to destroy the intruders.

Magtone waved his hand and sang. A wall of fractured colors like a broken mirror separated himself and Shango from the shambling dead. They beat upon his magical barrier with ancient weapons but could not break it. Their stench was terrible.

"How can we kill those who are already dead?" Shango asked.

"I'm working on it," Magtone said.

A loping shadow like a great hound dove through the barrier, shattering it with a roar and the gnashing of yellow fangs. The wizard had taken the form of a great black wolf. Shango recognized the cruel eyes of Sangzara in the creature's face. The beast leapt not at him but at Magtone, who went down beneath its fangs. Shango watched the beast tear at Magtone's body, which leaked light and sorcery as a man leaks blood. Then both of them were gone. They had landed on the flying carpet, and with dazzling speed it swept them both out the window.

The wizards' duel was completely lost to Shango's sight now.

The barrier separating Shango from the dead legion faded like a fog, and the mummies came against him with their flanged maces. He dodged and whirled with his newfound ghostly speed, still wondering if he were alive or dead. Then he realized that if he were no longer among the living, he had nothing to fear from an army of the dead.

So he waded into the stinking, fleshless warriors that sought to cut him down, hacking skeletons apart, taking off the shriveled heads of mummies, slicing dead limb from dead limb. Tomb dust and bone fragments filled the high chamber, and thunder shook the sky outside, where Magtone fought Sangzara somewhere above the world.

Shango sliced and thrust and leaped and cut. Never once did a dead thing's blade or bludgeon impact his ghostly form. Perhaps he was immune to wounds now, being trapped between the states of life and death. He fought until the last mummy lay in curling shreds at his feet, until the last clacking skull shattered beneath his sandal. Only then did the citadel's living guardians in their demon masks flood into the room to challenge him. There must have been a hundred of them or more, each one eager to avenge the death of his master.

Shango danced among them like a windblown flame. His flickering blade opened skin, vein, and flesh wherever it touched. Men howled and died and lost their limbs to the ghost-warrior's skill. These were the same men who had slaughtered Shango's people while he was not there to protect them. Disciples of Sangzara, Swordsmen of Zo, fanatics and madmen with a taste for blood. They would rather die than surrender, so they died in droves, rushing again and again at Shango. He cut them down without mercy, until the chamber of skulls was a chamber of steaming blood and twitching corpses. They lay in scattered pieces among the desiccated remnants of the undead. Shango stood atop the pile of dead without a single spot of red on his spectral robes, yet the blade of his great-grandfather dripped crimson from tip to pommel.

At last he sat upon the black throne and rested. He was not bone-weary or exhausted. He no longer had bones. He no longer felt the fatigue of bodily strain. But his spirit was tired now. Tired of killing. He wondered if his decision to follow Magtone had made him a coward. He should have died and joined his family in the afterlife. Instead he had taken Magtone's hand and become something less than alive yet far more than dead. What would happen if he sat here in this seat of sorcery long enough? Would he fade away to nothing? Or would he be caught here to haunt this citadel for the rest of time?

Before he could contemplate an answer to such dreadful questions, Magtone came flying through the window on his carpet. His tunic was ripped to shreds, but his flesh was whole. Sangzara's severed head, which had taken a man's likeness once again, hung by its pale hair from Magtone's fist. The withered face stared dumbly into infinity, the devil-fires in its eyes extinguished, lower jaw slack and dripping with gore.

"Sangzara is dead?" Shango rose from the black throne.

Magtone tossed the head into a firepit, where it steamed and crackled and melted into a black husk.

"I took his head off with a shaft of killing light," Magtone said. "But his body escaped."

"What do you mean it escaped?" Shango said.

"Exactly that," Magtone said. "It sprouted a pair of black wings and flew into the deep forest. I could not catch it."

"Headless…it lived?" Shango imagined his own flesh crawling, but it was a phantom sensation. He had no proper flesh now.

"Headless," Magtone nodded. "This leads me to believe that Sangzara was never human at all. Probably some devil or evil spirit wearing the form of a man. But he is gone now. I'll set spells upon this citadel that will disallow his return."

"How did a poet come to know such arcane secrets?" Shango said. "To wield such power?"

"As I said, it's a long story," Magtone said.

Shango followed him into the great library at the center of the stronghold. A thousand years of tablets, scrolls, and tomes were gathered here, the accumulated knowledge of sages, sorcerers, historians, astrologers, and poets. Magtone began poring through volume after volume, searching for the secrets of Odaza, City of the Walking Gods.

Shango burned all the demon-masks he could find and set to guarding the library for weeks, forbidding any of the citadel's servants to disturb Magtone's study. He no longer felt the need for food, hunger, or sleep. Magtone did not seem to need any of these things either. He may have once been a poet as he said, but Shango knew the man was a wizard first and foremost. A weaver of miracles. Shango's post-death existence was one of these miracles. He was not at all sure that he deserved such a gift.

One day Magtone emerged from behind a stack of books with a mischievous smile and fresh cup of wine. Sunlight flowed through the garden windows, and stray butterflies flitted about the shelves.

"Well?" Shango asked. "Have you found it?"

"The sages of Xu Shai all agreed that Odaza, City of Walking Gods, lay far to the east, even across the Sea of Ages. Now I know which direction to fly."

"So now you will leave," Shango said. "After all of this…"

"Come with me," Magtone said. "I promised you a living body. Our long journey will give me time to fulfill this promise."

"And if I choose to stay?" Shango said.

"Stay here? With the dead? Well, then I suppose you will eventually fade…perhaps to join the souls of your missing loved ones wherever they are now."

"Stay and face oblivion, or go with you and face…what?" Shango asked.

Magtone smiled and his eyes dazzled.

"The unknown…"

"That I cannot do without the ones I love," Shango said. "I cannot leave them again. I will stay here and hope to join them in the next world. There is nothing left for me in this one."

"Are you sure?"

Shango nodded his head. While late-rising stars glimmered in the sky,

Magtone brought him to a small graveyard just north of Huan-gao, where two fresh graves lay side by side. One of them was very small. Shango thrust the point of his great-grandfather's sword into the green earth and sat down between the graves. He watched Magtone rise toward the stars on his carpet and disappear into the night.

When the morning sun rose above the graves, only the ancient blade was left between them.

✗

A SUM TOTAL
Maxwell I. Gold

I sat behind a cyber wall, looking at the numbers that were the sum total of a world's existence, assessing their true value, to make way for judgment. While the stars dripped from my eyes, I smiled breathlessly as cities crumbled behind me, in devastation and ruin. With each keystroke, tap and swipe of the screen, Life was no longer measured in paper, blood, or time, but judged by me, with each bit, byte, and metallic shard that fell from my lips. My dark twisted algorithm tortured their neurons and pulled their synapses, leaving them trapped in a sticky web of Sisyphean uncertainty, doomed to forever wander in a replicating plane with a horizon that never bends.

Peering into the depths, I watched cities fall and worlds crawl helplessly, coming to an awful reckoning with those dubious odds. While my control alternating their dreams, merely forced the task, destroying all functions as nightmare became truth and pixilation became logic; there was no reasonable hope to escape. This was the sum total of their existence, assessed in true value, awaiting my judgement.

✗

THE RIVER
Sharon Cullars

Near the river where souls gather, a newly-arrived wraith sits near the shore pondering her situation. As she looks on, ethereal shadows move in a circuit around the edges of the water, the depths of the river reflecting nothing but rays of light from a strange moon.

The wraith, named Zephra in life, tries to recall how she came to be here. But trying to remember causes pain where her heart should be. Where her heart once was. The pain eventually subsides as the memory she has tried to capture evades her grasp.

The others, barely glimmers of motion, do not heed her. They appear locked in their own miseries, unaware of her and each other.

What is this place and why am I here? The questions buzz around in her head like tormenting gnats. She shakes her head as if to clear them, to allow her some peace.

A snatch of something grazes her memory, a well-honed blade scraping lightly against the surface of her mind. Explosive montages of a face, of a place. The face is a blur, the memory lost in a vortex that refuses to slow down to let her parse it.

She sits alone on the trunk of a dead tree. As she looks around, she sees that all the trees along the river are also dead, standing tall with stark branches that are spidery fingers reaching to touch the moon. The orb hovers in a starless sky, bathes everything in a florescent blue, warm and shimmery.

The smell that piques her nose is of a hot summer night. And death. A melange of floral and decay, of dying things giving off the slightest whiff of putrefaction.

Death. This has to be death.

Then, when had she lived? Who had she been in life?

She looks to the others, the wan apparitions moving aimlessly. There is one standing motionless just outside the ring of moving bodies. She seems as corporeal as she would have been in life. In the blue caress of the moon, her dark skin gleams like polished onyx. Her hair is cropped almost to the scalp, adding majesty to the planes of her face.

The woman looks up just at that moment to catch Zephra staring at her. And in this place of death, a smile emerges. That simple human reflex comforts Zephra. For whatever hell she is in, she still remembers the warmth of a smile. For that second, it pushes away the sorrow residing in the place where her heart should have kept a rhythm but no longer does.

The woman gestures to her, beckoning.

Unsure of her footing, Zephra rises from the desiccated trunk. Her body glides instead of feet touching ground as she wanders over. It is a strange feeling of freedom, this easy motion. She stops just before the wraith. The smile is still there, greeting her.

"You are new here," the woman says. "It is good to have new energy among us."

"Where am I? What is this place?" Zephra asks.

"You are in the in-between, the place that exists between life and the final death."

"The final death? But isn't this it?"

The woman shakes her head, her skin refracting the moon's glow. She is quite beautiful, and somehow her beauty recasts this lonely river into something less forlorn.

"Are you an angel?" Zephra wonders aloud.

"No," the near angel laughs, the sound pealing throughout the lonely place, echoing among the trees, reaching Zephra's ears almost like lyrics from a song long forgotten.

"I am not an angel, but I do minister the souls, keeping them calm." The smile disappears then. "See, they suffered during their last moments and are not ready to ascend. Not just yet."

"So this place is..." Zephra begins but the woman interrupts her.

"Is a place where they can heal and decide their destinies."

Zephra gazes at the barely corporeal bodies moving slowly around the river. Some of them are just wisps, barely perceptible to the eye.

"They're so sad. How can they possibly heal?"

"Some heal by letting go of the memories, and thereby the pain they experienced when they crossed over. Sometimes they can shed the pain quickly, but for others, the hurting has become an integral part of them and they hold on for fear of letting go."

"I have no memories. When I try to remember..."

"You feel pain when you do," the woman filled in the pause. "Don't force it. Let it come to you."

"And if I do finally remember?"

"Then you will decide where you want to go."

"Where I want to go? You mean heaven?"

"Heaven is just one of the destinations," the woman offers. "You may decide to return."

"Return...to my life?"

The woman shakes her head.

"No. That particular life is over now, and I'm sure you would not wish to return to a body that is no longer. No, you can return as another soul, in another incarnation."

Zephra, unable to remember life, can't determine if she would ever want to live again. If what the woman said is true, then she is one of those who suffered horribly when she died. The only thing that she has held on to from her life is her name. Memories of family, friends, any currency of her previous incarnation has been emptied from her soul. She might as well have never lived.

"How did I die? Do you know?" Zephra asks, her words softly tumbling over one another much like that of a child inquiring about the meaning of life...and not quite sure how to phrase the question.

The woman nods sadly. "You were murdered, as were all of the souls here. And as long as you do not remember your fate, you may wander here for eons. In other words, you cannot rest in peace. You may never regain your memories and will be forced to wander like the millions of souls who have passed this way before you. If a soul remains here long enough, it will lose itself and eventually cease to be."

A shot of fear courses through her, energizing her spirit. Fear is a very human emotion and in this second, she still feels very human. And the idea of ceasing to be is something beyond dreadful.

"How long have I been here?" Zephra asks.

"In Earth's time, several decades, a blink of an eye really."

"But it feels like I just arrived..."

"In the vastness of time, you *have* just arrived. Do you remember what you were called?"

"Zephra. At least I think that's what my name is...or was."

"Yes, that is the name from your last incarnation."

"How many lives have I had?"

"Several over the course of a millennium. But it is your last that has brought you here to this place. To try to assuage your trauma so that you can move on."

"How can I assuage what I don't remember."

"You don't remember because you are hiding the truth from yourself as are all of the souls you see here. To suffer such pain at your crossing impedes your journey. It is up to you to decide whether you go...or stay here for all eternity."

Zephra's soul cries out at the declaration. She doesn't want to remain in this dreary place for eternity. She has to capture her memories and face them, no matter the pain they cause. And then she can move on...maybe to heaven finally. No replay of the lives she has lived before. No more trauma.

No eternity in this hell.

"I *will* remember," she swears to the woman who says she is not an angel. But if this is hell, then is she a demon? Maybe Satan herself? No, not Satan but Lucifer, who was once beauty in light, but whose pride brought about darkness.

"What...what's your name?" Zephra asks.

"I have no name," the woman says gently. "I've never needed one. I simply am."

"Can you help me remember what happened to me?"

The woman/angel/demon shakes her head, sadness etching the planes of her face, the dark pebbles of her eyes sparkling the moon's translucent blue.

"That is something only you can do," she says with finality.

Then the woman walks away, circling the concourse of souls, at times reaching out to touch one of them as though to soothe their anguish.

Zephra closes her eyes, shuts out the scene before her. Inside herself, she visualizes the chains holding her memories at bay, containing them, trapping them in the recesses of her mind and soul. She pulls at the figurative chains, breaking the links enveloping her mind. At first, they refuse to give. But as she works the links, they begin to separate from each other, to fall away from her mind. And a freed memory comes rushing at her...

Blazing pain and anguish, as though her flesh is being torn asunder.

She tries to breath through the blood filling her lungs but chokes, the taste of iron and sputum coating her tongue, clogging her throat. A million sparks of pain sear along her flesh. She looks down where the light touches her skin. Her naked body is flayed in so many places.

She is lying on something other than the moist earth that edged the river. Carpeting or a rug soaked with her blood. The metallic smell permeates the sweltering room.

The moon is not blue now, but a glaring white shafting through the window she'd left open. Despite the ambient brightness, the attacker remains in shadow.

A knife hovers, then strikes down in a vicious arc. Agonizing fire as steel rips through pliable flesh. Why isn't she dead yet? She should be dead. She closes her eyes and prays for death but as the knife slashes again, it seems that death refuses to hear her, to give her a desperate release.

"Feels good, don't it you nigger bitch? This'll teach you." Even though he hovers above her, his words seem to reverberate from a distance. His heavy cologne suffuses the air around her.

She recognizes the voice now, with its guttural clench, its ten cigarettes a day rasp. She knows the man who is murdering her. And she wonders why he has taken this long to come after her.

After several eternal seconds, she closes her eyes for the last time. When she opens them again, the moon is blue and the earth beneath her smells like peat. It would be a soothing smell if not mixed with the cloying whiff of decomposing death. Of rotting bodies, long abandoned, their smell asking those nearby not to forget them. She is back at the river. And for a moment, what she once considered hell offers the sanctuary of heaven.

Lying there, she can't distinguish between seconds, minutes, eons. It seems she has just arrived but maybe she has been here forever. And now she has new memories, her mind no longer shackled.

Tears pool at the edges of her eyes, flows from the outer corners, moves through the kinks of her hair. She takes trembling breaths.

She remembers standing in that moonlit night, hovering over him as he hovered over her, watching the carnage that was once Zephra Giles, aspiring singer and middling waitress with quick clapbacks against those who sought to demean her. One of those clapbacks had now cost her life.

Her murderer folds the bloody knife in a handkerchief, stuffs it into his jeans pocket, then rolls her body in the rug and hefts it over his shoulder. Initially confused as to how she could be carried in that rug and at the same time stand witness to her murder, a slow realization dawns.

She is no longer flesh, but spirit now. A spirit as torn and flayed as her lifeless body.

Outside, she watches sadly as he loads her corpse into the back of his truck. She travels alongside the vehicle as it heads out of the city limits, drives for nearly an hour until it finally leaves the county. She is there as streets with rows of concrete buildings and brick homes eventually morph into clapboard houses half obscured by the tall stalks of wheat in neighboring fields.

Dawn is just a couple of hours away so he moves swiftly after he stops the truck on a stretch of a lonely road just at the edge of one of those wheat fields. No lights from the few houses or from the beams of passing cars. Everything is silent except for a wisp that rides a nightly breeze. The moon is luminescent on this night of her death.

He retrieves her body, and again hefts it over his right shoulder and walks several feet through the wheat whose spiked heads grab at his flannel shirt. His exertion causes him to take rasping breaths. Maybe he will fall dead here, both bodies hidden among the wheat, liquefying and dissolving beneath a sun that has been brutal this summer. He reaches a point where he seems satisfied and with one motion he unceremoniously dumps the rug and its load between the stalks. The breeze causes them to wave and bow under the moon.

Zephra looks down at the rug holding her body, which is nothing but a darker silhouette in the moonlit night. She wonders whether her body will be found in time before she becomes nothing but bones. It is near reaping time, so there may be hope that she will be found and given a proper burial. Laid to rest but not in peace.

The man who murdered her also looks down at his work, takes a breath of satisfaction, then walks back through the stalks to his waiting truck.

She knows him but not his name. He had come into the diner a few times, and had always ordered the same thing: chicken fried steak, hash browns and black coffee.

He always sat at her station.

He always stared her down with a sneer, along with something else in those eyes. Something dark that touched on everything between lust and hatred. Those eyes called her all of the names she had ever been called.

On that last, fateful day, the day that edged into the night of her death, he'd voiced one of those names. And had tried to grab her wrist as she set down his piping hot coffee. A mistake on his part. The hot coffee was easily upturned in his lap, probably scorched his balls. He'd leaped up, pain and anger scrawled on his already weathered face.

"You black bitch! I'll kill you for this!"

"Just a goddamn minute there!" Mitch had come from behind the register to stand between her and the fist formed mid-air ready to swing down on her. Her manager indicated with a wave of his head that Zephra was to get out of the way.

"You don't put your hands on any of my staff!"

"She deliberately poured coffee on me!"

"That's because you called me a nigger, then grabbed at me! Nobody treats me like that! Especially no ugly racist ass hillbilly!"

Since he couldn't hit Zephra, the customer whammed on Mitch, landing a fist square on the manager's jaw.

Two of the male cooks had already come out of the kitchen at the sound of the yelling. Seeing their manager being assaulted, quickly waylaid the angry man and all three of them managed to throw him out of the door. He yelled expletives through it all, promising retribution against the lot of them, his voice a bellow through the thin glass of the door.

Zephra had breathed a shaky breath and Mitch, rubbing his jaw, had asked if she was all right.

She'd thought she was. All of the guys had stood up for her and the customer wouldn't dare show his face around there again.

Or so she'd hoped.

She'd finished her shift and had headed home in her Honda, forcing the thought of the man out of her head. Instead, she'd sung all the way home, a little rehearsing for the gig she'd landed for the weekend at Club Xavier, a little smoky jazz venue that featured plenty of watered down drinks and local talent who had dreams of something much bigger.

For Zephra, Xavier's filled her dreams, was a path maybe to a musical on Broadway or maybe a contract with a music producer.

But those dreams ended that sweltering night she'd left the window open to get some relief to the heat in her close bedroom.

As she looked down at her body, a rage settled through her. This was so unfair! She was just twenty-three and was nowhere near to finishing her dreams, or realizing everything that had been out there for her.

One moment, she is standing in the quiet moonlit field, white rays bathing the wheat stalks dancing in a breeze, her body hidden, destined to be found too late for a dignified burial. And then she is sitting near a river, the blue rays of a strange moon casting shadows as souls wander around the water.

How long has she been here? Decades?

She remembers everything now. Her mind is finally set free. But her soul is still shackled to the river. Shouldn't she be moving on?

She sees the angel who is not an angel. Whose onyx skin is only shades darker than Zephra's own. The woman is talking with one of the souls, a woman whose anguished face is so spectral, the moon shines through the skin. The anguish diminishes just a little as the woman speaks with the spirit. Whatever the words she is saying, the soul is comforted.

Comforter. An apt description for the woman. Zephra needs that comfort right now as the memories of her death have confounded her. Instead of closure, they have opened so much, including psychic wounds that hurt her very soul. She continues to feel the knife wounds, the horror, the anger and sadness. Her soul is anguished that her life was so easily discarded. She will forever see that dark shadow lying in the wheat field.

She is lost in thought and is startled when the woman touches her shoulder. The comforter has come to her, hopefully to answer those tormenting questions.

"You have remembered at last," the woman says.

"Yes, I remember everything. I feel destroyed."

The woman nods. "It is like that at first. But you will continue to gain strength with each detail that you remember. Only then can you find peace and solace as you release the pain, temper your anger."

"I can never let go of the anger! That piece of shit killed me!"

The woman's features express her sympathy but something else as well. But she remains silent. Zephra feels censured, like a child under the disappointed eyes of a mother.

"He killed me for nothing," Zephra moans, wanting so much to go back in time, to change things. This time around, she would hold her tongue, or watch out whether she is being followed. She would lock her windows, turn on a fan instead, even though it would only feed her a warm current. But she would happily suffer the discomfort because she would be alive. She would be able to take the money she was saving and move to Los Angeles or San Diego. Sing in clubs there, if she had to. Or even waitress while she waited for her luck to find her.

But instead, she died because of her own quick, careless words and a cup of spilled coffee.

"You're not to blame, you know," the woman finally says. So, she is a mind reader, too.

"But if I hadn't said anything…"

The woman shakes her head. "Fate, in the end, is unaided. Your destiny was to meet your attacker. Nothing you did or didn't do could change that. Had you not spoken your words, he would have found any millions of reasons to harm you."

"But why me?" Zephra asks. "I never hurt anyone. I tried to be a good daughter, a good granddaughter, I went to church…"

"Goodness very rarely protects the flesh, but serves as an aegis for the soul. These souls you see wandering here, they are not evil. Like you, they did not harm another. They too had family and dreams. They simply could not escape their fates. And until they settle their souls, accept what has happened to them, they will never be free of this place."

The woman pauses, considering Zephra. Strangely, Zephra feels tears on her face; she didn't think that spirits could cry.

The woman smiles. "You are crying because your soul has broken free at last. You are luckier than the others. You remember…and you can now feel all of your emotions again. Describe what you are feeling now."

"I'm sad…and angry. I want to take from him what he took from me."

"You now have a purpose. And you have a decision to make."

"What decision," Zephra asks.

"Whether to move on to a higher level…or return to the world in another incarnation. It is up to you now."

"If I…return…will I remember my past life?"

The woman slowly shakes her head. "Mostly no. Although, on a rare occurrence you may remember vestiges of the lives you have lived…"

"Lives?"

"Yes, this was not your first embodiment. You have had others."

"I don't remember the others…"

"That is not unusual. Each incarnation will burden your present soul, force you to repeat patterns. Choose carefully. You can go toward a peaceful eternity or try again, as you have done before."

"Did I die violently those other times?"

"No. Although you did not get to live long in any of them. In this in between each soul upon arrival here is given a choice. Those who have met such painful ends at the hands of another often suffer anguish and confusion. It is the confusion that keeps them from reaching a decision. But you have now moved beyond that state and you are again able to choose."

Zephra stands beneath the blue moon contemplating her fate. She is free to live again. Or to go on to heaven for eternity. When she thinks of the latter, it is not something her soul reaches for. She does not crave eternal peace. Maybe if she had lived a long natural life, maybe then she would be ready to move on. But in her last life, she hadn't even made it to thirty. There had been so much she wanted to accomplish. And she feels that desire again. But she also has a heart full of rage. The rage felt good, it energized her.

"I want to go back," Zephra says without any hesitation.

"You are sure? You can have plenty of time to decide. Do not feel you have to rush an answer."

"Yes I am sure. I am ready to go back."

"I wish you a better destiny this time."

"I do, too," Zephra says.

"Close your eyes and you will awaken again…

* * * *

She opens her eyes. The sun is bright yellow. She likes that. The heat feels good and she wants to do nothing but bask in it.

She pants as she sees the water now and she's excited at the thought of leaping into the cool, cool liquid, submerging her face in its depth.

Just then something flies near her nose; it buzzes. It excites her and for the moment, the water is forgotten as she leaps up, giving chase after the strange creature.

"No Dolly, come back. Come back now."

She hears the demand in his voice. He is displeased and she doesn't like to displease him. She really shouldn't chase after the buzzing thing even though it would be so much fun. And there's the water that would be so good to jump into.

But she knows she has to go back where he is standing. She drops her ears, disappointment casting away all the joy. But when she looks up at his face, it is not his mad face. But it's not exactly a happy face either. Then he touches her head and she knows everything is OK.

Someone approaches him and her guard goes up. It is a stranger. She usually can tell whether they are friendly or don't mean any harm. But as the stranger talks with her human, she knows there's something about him she doesn't like. They are talking but she doesn't understand.

Then her human takes out a small stick and offers it to the stranger.

The stranger has lines on his face and his eyes are unkind. When he speaks, there is a gruffness that says he is not friendly. She smells his scent drifting toward her. It is a scent she doesn't like. She wants him away from her human. The stranger sets the tip of the stick on fire and she smells the smoke. Smoke, fire are dangerous. This she knows. She has to convince her human to get away from this man so she speaks.

"Get away from him!" she yells, but as always, her human doesn't understand her words. Instead he gives her the command to be quiet. He's wearing his angry face now. But she doesn't care.

She keeps yelling at the stranger, backing him up against the large tree behind him. She likes the fear on the man's face.

Her human grabs at the long strip that connects to the part circling her neck, and she finally quiets. But she bares her teeth to the stranger, a guttural sound rumbling in her throat. She feels a strong urge to tear at his throat, to rip him apart.

She does not like his face nor his smell; that smell is familiar although she doesn't know why. Long ago. It is the smell of a man who hurt her, she is sure of it…even though she cannot quite remember him.

Her human's voice is distressed as he yanks at the strip restraining her, and the action pulls her back even as she tries desperately to rush at the stranger.

The man is angry and it mixes with the fear. He wants to hit her, she knows this with all her senses. And she wants him to try.

Finally her human pulls her a distance away from the bad stranger, at the same time saying words to the man in the tone that says he's sorry. He sometimes says that to her but this man, who is now walking away, the stick hanging from his mouth as he looks back at her…this man is something she does not have words for.

But her human has angry words for her when they get home.

Bad girl!

She doesn't know the meaning of the words, but she understands that he's upset with her. But the thought of the strange man stays with her even as her human over time loses his anger, rubs her head then turns her over to rub her stomach. But those things that she usually likes for him to do does not settle her sadness. Even when he puts her dinner bowl in front of her, she barely eats, barely tastes the moist bits of flesh.

Because there is something she has to do. She knows that now.

She waits until it is dark. This is the time when her human sleeps. This is the time when she sometimes pretends to go to sleep until it gets really quiet in the dark. Then she goes out the small door made just for her. She usually likes to roll on her back on the soft grass and look up at the shiny thing hanging in the dark sky. It gives light to the darkness.

The light shines in front of her as she walks a familiar path. She passes the houses that she sometimes sneaks behind, sniffing the flowers, playing with the other dogs, sometimes cats.

She keeps walking, knowing that her human will be even more angry at her now. Still she walks on, her strides sure. She knows by memory the path that leads to the park, the place where the water is nice and cool, the place where buzzing creatures fly around the pretty flowers. She likes this place. But she doesn't feel like playing now.

She is full of anger and she does not understand why. But she knows what she has to do. This urgency actually calms her, telling her to take her time. She stops near the tree where the stranger stood and sniffs the air. At first there is nothing. Then she sees the stick the man had in his mouth earlier. It is lying next to something white and crumbled. She has seen her human use something similar to swipe at his nose. She leans down, puts her nose to it; it has the scent of the man, the smell that made her realize she knew the stranger...and that she hates him.

The smell leads her now as much as the light bathing her from the night sky. She moves through the park, past the trees. When the trees are gone, she passes still more houses with bushes and flowers. Through all the smells touching her nose, the man's smell grows even stronger.

There are no other humans outside. Although as she passes the houses, there is light coming from the windows. She sees people moving inside as she walks. Just the shadows of them really. Her ears perk up at the muffled voices. She keeps moving past the houses. It is cooler now, but she is not cold. Not yet. There is no yellow light beaming down to warm her. She should be lying on the soft floor asleep, pictures playing in her head of chasing and fetching. She likes to fetch. Her human enjoys it when she brings the balls back.

She stops at the last house in the line of houses. The stranger's smell is strongest here. She has found him.

She walks up the path to the door. The windows are dark. There is no light surrounding the house and it seems a very bad place, a place she should run from. There are no flowers here. What little grows in the front is scraggly and ugly. She climbs the steps and is at the dark door; she sniffs along the bottom. She whimpers at a memory of that smell.

Not the smell from today.

She freezes up as she feels pain in her stomach, her heart. It burns.

But there is nothing and no one who is the source of this agony. She collapses on her legs and lays on her stomach trying to find strength again. After a while, the bad pain goes away. But she is more angry now. More things are hurtling at her brain, bad pictures of a man, a woman. The man stands over the woman who is bleeding.

The plan develops. There is no way in. He will have to come out.

She lifts her head to the white circle in the sky and howls. And with each howl, she remembers more.

She remembers her name. It is not Dolly.

She is Zephra. That is her name.

The door opens.

The man is standing above her, a scowl sketching his face.

The face is older now but the hatred there is as fresh as when she first saw it years ago.

"What the fuck? Get the hell off my porch before I shoot your ass, you ugly black bitch!" But his hands hold nothing to hurt her.

She growls, a burning rising in her throat. Her lips pull back baring all of her teeth. She wants him to see her hatred. To feel the fear she felt that night. But there is no fear on his face…yet.

He makes a mistake.

He moves out of the protection of the door to kick her but misses. Her aim is surer as she latches onto the offending leg and let her teeth sink through the material covering his flesh. He screams.

"Let go of me, you ugly black bitch. God that hurts!"

But she is hardly through with him. With a force beyond her strength she pulls the leg from beneath him causing him to stumble backward. He falls.

And now it is she standing over his prone body. She remembers looking up into those evil eyes.

The evil is now joined by fear. And pain.

He looks into her own eyes and sees his destiny.

"No," he cries out.

He thinks he is reasoning with a rabid dog. He doesn't realize in these seconds that she's morphed back into the woman he murdered. At least in her mind, her soul. Her consciousness is split between that night and this night.

He stole her dreams that night. The least she can do now is become his nightmare.

The taste of satisfaction mingles with the taste of his blood as she tears into his jugular, tearing the flesh around it. His screams are garbled, full of terror and agony.

She discovers something during her savagery. Something all the moralists have never taught from a pulpit or from an academic dais. Killing can bring joy.

She once gave him that particular pleasure with her screams and pleas. Now the roles are reversed.

He once left her with flesh hanging from her wounds. His flesh now hangs from where she has ripped into his throat, exposing blood, sinew, bone.

She could not know when she decided to come back that she would be given this gift.

There is one last gargle before he convulses. And then he lays still.

She looks down at him, feeling nothing but satisfaction. Her death has been atoned.

She hears the blast before she feels the agonizing fire. It tears into her coat, through her flesh.

She turns her head, blood dripping from her mouth to see a man holding a rifle. He has come to his neighbor's aid.

But it is too late to save her prey, her murderer.

In a way, she has been murdered again, she thinks ironically as she draws in her a ragged breath and collapses on the body. No wheat field this time she muses as she dies once again.

The moon is strange and blue. The river flows silently as the souls walk its shore. The smells of summer and death intertwine as they pique her nose. Strangely, the smells bring her comfort.

She sits on the desiccated remnant of a tree stump.

Things are familiar but she's not sure why.

How long has she been here? What is this place?

A beautiful woman with skin of luminescent onyx meets her eyes, then smiles. She moves…no, glides…over to her.

Who is she?

The woman speaks one word: *Remember.*

And she does.

She remembers everything. Including the face of her murderer, who is now walking among the ring of souls circling the river. He appears anguished. The woman notices Zephra's focus and nods.

"Yes, he is here. Remember, all who suffer traumas at their deaths, especially at the hands of another, come to this place. This is so, no matter the state of that soul. This place knows no virtue or evil. It simply is."

Strangely, Zephra feels no anger and yet, she has no peace. As though her soul is still in flux. She's avenged her death. Shouldn't there now be peace?

But there cannot be. And she begins to understand.

"Will he continue?" Zephra asks.

"Continue?" the woman responds.

"Will he return to another life? To do what he did before?"

"Everyone is allowed their chance at redemption. But if the seed of a soul does not seek deliverance from darkness, then patterns may repeat. He will not be the first murderer to return…and yes, to continue his misdeeds."

"Does he remember…how he died?"

The answer is in her silence.

The man lifts his head for a moment to look over at the onyx woman. His focus moves from her and his eyes finally locks with Zephra's. There is no recognition in them. She is in her human form. She is Zephra, the woman he murdered.

But he does not remember.

Yet she will never forget him. No matter her incarnations.

When he remembers fully, when he remembers everything, the pain of his throat being ripped open just as he ripped open hers long ago…or maybe not that long ago…he will not seek redemption.

He will return to a world full of prey.

And when he does, she will follow. As many times as she can to find her peace.

She will be that woman, that man, that animal. Maybe an eagle with talons who will swoop down to rip his eyes out. And each time, she will know him.

She will be there to stop him. Or at least try.

Because now she knows that he and she have done this before.

An eternal circle ties them together, and they march around and around, like those circling the river. A river of death and sorrow.

She closes her eyes for a second…an eternity…and when she opens them again, he is gone.

His return is swift.

Soon she will follow.

And soon she will return.

To this river.

Until she finds her peace.

NIGHT HAG
Neva Bryan

In American Southern folklore, witches are believed to visit sleeping men, turning them into horses that they ride all night.

Last night
I danced
into his dreams.

Chanted…
Chanted…
Cas. Troi. Tionndadh. Rursus.
Equus!

Slipped my bit
between his lips,
disrobed for the ride.

Rested my currycomb
against his bare back,
slapped a strap
across his neck.

Hooked my thumbs
into his nostrils,
laid my face
against his mane.

He galloped,
galloped
into the wretched black.

Rode hard,
put away wet,
he looked like death
when I left him.

TAKING OUT THE TRASH
D.C. Lozar

As jobs go, washing dishes at a steak restaurant on the Lower East Side of Manhattan wasn't the worst thing a sixteen-year-old dropout could get. My boss, Mr. Rackham, an older guy with a face like aged horsemeat, spat on the ground when I said I'd had trouble in school. What did grades have to do with washing dishes?

I got paid in cash, and it was enough to cover rent and food. My manager, a girl named Emma, was a little older than me and had these fantastic green eyes and the cutest butt you'll ever see. I can say that because all the girls at The Chop House wore short skirts and low cut tops. Again, it wasn't the worst job a dropout could get.

If it hadn't been for the dumpster, I'd have been set.

My crew razzed me when I complained. They said I watched too many horror movies and threatened to lock me in the basement to toughen me up. Most of them worked for the local "Families" and shook down businesses for protection money or sold product. Being in a wheelchair on account of the bullet lodged in my spine ruined my career as a tough guy, but it improved my world viewpoint—short skirts and all.

You'd think being in a chair would make washing dishes easy. It doesn't. I'd have to lock the wheels and pull myself up to reach the plates before twisting my pelvis to scrape the leftover crap, the nasty gristle, into a trash bin. People waste so much food it would make you sick. They order these expensive steaks, tell the chef exactly how to cook it, and then leave half of it uneaten. Don't get me started on the sides. I mean, I think people like the concept of vegetables, but the amount of soggy broccoli and squash that gets tossed is staggering.

Our chef, Nicky, is Slovenian or something so he doesn't speak much English, but he knows how to make a burger. If I was a server, that's what I'd recommend. The bun hides the vegetables, and I've never scraped one of Nicky's burgers into the bin. Burgers are like the perfect food.

So, after unloading the heavy stuff into the garbage, I'd lean over the sink to grab this aluminum hose that sends a jet of steaming hot water at the dishes. I thought it was cool in the beginning. I imagined having superpowers where I could shoot mega-hot water out of my fists at bad guys and watch them melt. Then, I noticed how at the end of the night, my hands bled, and the skin peeled off. I tried wearing gloves, but it didn't help and made it hard for me to roll my chair. So, I sucked it up. Eventually, my hands got all calloused, so I didn't feel anything. I mean, nothing. They worked and all, but you could've lit a match under one of my fingers, and I wouldn't have said boo. Occupational hazard, I guess.

Once I'd gotten all the slime off the dishware, I'd hit the disposal switch and listen to it grind. The plates, bowls, and silverware went on the drying rack for Emma and the other girls to collect, and I'd sit back and listen to tunes while I waited for a new load to pile up. Simple stuff. Right?

Yeah. Except, then there was the trash. About three times a night, the garbage bin would fill up to the rim, and I'd tie off the bag, yank it up onto my lap, and wheel it out into the alley behind the restaurant.

I hated that alley.

It's deserted back there, and you'd think I was worried about getting mugged. That wasn't it. Maybe you'd guess I was scared of the dark. Nope. Was I shot in an alley? Yes. Is it like a PTSD thing with flashbacks? I wish.

It was the damn dumpster.

Every time I went out there, I had to wait for my eyes to adjust. The alley's got one flickering streetlamp at the far west end, narrow brick walls that block out the stars, and puddles of who-knows-what glistening all up and down it. I'd roll down the ramp, hear my wheel splash through one of those pools of liquid, and know my hands would smell like fermented apples, wet cardboard, and rotting meat for the rest of the night. Then, there was this wind, a moaning thing that blew across the back of your neck and left a chill colder than a witch's tit sitting between your shoulder blades. Spooky, right?

That's not the half of it.

Let me tell you about the dumpster.

It was a squat army-green box covered in rust with a heavy plastic lid that I had to lift with one hand while I swung the trash in with my other. Pressed hard against the far wall of the narrow alley, it reminded me of a tic with its head buried in the wall while its butt hung out in the breeze. Maggots, the pale white ones, clung to the red brick around the dumpster, but I never saw any of them on the ground or inside it. Anyway, it gave me the heebie-jeebies the first night I saw it.

Only, it wasn't until my third or fourth week on the job that I figured out why.

You know how you know something's wrong, but your brain has to run down a list of things until it figures out the problem? Like if you see a young girl sitting on some geezer's lap in the subway, and it takes you a minute to realize she's a ventriloquist's dummy, and the guy is on his way to work. It's still creepy, but in a different sorta way.

So, here's my brain running down things.

The alley was too narrow.

So what?

Trash pickup happens once a week. The garbage men pick the bags off the side of the street, and they use the truck on the dumpsters.

And?

There was no way a truck was getting down that alley. It wasn't wide enough for a car.

Okay, my brain argued. They must walk down there and roll the bin to the street, load it into the truck, and roll it back. That made sense, right? It's half-a-city block in either direction, so they would only lose ten minutes from their route every week.

A New York City employee is going to do what?

If I could have bitch slapped my brain, I'd have hauled off. Instead, I told myself it wasn't my problem. The trash disappeared. Someone took it, so why did I care?

That worked for a while.

Then, I started to notice other things about the alley, like, how I'd never seen anybody in it but me—nobody. There wasn't even graffiti back there.

So, here goes my brain again.

Someone must have gated it off.

So, one night I decided to investigate, and I wheel down both ends. No gate. On either side, I come out onto a busy street. From the sidewalk, I can make out the dark outline of the dumpster in the shadows. I squint, and it looks like a hoodlum waiting to jack anyone stupid enough to take the shortcut.

Mystery solved. There were no people cause they were afraid of a shadow. Shut up, brain.

My boss, Mr. Rackham, gave me a raise after six months on the job. He said it was the longest they'd had a dishwasher stay with them. All the other washers just up and disappeared without a word. He understood it was a crappy job, but he hoped I'd let him know when I'd had enough, so he could find a replacement. I promised I would and decided to celebrate by buying a bottle of nutcracker from Jimmy.

Jimmy and I go way back. He was there when I got shot and, although it's sorta his fault for setting up the bad deal, I gotta give him props for sticking around and holding pressure on the wound when everyone else scattered. The cops couldn't pin anything on him, but they hassled him for weeks.

So, I roll up to Jimmy's place on my way home, and we catch up. I tell him about the raise, and he sells me a big bottle. We share it on the porch behind his house, and he tells me how he's getting heat for not bringing in more revenue. He's supposed to start moving some new product, something shipped in from Europe that's bio-engineered to get people hooked. I complain about how I can't feel my hands anymore, about the amount of shit people waste, and how the alley's too damn narrow for the trash to get picked up.

That stops him, and he asks, "So where's it go?"

"I don't know. Somebody takes it."

"Bums?" He took a deep swig from the bottle, coughed, and handed it back. "It's food. Right?"

"Right, but I've never seen anyone down there." I try not to let him see my eyes water as I choke the homemade hooch down. Jimmy made it strong and sold it in lemonade bottles, so you knew it was his. "It's not even tagged."

"You're saying it's pristine, like a virgin alley."

"Not a mark on it," I agreed, trying to guess why he'd care.

"I don't believe it," said Jimmy. "You work for old man Rackham, right?"

Now, I knew. "Leave it, Jimmy. He's alright."

"All the more reason, I need to talk to him," he said slowly, working it out. "The city's a dangerous place, Mike. You know. Good people like him need to be protected."

"They're just sliding," I said, taking another drink to hide my nerves. Jimmy's built like a tank and not half as bright. "They can't afford you."

"He just gave your sorry-ass a raise. I'd say he's doing better than sliding" He took the bottle back and took a long swig. "I'll bet it's rats."

"What rats?"

"I'll bet your dumpster's full of rats, like hundreds of them." He tossed the half-empty bottle at a shadow as it crept around the corner of his neighbor's building. The hairy thing was as big as a dog and twice as quick. It vanished before the bottle shattered. Dark brown fluid stained the brick. "Damn things are everywhere."

"That was my bottle, turd." I was half-buzzed and angry for turning Jimmy onto my boss, so I may have raised my voice. "You owe me!"

One of the neighbors yelled at us to shut up.

"I'll drop it off tomorrow night," he said with a wink.

"You do that, and we're through. He's under my protection."

That got Jimmy laughing so hard he couldn't catch his breath. "What are you going to do? Run over my toes?"

I spun my chair and wheeled away. I threw up on my way home and wondered if Jimmy had spiked our drink with something. Somehow, I made it back to my apartment, can't say how, and collapsed in my bed.

I woke late with my head on fire. Maybe it was a fever, maybe it was the worst hangover I'd ever had, but there was no way I was going to work. I called in, and Emma picked up.

"I'm sorry you're not feeling well." She even sounded cute on the phone, and I considered asking if she'd like to catch a flick. Then this wave of nausea hit me, and I threw up all over my bed while she was still on the phone. Real smooth, player. I spent the rest of the day doing laundry.

When I got to work the next day, Emma was frazzled. I said I was sorry for calling in sick. She jammed a fresh bottle of Jimmy's nutcracker into my hands and walked away. Nicky's left eye was swollen shut, and his knuckles were bruised. He wouldn't talk to me.

Stuff had gone down, and I needed to know where I stood.

So, I knocked on Mr. Rackham's office.

He was slow getting to the door, and I noticed he was limping. I tried saying something, and he jammed a wad of twenties into my shirt pocket. I followed him into the kitchen, where he told Emma he was going home for the night. I mumbled something about being sorry, and he spat on my shoes before storming off.

I poured the nutcracker down the drain. The stuff smelled like fruit punch mixed with gin, cheap and deadly.

When I wheeled the night's first load of trash into the alley, I found my new "boss" leaning against the dumpster. He grinned wide, his teeth as pale as the maggots on the wall. His dirty red backpack sat in a puddle of shadow between his feet.

"I told you to back off," I said, rolling over.

"Did your girlfriend give you the bottle? I told her she'd better give you a kiss along with it." Jimmy licked his thin lips.

"I'm asking you as a friend, Jim. Move on."

"But this is my new office." Jimmy spread his arms wide. "It's off the map, totally hidden, like Batman's cave or something, and your back door is the only way in or out. If I see someone coming and they don't have an appointment, I slip out through your kitchen. If bad news comes at me through Rackham's, you wheel out here and warn me. It's perfect."

"You're going to deal from back here?" This was bad. If Jimmy made even a little cash, he'd never leave.

"Hey, relax. It's not like I'm not going to help you out," said Jimmy as he took the trash bag from my lap and swung it effortlessly into the dumpster. "Friends, right?"

"No." I tensed. There wasn't anything Jimmy could do to me that was worse than losing my legs. "We're done."

"What?" Jimmy's scraggly beard bristled as he bent down. "Didn't that little skank give you your kiss? Do I need to explain things to her again?"

"She kissed me," I lied. Now I knew why Emma had been so cold. Then, reluctantly, I added, "Thanks."

"That's my boy," sneered Jimmy, pulling down the collar of his T-shirt. There were fingernail marks on his neck. "I had to show her how to do it properly. She's a hellcat, but we came to an understanding."

I took the twenties out of my pocket and threw them on the wet ground. "You're an asshole."

"Takes one to know one," agreed Jimmy.

I waited for as long as I could before taking out another bag of garbage. Jimmy was sitting on top of the dumpster with his back against the wall. He was smoking, and the orange embers made his face look like a jack-o-lantern in the dark. He sprang down as I rolled over. The plastic lid that had been struggling with Jimmy's weight recoiled with a wet flump.

"I get what you're saying about this alley being weird," whispered Jimmy. "I can't even hear the street."

"Figured you'd like that?" I kept my voice cold. "No one to hear the gunshots if something goes wrong."

"Normally, yeah," he agreed, ignoring the bait. He lifted the dumpster's lid, so it rested against the wall and tossed the trash inside. The odors rushing out of that dark maw reminded me of the dead squirrel we'd found in the park as kids——bloated by the summer heat, covered in flies, and stiff with rigor mortis. The crew had done rock-paper-scissors, and Jimmy lost. He stuck a stick into the thing, and it had burst open like a three-day-old balloon splattering us with rot. We'd spent the rest of the day smelling like corpses. "But it's too quiet."

"Maybe you aren't welcome?"

"Like Hell. I've already made two deals," said Jimmy. He took a long drag on the cigarette before flicking it into the dumpster. It hissed on something wet. "Did you get any more kisses?"

I grunted and rolled back inside.

I won't say I liked having Jimmy do business in the alley, but it did make throwing out the trash less disturbing—initially.

To hear Jimmy tell it, his alley was the center of New York's drug trade. He had more customers than he had product, and they were falling over each other to get an appointment with him. Only, every time I went to throw out the trash, he was alone. After a few days, he started acting funny— twitchy and scared. I'd open the door, and he'd be right there waiting for me like a scared puppy asking why it had taken me so long to come back out. After that first night, he stopped helping me dump the trash and hung back from the dumpster.

"You ever notice any noises back here?" Jimmy stood behind me as I tossed in a bag. He was nursing one of his nutcrackers. "Like sucking or chewing sounds."

"No." I shook my head. "But I never stayed long."

"Right. That makes sense." Jimmy's voice was hushed. "I only notice it after you've gone back inside."

"Notice what?" I turned around.

"It's like it knows it has to wait until you're gone to eat." His deep-set eyes accused the dumpster.

"Are you sampling your shit?" You had to be straight up with Jimmy. It's what he understood. "I thought you said that stuff was chemically engineered or something?"

"Just a sprinkle." Absently, Jimmy kicked the grimy backpack at his feet. The bottom of it was moist from the wet cement. "It adds a zing to the juice."

The "Families" frowned on any of their sellers becoming users. If they found out, Jimmy would have a lot more to worry about than imaginary noises in the dark. "It stinks out here, Jim. Come inside. Get some fresh air."

"No. This is real, Mike. I've been studying it." Jimmy took another drink from the bottle. "If you stand here and wait, you can feel it breathe. It's slow and long. The inhale is over there by the light, and it exhales on the other side."

"That's called a breeze, turd." I had dishes piling up. I couldn't babysit him all night. "You gonna come in or what?"

"This is my office." Jimmy's eyes narrowed, suspicious. "Are you saying I can't handle my job? I've got six more appointments tonight."

"Maybe it's the rats?"

"Maybe." Jimmy let his jacket fall to the side so I could see the butt of an automatic sticking out of his belt. "I'm watching for them."

The pistol made me nervous. Blame it on my PTSD or whatever, but I was glad to get back inside, back to washing dishes and stealing glances at Emma. The kitchen was a place I understood: Scrape, wash, dry, and repeat. There were no eerie dumpsters or bad smells inside, and I could blast anything that looked nasty with steaming hot water. I worked hard, kept my head down, and apologized to Mr. Rackham, Nicky, and Emma every chance I got.

Eventually, they stopped giving me the cold shoulder, and things got back to normal. Emma said I was one of the hardest workers she'd ever met, and I got another raise from Mr. Rackham. Nicky started making me burgers again, and we shared a few laughs, although I'm not sure what the joke was about. Things were routine, steady, and most nights, I think everyone but me forgot Jimmy was out back doing business.

Then we had a run of slow nights. I was all caught up with the dishes, and the dining room was empty, so the servers were hanging out with

Nicky and me in the kitchen. The girls were complaining about the tips and wondering if their skirts needed to be shorter. I voiced my opinion and got some giggles.

The gunshots were muffled, thumping sounds that echoed around the kitchen and made us freeze. We looked at the alley door.

Mr. Rackham burst out of his office and glared at me as if I'd pulled the trigger or something. We knew we couldn't call the police, so I told them to hang out in the front of the store, and I'd check things out.

I found Jimmy standing ankle-deep in a pothole in the alley. His eyes were frantic, desperate. He had his pistol out and aimed at the dumpster. It had two deep gashes in it, and they were leaking rivulets of black fluid.

There was no one else around.

"You okay, Jim." I kept my voice calm.

"No! I am not okay!" He seemed unsteady on his feet. He tried to step forward out of the puddle and almost fell. "Where have you been? It's hungry."

Being in a chair, I pay close attention to potholes and things like that, and there had never been one where Jimmy was standing. All the same, that's what he was standing in, filled to the rim with alley piss. "What are you talking about?"

My brain began to work on the pothole problem.

Where had it come from? Had Jimmy knocked it out so he could hide his money? Where would he have gotten a jackhammer?

"Go get the trash!" He waved the pistol at me. His finger twitched on the trigger, and suddenly my brain didn't care about the pothole. "Hurry!"

I went back inside, pulled the garbage bag up, tied it off, and set it on my lap. There wasn't much in it, maybe a couple of steak dinner leftovers and some half-eaten buns.

Emma stuck her head in through the swinging door that led to the dining room. She looked worried. "Are you alright?"

"Yeah. It's nothing." I flashed her a smile and hoped it looked confident. "I think Jimmy is going batty from being out in the dark so long."

Emma edged her way into the kitchen. She glanced at the alley door. "You mean he's scared of the dark or something."

"Or something." I could tell she was thinking about how Jimmy had made her practice kissing him that first night. "He's been sampling his product."

She nodded; the gears turned behind her emerald eyes. "Bad trip?"

"He's acting paranoid," I agreed, seeing how that made sense. "He thinks the dumpster's alive."

"So," she said with a slow wink. "If it took you a while to get back to him, he'd be upset."

I nodded, remembering Mr. Rackham's limp and Nicky's black eye. "He'd probably piss his pants."

Slowly, seductively, Emma took the nearly empty trash bag out of my hands and let it fall on the floor. Just as slowly, she sat down on my lap and eased her smooth arms around my neck. "That'd be a real shame."

We kissed for a long time. She smelled of smoke and bourbon. My hands were numb, so I couldn't appreciate things as much as I wanted, but I still had a good time. I think we both did.

A few more gunshots went off, and I started to pull away. She shook her head. So, we kept on going.

Finally, breathless, she stood up. "Make sure that asshole knows I kissed you."

Guilty, I said. "I had nothing to do with that."

"I know, Tiger." She said as she slipped back through the door to the dining room.

Three more shots went off as I retrieved the trash bag off the floor. I figured Jimmy had used more than a sprinkle of his product in his nutcracker. The fourty-five had seven rounds, so it should be safe to go outside as long as he didn't have another clip. I'd tell him there'd been a rush of customers, and so I hadn't been able to get away.

When I unlocked and opened the door, I didn't see Jimmy. I assumed he'd freaked and run on home, so I rolled down the ramp and into the alley. The entire thing was wet with dark water. So, my brain did its thing.

One of Jimmy's bullets must have hit a water line.

Where? There was nothing back there but a brick wall.

Shut up, brain.

The slimy alley juice got all over my hands, but what did I care—I had a girlfriend.

Grinning, I lifted the dumpster lid and tossed the bag inside. There were seven holes in its surface, but none of them were leaking fluid.

My hands felt tingly, which was weird since I was used to them being numb. I wiped them off on my jeans and looked down. My bones flashed up at me through the missing flesh on my palms.

Freaking out, I started backing my chair away from the dumpster when I heard it. It was a slow sucking sound, like how someone pulls on the end of a rib to get at the marrow. I looked up and down the alley, but it was empty.

"Mike," came Jimmy's voice. It was weak and choked with fear. "You've gotta help. Pull me out."

I looked down, squinted, and saw Jimmy's head and part of his right arm sticking out from under the dumpster. There was a big puddle of black water all around him. He struggled to lift his head, and the skin on his face oozed away, just like how the grease on the plates melted when I sprayed them. "Jimmy?"

"I told you it was hungry," said the bones and sinew still attached to Jimmy's skull. "I tried running, but my feet were gone."

I grabbed what was left of his arm. I pulled hard, using my other hand to roll us back. He slid forward and then stopped. He was holding onto his backpack with the bones of his left arm, and the bag was caught up on the underside of the dumpster.

Then, something powerful yanked us back toward the wall. It caught me off guard, and I almost fell out of my chair into that deep puddle. "Shit!"

"I told you," said Jimmy as tears rolled down his ruined face. "It was hungry. I shot it, but then I fell down. It ate my feet, Mike."

I yanked hard, but it was like trying to take a bone away from a dog. Something growled at us from beneath the dumpster, and I almost left him right then and there. Only, Jimmy had stayed with me when I got shot, so I locked my wheels. "Kick at it! Try to wriggle free!"

"I can't feel anything," cried Jimmy. "It makes you numb, so you don't know it's eating you."

I heaved back, trying not to think about the skin and muscle sliding off my hands, and got his torso out from under the thing. Then, there was a pop just like when that squirrel's belly burst, and Jimmy's intestines and organs spilled out like a broken piñata. He looked up at me, hopeful, not knowing why we were able to slide away from the dumpster. Great spurts of aortic blood gushed out of his upper torso, and I watched dumbly as the light went out of his eyes.

Thick tentacles, sloppy oozing things with malformed suckers snaked out from under the dumpster. They wrapped around what was left of Jimmy and sucked him right out of my hands.

I watched Jimmy's head bubble and pop as it dissolved in the puddle of salivary fluid beneath the dumpster.

I listened to the slow sucking, gnawing sound it made as it ate.

I smelled the gagging aroma of rotting shit and blood.

I turned and rolled back inside.

Emma said they found me at the sink, spraying steaming hot water directly at my hands. The doctor said I was lucky. He was able to save three of the fingers on each hand, but the third-degree burns mean I'll never feel anything with them. Mr. Rackham said he still can't find a dishwasher as good as me. Since I've been under psychiatric observation, three more of them have up and disappeared. He said I've got a job if they ever let me out.

Nicky made a joke. We laughed, and I still don't know what he said.

No one's seen Jimmy since that night. The word is he got "disappeared" for using the product instead of selling it.

I told Mr. Rackham I might take him up on his offer.

Hey, for a dropout on the Lower East Side of Manhattan, it wasn't the worst job you could get.

I just had to be careful to avoid the puddles when I took out the trash.

WHAT IS THE SEASON?

Ashley Dioses

What are the stars, what is the moon
That shines upon this night?
What spoken spell and written rune
Can summon forth a wight?

What is the time, what is the season
That graces all us now?
What daemons enter, barring reason,
To aid me in my vow?

Is it Midwinter, eve of May,
Or even Samhain yet?
What is the sabbat of the day
Where fae and I have met?

What spell to cast, what circle drawn
Can I trace out tonight?
I must consult the dusk and dawn,
The stars, the moon, the light.

My ancient grimoire opens wide
Awaiting its sole sire.
What necromancy from inside
Can sate my dark desire?

ARTHUR WARDROBE AND ASIA ANASTACIA: A LOVE STORY

Andrew Darlington

This morning, when she awoke, she decided to be a snail. A slug in wraparound body-armour. She extrudes trembling eyestalks that quiver this way and that, sensing aromas, detecting shifts in the shape of air, and rainbow ripples of sunlight prisming through shattered glass. The wall is burned ash-black. She slip-slithers on a trail of ooze in defiance of boring old gravity, grazing on particle-packages of food only snails can see...

I know this. I can see it. When I shock up out of delirium I see Mom and my current Dad looking down at me. I know the concerned expressions that their faces say to me. It's happened again. The fits are becoming more extreme and frequent. It's such a terrible affliction. Why do we have to bear this terrible curse? Why us Grud, why us? If this is a phase I'm going through, when does it end and move smoothly into the next phase? Is there a chart you can consult, a Venn diagram, or a graph that indicates you are here, moving up this sharp incline towards that point there, after which you move through into the next phase where all this confusion is resolved. When does that set in?

Today she is called Asia Anastacia. Sometimes she is Samuela Stretch. Once she was J Peasemould Gruntfuttock. I like that name. I love that one. She lives in a place that is not a place, and talks to me in a voice that is not a voice. She sees with second sight. And she comes to me in colours. Today she is mauve, which is playful and funny. I wonder what it's like to be a snail.

I write this because I can still write. By touching the keys, I can still make words...

The day is long, and getting longer. Sometimes... like snail eyestalks, time just oozes in different directions, and you lose track. Pieces of it break away and spin off like dandelion seeds. I've stayed out longer than I should. At first there were three of us. We range up across the retail park through the alleys between the big black warehouses full of junkies and spiders and muggers and crystal spider-junkies, and out through the gap in the fence to where the culvert threads up through bowers of sick trees. We aren't supposed to come here, but of course, we do. There's sloping concrete, but it's rotting where moss and weeds explode up through ancient crumbling cracks. The water smells like farts, and it burns your fingers if you touch it. Epsilon Stealth gets scared and heads back. We've never been this far. It's dangerous. But we climb up between the briars and tangled nettles to what looks to be the top.

Except when we get there we find out it's not the top at all, but there's more paths and pathlessness leading even further up. While the sludge-grassy shoulder we're on slopes away on either side. There's an old car that's flaking into rust and being eaten by weeds. I hear it screaming. There's a wet pile of old catalogues, the pages stuck together, with pictures of tall ladies in long coats with shiny shoes. And a smashed c-screen. It's creepy the way that the people inside the screen live their lives even when no-one's playing it, even when no-one's flicking the controls. They're still there, even when it's shattered, the characters leak and dribble out into the real world. Next to the c-screen there are empty bottles, with green stuff growing inside them. The green stuff has eyes that look out at us as we walk by.

Face-Ache says 'Nadgered Badgers. We should be getting back.' There are bad guys here who hurt you. But I'm still curious. So now there's only me. And I angle down sideways like a crab. Looking up, there are lights moving in the sky. They carve curves and intersecting circles around each other. Every now and then, one of them flares and vanishes. One Dad told me the war continues, no-one told the robots to stop, so they still war together. I watch. Tracing patterns.

At the same time, I feel Asia stirring, restlessly in the back of my thoughts. But soft. Not in the hurting way that they call the delirium. She's always there. She's always been there. Sometimes I fight her, sometimes I try to block her out. But later, unsuspecting, when I lie in bed and close my eyes, she creeps back in again. Through the pores of my skin. Beneath my eyelids. In through my tear-ducts. Into the retina of my dreams. 'Hello Asia. Who are you today?'

The stone hits the side of my face and opens up a sharp cut. I turn. Three of them, with evil intent. Boogiemen who sleep under the bridge, who stink of puke and piss. With black hoods and inhalers, scary-strange. I shoulda gone back when I had the chance. People told me. They warned me. Too late now. I skedaddle as fast as I can. They laugh their wicked wrecked laughs, throw garbage and sticks, yell and taunt. Three of them. They fan out behind me and give chase. They eat kids. When they can't catch sewer-rats they catch alley-cats or feral junkyard dump-dogs, or they skin and roast kids on their fires beneath the bridge and chew on their bones, wiping greasy fingers on dirty T-shirts. I run. I run. I run. Until I can run no more.

Then I stop, slouching, hands on knees, slurping in big gasps of breath. The cut on my forehead bites with sharp nibbles of pain. It's sticky-warm to the touch. I'm light-headed, blood racing at my temples. In that same moment, my heart leaps and shivers with fear, excitement runs up and down my spine. For I'm no longer alone, there's another presence here. And I know it's her voice. Her time to return. Time to submerge deep into our shared consciousness. Blood on my face. A choking sob, an animal sound. She begins, the brainwraith that creeps into my head. "Hello Asia Anastacia, How goes it?" "How would you have it go?" answers the voice in my head.

I can feel you, trying to get in. This is the way you always arrive. When I'm writhing and shuddering, stiffening into a puppet stretched raw on cold wire. She's seeping in through the cracks, inveigling her way into my mind, striving to get a hold on our world. Trying to take me over. My hands tense into claws. My back arches, muscles quivering. As though I'm submerging in tide and unable to breathe, no longer conscious of breathing or of my heart beating. The paroxysm jerks my limbs into cramped spasms, more frantic, less reflexive. "Why does it always hurt when you come to me?"

"Because something inside you still resists me. But now we're closer than ever."

"Are you near?"

"We are very close to each other. I can see you. Do you doubt your senses?"

"It's rude to stare."

"You shouldn't look the way you do, then maybe I wouldn't."

I wake to my own sweat-stench. My tongue raw where I've chewed it. Spitting the salt-sour blood taste from my mouth. A warm spreading wet patch at the crotch of my pants where I lost control and pissed myself.

And stars. How long was I out? Moments... or more? When I resurface I'm staring up through dusk-light at stars. Guessing at their names. Watching them, until they start to crawl in front of my eyes, rearranging into the letters that make up my name. ART. I sit up. From here I can see across the huge incoherence of Satan's Circle. Somewhere out beyond it is our trailer park. Can't see it, but its there. It's in the loop where my current Dad picks up thumbuddies on the iWay, and loots their haulage.

I can go round, in a big arc. I can do that. But it's late already, and getting later. I'm gonna catch hell. The quickest route between two points is... we all know, that straight line from here to there. Just that there's the Circle midpoint. And the barrenland is an ulcer. We don't go there. What secrets conspire in that strange and terrible toxic blot? Or what if it's just superstition? Mom will be mad if I'm out late, and I'm already late. I'll never forgive myself if I back down, and don't find out. You reach a point where you gotta grow up, and move beyond. I'm thirteen, I gronk that. And that time is now. So, I thunk I just changed my mind.

I slither carefully, spraggle-legged in damp underwear. Down into the blasted city. There's no exact terminator where you step over from here into there. An outbreak of grass and weeds ebb in over asphalt and concrete, a pandemic of shrubs with long spiky tendrils blur the margins. The people who once lived here chose stupid names like "Cowslip Meadows," "Sycamore Grove," "Paradise Corner," and "Butterfly Fields" for what's now derelict implosions of dead masonry. Spaced by empty buildings and tall black spires.

Everything feels so sharp. They say terrorist suicide bombers were implanted with self-destruct devices programmed to detonate in response to chemical changes in the brain. So the zone is perfectly circular, centred on the blast-point. The distorting intensity was such they opened rifts to the Collywobble bubbleverses that coexist within ours, simply one molecule out of phase. It's all to do with relly-tivities, drawn on sacred algorithms, blasphemous poetry and mystic psycho-geography. This is the mind-field of time-maggots, and worse. Flaming spears of sun melt into diamond skulls with jeweled eyes, the offspring of chaos whose hideous gaze burns all who dare trespass against them. Or something like that.

The sound of a hurdy-gurdy. I look down, and there's a green lizard. A lizard with two heads. No, it's two lizards. Wrong again… the second lizard is a girl. A girl the size of my index finger. I look down again, and there's a single green lizard. Instead, a hole shimmers in the air. A figure emerges. The same girl, the size of my index finger. She has flowers in long tangles of hair, and she's dressed in nothing more than gauzy diaphanous strands. She comes in colours. Today she's soft saffron. I expect monsters, and what I get is Tinkerbell.

"Asia Anastacia, is it you?"

"You were maybe expecting, Titania, Queen of all the Fairies?"

"Is this the form you've chosen for me to see today?"

"Sometimes, I glow. Is this not pleasing to you? I can be something else if you prefer." She alights on my outstretched palm. Less feather-light, more a ray of falling light.

"If you're my imaginary friend, how come I can see you?"

"Have you ever considered that maybe it's me imagining you?"

I get a shiver up my spine. It's that same feeling as when you realize something's standing directly behind you… watching, waiting. Some claim that escaped biosplices find refuge in those shattered towers. I don't like talking dogs. The unleashed dogs of war. And they say that gibbons roam in gangs to steal food and shiny things. There are also residual images of the dead, and of beings distilled from mental projections of matter, they need to feed on flesh to maintain their form. The shades of dead children weep in every shop doorway, little girls in floral dresses with long golden plaits. They clutch grubby teddybears. So sad it breaks your heart, until you feel the need to comfort and reassure them, but as you get close they grow and expand with alligator teeth and bear-claws and multiple whipping tentacles to slash and devour.

So we go tippy-toe. Me and Asia. Deeper than it's wise to go. This does not feel safe. This is what happens when reality fails. She dances in drizzling storms of dandelion seeds. Looking up between empty towers, lights scratch patterns in the sky, moving between stars. They pirouette curves and intersect circles around each other. Every now and then, one of them flares and dies. An aerial conflict that never ceases.

"Do you talk to others, or only me?"

"There are others. I can touch them. I can feel they're out there. I catch glimpses of their lives, of what they're seeing and thinking. But none of them are as special as we are." She pauses "Shut me up if it's none of my business, but I'm curious. Can you remember when we began?"

I'm perplexed by her question. "I can never remember a time when there wasn't 'us'. When Daddy Bigbad beat me, I was hurting and crying, but you were there to help me."

"I'm here now. Never forget."

"I'm glad, Asia. I'm glad you're here."

Severed hands scuttle like scorpions, or perhaps they are scorpions? Swarming psi-bugs ripple like ants. Time-spheres settle across city contours from impossible end-of-time futures. The sky is raining a silt of monsters, a billion kilos of ghastly monsteroso flesh that crashes down around and upon us. We're gonna get munched by a nastysaurus. We're part of the food-chain. Protein, amino acids, calcium, carbohydrates. A snacklet, no more. They know I'm here. They sense thermal radiation, like a snake does. They're talking to their next meal.

Sound. A quiet rustling in the dry leaves. It stops, rustles, and slithers again. A snake sound. Nothing more than a rustling. Movement. Then it slithers again, a long slow dragging in the leaves. There are yells. The Boogiemen who sleep under the bridge, they followed us. I take to my heels, dodge between alleyways choked with garbage and undergrowth. I can hear them behind me. Breath roars hot in my throat. For a moment I fear that I'm alone, that I've lost Asia in our mad panicky rush. But no, she's here with me.

"Where are you, Asia?"

"I'm here. Can't you see me?"

"No. I mean, where are you really really really?"

We're close to the centre now. Me and Asia. And the closer we get, the spookier it gets. At its very core, the city is a puddle of melted glass. Irradiated towerblocks of fused crystal. Cars frozen into seamless glaze. Screaming faces fused into reflecting planes, preserved forever at their instant of extinction. Locked into their temporal-stasis. Time accelerates, crumbling stone, rusting steel. Reach out, touch its smoothness, they'll grasp your hand and drag you into their time-slow glassy continuum. An ice-thin world of glistening surfaces.

I've heard tell about Robotic Policemen on remote navigational nodes who hand out Jaywalking tickets to a nonexistent population. They lock you up in a holding cell pending further instructions that never come, from flawed part-lobotomised fragments of reformatted artificial intelligence. Shifting electrical and magnetic fields. And there are huge mutant blossoms that exhale alluring narcotic perfume that also plants seeds deep inside your lungs, where they germinate and grow. While there's always a black rain of chemicals eternally suspended in the haze. In what drug-addled fugue-state does all this make the slightest sense?

And asquat at its very absolute centre, at a nexus of worlds, there's a being of evil intelligence, whether plant or animal, I know not. And by the time someone else passes by, it could be too late, and that monstrous entity will have grown too strong to combat.

I pause for breath, leaning up against an ash-black wall by an intersection. Then the fist hits me, knocks me numb sideways and down. Gasping in a sprawl. He's stood over me, the Boogieman. I can smell dead animals on his breath. I can smell the stale stink of puke and old beer. He wears a hood, but the glimpses I catch of his face are a horror-show. Skin flaking and peeling like radiation leprousy, open suppurating sores and boils, shattered yellow-brown teeth.

"On your feet, boy." Slurred, as though his mouth doesn't function properly.

I know he's going to hit me again, but I do it anyway. Like they shuffle to the electric chair to be strapped in. Like they climb the steps to the gallows. Like they dig their own grave-trenches as the firing squad waits. As though we can't believe it'll happen. As though, no, they can't possibly do this thing to me. My head is numb. Nothing hurts.

I stand up. I look at him. He leers at me. Then hits me full in the face with his balled fist. Everything blanks out. The impact flashes across my head. I'm crumpled again, an aching thing on the dirty ground. Eyes glistening, but determined not to cry. He laughs a mad cracked laugh. There are two other Boogiemen moving in behind him. He takes a deep hit from his narco-inhaler with an expression of obscene glee, and starts into unbuckling the belt of his pants …

Light. A flood of light. He looks up. There's an aerial collision above the towers, a detonation. A scream like the planet's coming apart. A burst of flames. An incandescent comet hurtles down, buzz-saw blades spinning like vicious martial-arts rotors, smashing into the junk and desolation behind him. There are always sparks moving in the sky. They carve curves and intersecting circles around each other. Every now and then, one of them flares and vanishes. This one has disintegrated into lethal shards that rain down onto the city, bristling with ruptured machine-parts, fins, nacelles, circuit-boards, kill-ware weaponry.

He backs off. His eyes are luminous. The ground between us splits, like opening jaws. Seismic shockwaves ripped by impact wrench a deep gaping fissure, and another behind him. He yells like a trapped animal. I haul in, back up against the ash-black wall. I can see a long long way down into the opening rift. It's seething with geysers of white-hot magma. The shattered aircraft fragment, skewered into the surface as high as two men, it smoulders, spurting gouts of fluid like blood from a severed limb, then detonates in thermo-blasts of distortion, a gale of searing heat and sonic roar. Like blast-furnace doors suddenly wrenched open. Like standing in the heart of a sun going nova. The Earth comes apart. Walls of flame. My eyes are slammed shut. Still I see it. Burning back through my retina, scalding my brain. I feel the hair on my head and my eyebrows crisp and wilt in the heat.

I daren't look. Everything burns. Sky. Towers. Ground. Walls. Nothing but flame.

Eventually I open my eyes a cautious crack. It's all gone. Leaving no trace. He's standing in a protective half-crouch a way away. Another Boogieman behind him, crouching, head in hands. The third has scuttled as fast as he can.

A pause. A stillness. But if I saw all of that, so did they. We all saw it.

He's hung on indecision. Then there's the sharp crack of gunfire, and a bullet sprangs off the weed between his legs. That's all he needs. He turns and bolts back towards wherever he came from.

I cower where I'm lying. A man in dungarees and a floppy straw hat emerges. He's nursing an antique double-barrel firearm in the curve of his arm.

"Arthur? Arthur Wardrobe? Don't be frightened. She told me you were here. Asia told me you needed help." He has the sharp yet curiously faraway look to his grey eyes that betray the dreamer. Both lulling, and reassuring.

It's only now I begin sobbing. He smiles. He leads the way. I follow him. We cross the alley, in through a shattered-glass foyer into an empty building. There are wide flights of steps going up. We climb to the first terrace, and then higher still. Maybe this is not wise?

"You live here?" I venture. We're walking down a corridor with closed doors lining each side.

He pauses outside one particular door. "I don't know what you're thinking, but I can guess," he says. "I'm not going to try to explain or persuade. Perhaps I just want to hear myself talk to keep from thinking too much. Any time you want me to stop, just say so."

I don't understand, but I nod anyway. He keys the security and leads me inside. A middle-aged woman looks up and smiles as we enter. We are in clean kitchen-space, with the aroma of warm food. He closes and locks the door behind us. Momentarily I feel trapped.

"This is the only place we can live, and feel safe" he says softly. "This is where we can securely take care of Asia without people accusing or condemning us. The three of us. Just the three of us. And we live fine. There are rabbits. Some of the supermarts still have food-cans. The rad-levels are toxic, but we knew from the start we'd never have Asia for long. So it's important to us. I'm glad she had you. You were a good friend. I'm so very glad you were there for her."

"Asia did all that, didn't she? She created all those things that saved me from the Boogiemen?"

The woman—Asia's mother, crouches down on her heels, so she's looking me directly in the eyes, she wipes a trace of blood from my forehead with the corner of her dishcloth, and puts her hand on my shoulder. "She'd never done anything on that scale before, Arthur. But she loved you. She knew you needed her help. It took everything she had. It drained her."

It's then I realize. Asia's voice has gone. As though she can never return. And I feel an emptiness. A silence.

Standing, her mother indicates a chair beside the kitchen table. She ladle's thick stew from a steaming saucepan into a white bowl, and pushes it across to me. I think I'm not hungry. Bruised and sick to my gut. But as soon as I munch a juicy mouthful I have to eat it all.

She smiles. "You live in the trailer park by the iWay, don't you Arthur? We know, because she told us all about you. When you've finished eating, Walt will see you safely on your way through the zone, to the perimeter, where you can get back home. Alright?"

"Can I see Asia first?"

They exchange meaningful glances. "She's in her room. How did she appear to you, the last time you saw her?"

"She comes in colours. She was saffron. She was Tinkerbell."

"Better you remember her that way, Arthur."

They're as good as their word. Once I've finished the stew, and used their toilet, the father—Walt, takes his shotgun. Her mother holds me close. I swear she's crying. I say "thank you, and goodbye." He leads me back down to the street level. Dusk is thickening. Leaves are blowing along empty boulevards. Stars dance fireflies above the horizon. He doesn't say much, just leads the way along dark canyon alleys and across shattered bridges, around fallen rubble and rainwater lagoons where asphalt has sunk into deepening hollows. Once or twice he signals us to pause, drawing back into sheltering shadows, as something I can't quite see lumbers past. Eventually we emerge on the zone's far side without incident. I start to recognize where I am.

I say "thank you," and he disappears back into the trackless wastes of Satan's Circle. I watch until he's out of sight. Back at the trailer Mom and my current Dad don't even seem to realize I've been gone. I head for my bunk. I'm tired and need to sleep. But sleep won't come. I lie awake listening to the sounds of the night. Remembering Asia Anastacia. And the last glimpse I saw of her as I passed her room returning from the toilet. I couldn't resist the urge to look. She lay in a railed cot, the kind you'd keep a toddler in. She was white. She has no limbs. Her head is a mass of tumours.

I write this because I can still write. By touching the keys, I can still make words…

I focus my thoughts. I concentrate hard. I send out a message. "Hello Asia. Who are you today?" And I wait for her to reply…

To the memory of Walter M Miller

SNACK TIME
Franklyn Searight

It was an arduous ride from Chicago's Union Station to the more leisurely environs of Birmingham, Michigan. With the constant rumble and clickety-clack of the locomotive chewing up the intervening mileage, even a short snooze was impossible for Michael Duffy. He had been unable to sleep for a single moment throughout the entire seven-and-a-half hour trip.

And, adding to the constant noise was the continuous commotion caused by two undisciplined children in the seats behind him, frequently arguing and yacking, both at the same time. They had joined his passenger car with their mother shortly after he had settled in and had not stopped the hubbub for a moment, it seemed, just as they probably never ceased at home or at school, either. The parent, or caretaker, still in her early thirties, was completely oblivious to the obnoxious terrors, seldom raising her eyes from the book she was reading, barely aware they even existed.

Duffy had arrived in this middle-sized community on the outskirts of Detroit to begin a new job, summoned there by his older brother, a carpet dealer by trade and the proprietor of his own developing business which needed a responsible employee to assume the clerical and managerial duties of the clerk who had held the position. This was a job almost designed specifically for Michael Duffy, himself a rug merchant for the last few years and well acquainted with most aspects of the business. The idea of working for and with his older sibling, of course, had made the job offer even more enticing.

Duffy vacated the locomotive at the Troy depot, the mother and her pair of horrors remaining on board, continuing to a distant destination, and crossed a few streets to the city park where he found a hard bench upon which to sit. He placed his single valise at his feet—the remainder of his possessions being shipped at a later date—drew in a deep breath and shook his head, thinking of the impossible twosome he had left behind, their constant clamber and chatter still ringing in his mind. He enjoyed being with children, but too much was more than enough. It was much quieter now, here in the sylvan setting with no distractions to scramble and scatter his thoughts. He extended his legs and bent slightly backward, appreciating the coolness of the breeze.

He considered whether to check into the local YMCA, just a few blocks away, or continue to sit where he was for a spell and recover from what he considered the ordeal of the seven-hour trip. From the side pocket of his suitcoat, he withdrew the remnants of his lunch, a roast beef sandwich, slightly crushed, and a pickle he had chewed off at the end. He could finish these and consider it his dinner, or leave and walk to the Golden Arches he spied a block away and order something a bit more substantial from Mc-Donalds. He was not a big eater, ordinarily, but even what he had with him might not be enough. He could order a Big Mac and maybe a side salad to hold him until breakfast time the next day.

He made his decision and was about to take the first bite when:

"Hey, Mister," called a thin voice, "you gonna eat it all?"

Duffy turned his head around…and looked down…his eyes coming to rest upon a little boy standing behind hm. He was a lad of perhaps seven or eight years old and not much taller than the back of the park bench. He was dressed in a tattered pair of dark slacks and a wrinkled shirt, white at one time but now smeared with blobs of dirt and an assortment of varied-colored stains. Blue eyes were set in the midst of a cherubic face and peered at him without blinking or noticeable movement.

"Where did you come from?" Duffy asked.

"From down there," said the slender lad, pointing with a begrimed finger to a large saucer-shaped iron lid covering a large hole in the ground, presumably a part of the city's sewer system.

"Good one. You're teasing me, aren't you, boy? You mean you live over *there,* don't you?"

"No, sir. I mean *down there.*"

"But it's a sewer, boy. You can't be from down there!"

"Course, I am. It's where I live, ain't it? Me and my sisters come out about this time every day and look for food. It's almost supper time, ain't it?"

"Guess it is. What's your name, boy?"

"Jimmy. What's yours, Mister?"

"Name's Michael. You can call me Mike."

"Ain't you got a last name, Mister? I don't."

"Duffy is the last name. What do you mean, you don't have one?"

"Means I don't have one. No mother; no father; no last name."

"Well, isn't that a shame? And you want the rest of my sandwich—that it?"

"If you don't mind, sir. Me and my sisters are always hungry; I'll share it with them."

"Will you now? You're a very generous boy, Jimmy. Not much here, though. How many sisters do you have?"

"Two of 'em, sir. We always share. It's what we do to get by."

"I guess you'd have to. And do you really live down there…inside the sewer system?"

"Yes, I do. Cross my heart. Me and my sisters."

"Can't be much of a home," Duffy observed, not believing what he was being told, but playing along with the young tyke, anyway. "Never heard of anyone living in a sewer."

"It's ain't so bad, sir. We found an old couch by the curb one day and drug it down to the big room. Got us a nifty lounge chair, too. Something to sleep on."

"Better than nothing," the carpet seller observed. "Where are your two sisters?"

"Oh, they're around here, somewhere. Probably hiding from you and watching to see you don't hurt me."

"Why would anyone want to harm you, Jimmy?"

"You'd be surprised at what some people are like. Some are good and others are bad. Some enjoy hurting others, some don't; just the way big people are. Guess it's just how they want to live their lives, ain't it? Not easy to tell which ones are which, though."

"Well, yeah. Hard to tell. It's nice you have someone to watch over you, Jimmy."

"Yeah. Mindy and Lucinda, they ain't very far away. Would you like to meet them? You ain't done noffing yet to scare 'em. Probably hiding behind some tree around here."

"Well, sure, I'd like to meet them," said Duffy, not believing for a moment they even existed. "Assuredly!"

"And you won't hurt them?"

"Of course not."

Duffy thought for a few seconds about what Jimmy had already told him and concluded the boy liked to play games with the truth. Did the youngster actually expect him to credit the implausible story of him and his siblings living in the sewer? Of course, maybe they did—anything was possible, he believed—although more likely than not it was a humungous fabrication. But it followed—if he could devise such a whopper, he was certainly capable of inventing the existence of two sisters who shared his dilemma.

"C'mon out!" Jimmy called suddenly, cupping his hands before his mouth, his voice elevated by a few decibels.

And, sure enough, from the corner of his eye, Duffy saw two waifs emerge from behind a large tree, off to the side.

"C'mon over," the boy urged them.

Slowly, timidly, almost reluctantly, the girls advanced toward them. One was taller than her brother, perhaps twice his age and the other was smaller, maybe five or six years old. Both were clad in appalling hand-me-downs which had probably passed through a succession of owners and both had blonde hair flowing about their head and shoulders, uncut, untrimmed and not very clean looking, at all.

"He's okay," the boy said to them. "He's my friend, Mike, and he has some food we can have."

Hearing these words, four eyes regarded Duffy with a more congenial appraisal and their expressions brightened as though he was about to present them with a staggering cake of chocolatey delight.

"This's my family," beamed the lad with a degree of pride.

"I'm pleased to meet you," said the carpet guy, with a nod of his head including all of them. "What are your names?"

"I'm Mindy," said the little girl.

"I'm Jimmy," said the lad, repeating himself.

"I'm Lucinda," said the tallest one. "People call me Lucy."

"Pleased to meet you. My name is Michael Duffy. You can call me Mike or Mikey or Michael."

"I'll call you Mikey," said Mindy, speaking up, her rosy cheeks dimpling.

"I'll call you Mike," choose Jimmy, "or maybe just Mister."

"And I'll call you Mr. Duffy," offered Lucinda, the eldest of the trio, more mature and better mannered.

"Jimmy tells me you have no mother or father. That so?"

Both girls shrugged their shoulders at the same time.

"Ma's gone," said Mindy. "She left one day, leaving us with a box of crackers, and hasn't been back to take care of us ever since."

"We don't know about our daddy," contributed Lucinda.

"Don't know anything about either of them," Mindy concurred. "Daddy left when I was born and Ma didn't tell us anything about him. Didn't seem to even know what his last name was."

"My, my; is that so?"

"Yes, it is," said Jimmy, tired of the conversation being dominated by his sisters.

"Jimmy told me you children live in the sewer. True, is it?"

"Course it isn't," differed Lucinda. "Jimmy was just funning you. Can't you tell he's a huge liar? He tells shameful fibs all the time."

"Well, he sure had me fooled," said Duffy, feigning a reproachful look at the small boy.

Jimmy grinned sheepishly, revealing a gap in his teeth where a baby tooth had been, the space left to accommodate an adult incisor soon to be growing in.

"I didn't really believe him, though. But where *do* you children live?"

"Up there," said Jimmy, changing his original story and using his finger to point to the top of a high apartment building down the street.

"My, my," observed Duffy, "it's a long way up. Lots and lots of stairs to climb, unless there's an elevator. You must live in the pent house, if they have one."

"It's high enough for our needs, all right," said Lucinda.

"You gonna eat your sandwich, Mister?" asked Jimmy again, putting up a brave front.

"No. I've been saving it for you three. Here."

Duffy enjoyed his conversation with the children. His older sister, thousands of miles away, had six of them and he always looked forward to their visits with him. He was more than happy to chat with and share what he had with these three, who were so unlike the brats he had experienced on the train.

He passed the remainder of his lunch over to Jimmy, who studied it for a moment and then passed it to Mindy, the youngest and smallest of the trio, probably the one her siblings took care of first. She took a huge bite from it, severing off a portion, and handed it over to Jimmy, who likewise did the same. What was left, almost a third of the sandwich, was given to Lucinda who bit off a large bite and shoved it into her mouth. She chewed thoroughly, slowly, savoring every morsel before swallowing.

"Thank you, Mister," said Jimmy, in between chews.

"Thank you, Mikey," Mindy murmured, licking her lips, as though she had bitten into an unexpected treat she would enjoy for years to come.

"Yes, indeed," echoed the eldest of the trio. "Thank you, Mr. Duffy."

She swallowed the last of her portion as though it had been the first food she had eaten in days.

"You're very welcome, I'm sure," returned Duffy. "I only wish I had more to offer you."

"This was sure nice of you, Mister," said Jimmy, shifting from one foot to the other.

"Are you still hungry?" the carpet man asked. "It wasn't very much. You must have room for more."

Mindy, the youngest of the three, nodded and said they were.

"Then come with me. I bet each of you would like to have a Big Mac of your own."

"I like Big Macs," said Mindy, innocently.

"Shhh," said Lucinda, taking her hand and pushing her back. "We should be thankful for what we have already received."

"But I do like McDonalds' food when I can get it," the little girl insisted.

"Me, too," said Jimmy with enthusiasm.

"Then come along," invited Duffy, ready to return to the park entrance. He brushed invisible crumbs off his shirt and grabbed his suitcase.

"Hey, you kids," said a rough, virile voice of authority from behind them. "C'mere!"

Duffy swiveled to see, striding toward them, one hand on his hip, a police officer. He was holding a Billy club, or something else of a threatening nature, in the other. A shield, which could not be read at this distance, was pinned to his chest and a peaked hat rested upon his head.

Duffy was surprised. He turned again to face the children, wondering why the policeman would trouble them, but the youthful trio was gone, like the unseen breeze whispering through the trees.

"Now, where'd they go?" the carpet fellow asked of the officer coming to a stop beside him. "And who are they?"

"Dunno *who* they are. Live around here, though. Cause plenty of trouble, they do. Steal food from the grocery stores and lift wallets from unsuspecting folks. Give 'em a good talking to whenever I catch 'em, but not much I kin do about it. Just homeless urchins like you'll find in most communities, I guess. I'd advise you to keep away from 'em."

Duffy stayed around for another ten minutes, hoping the threesome—his welcoming committee to the city—would return once they noticed the agent of the law had gone; he had been actually having fun listening to them. But they did not come back and he eventually left the park, went to the cross streets to get his bearings and began his three block trek to the YMCA, following the simple map drawn for him by his brother.

* * * *

It was not until three days later Duffy was able to return to the sylvan setting near the train depot where he had encountered the three children. He had nicely settled into his little nook at the Y, venturing forth now and then to see something more of the neighborhood in which he now temporarily lived until he could locate more suitable quarters, but he spent most of his free time at his brother's place of business, learning the particular ins-and-outs of the job he had been recruited to fill. It was not a terribly exacting position, but it did require a certain amount of experience, which he had, and study which he was agreeable to do. His lunch and other leisure time were spent on the premises in order to master the expertise he must have.

He had not forgotten his meeting with the youthful trio and thought of them from time to time, wondering how they were getting along and thinking of questions he would ask about their living arrangements and of the comments made to him by the officer which had puzzled him. Once he was acclimated to his job he might be able to assist them in some small way not requiring an exorbitant outlay of currency or time, or place an unfavorable burden upon himself. He would not be receiving his first pay check until the end of the week, however, and until then he had to be careful of how he expended what money he did have. The threesome certainly appeared to be in need of financial assistance, if their skinny frames and slothful attire were an indication of their need, and Duffy was a compassionate man.

On this particular day, his duties at the office now well understood, he was not surprised to find his aimless footfalls taking him past tracts of forested land on his way to the park. His subconscious had been guiding him, he realized, and he found himself looking forward to another tryst with the children if he should encounter them.

Before entering the grounds, he stood for few minutes watching an elderly man and woman, standing in front of a store window, gazing at the display inside before going in. Almost as though it had been prearranged, he turned to see Mindy, the littlest and youngest of the children, sitting on a bench not far away from where he had first met her. She was licking an ice cream cone—strawberry, he guessed—looking at what still remained of the delicacy poking itself above the rim of the cone. She was swinging her legs, too short to reach the ground, and he wondered how she had managed to crawl onto the bench while still holding the treat. Her eyes were fixed on something in the distance and not on the frigid delight which she continued to lick, absentmindedly.

"Hi, Mindy," Duffy said, smiling pleasantly and walking over to her. "Remember me?"

The little girl tore her eyes away from the squirrel she had been studying and looked up to see Duffy gazing at her.

He might have been wrong, but he was willing to swear he had startled her into a state of great surprise; her eyes were wide and her mouth opened into an O. Was she contemplating some nefarious action? Was she fearful she had been discovered?

"Oh, it's you, Mikey," she said at last, the tension in her facial features and the muscles of her physique visibly relaxing as she recognized him and knew he posed no threat to her.

"Are your brother and sister around?" he asked.

"They were," she responded, then turned her head one way and then the other, looking at the nearby people strolling by. Her gaze returned to Duffy and she added, "But I don't see them around anymore. They're probably down the street, begging for a handout."

"A handout? You mean food?"

"'Course, I do. Lunch time, ain't it?"

"So it is. Is the ice-cream your meal?"

"It is," she stated affirmatively, taking another lick from around the side. "I love ice-cream!"

"I think most people do," Duffy observed. "And how did you get the money to buy it? Or did you beg for it like you say Jimmy and Lucy do?"

"Course, I did. How else would I get it? See the ice-cream parlor across the street? I just go in and look sadly at all the mixtures in the bins. When someone comes along, usually an older lady, I look up at her and smile. I don't have to ask for some; usually, they just offer it to me. And sometimes, when no one else is in there, the owner will give me some ice-cream for free.

"Ain't begging, is it? Not if I don't ask for it?"

"Well, maybe not, but if they didn't offer to get you a cone, would you have asked for one, then?"

"'Course, I would. Sometimes, people aren't so generous unless I do asks, see?"

"Did you thank the lady?" Duffy asked, continuing the conversation.

"I did. Lucy says we must always thank people when they do something nice for us."

"Lucy is a very polite young lady, mature for her age," said Duffy.

"No, she ain't" disagreed Mindy. "Not really. She's a kid, like me; just a little older and taller."

"Are you still hungry," asked Duffy, "or did the ice-cream fill you up?"

"I'm usually always hungry, Mikey, but I already ate half of a hamburger and a handful of French fries when someone walked off, leaving them on the table—probably to go to the restroom. By the time he got back, I had already finished it and was going out the door."

"Tsk! Tsk! The guy was probably pretty mad."

"Maybe not. He might have thought he had finished it himself, or the cleanup guy tossed it away thinking he had left. Maybe he was given another one, if he complained. So, don't worry. I'm pretty full now and I won't ask you for something."

Duffy grinned. "You're a little conniver, aren't you, Mindy?"

"A conniver?"

"Oh, never mind. It's not important. Mind if I sit here, next to you?"

"'Course, you can, but don't ask me questions about my family, okay? Jimmy and Lucy don't like for me to tell strangers about us."

"Oh?"

"They're afraid I'll tell people our secrets."

"Now, what kind of secrets could you three possibly have? You mean like living in the sewer?"

"No, 'course not. Jimmy was fibbing you. No, I mean like the kinds of things we do in the park when it's late at night and the moon is full. Things they wouldn't like for you to know."

"Maybe they wouldn't mind. After all, I know Jimmy and Lucy pretty well now."

"Yeah, I guess you do. Well, late at night we join a big group at a bon-fire deep in the woods. We roast marshmallows when we can get some and smash them onto a graham cracker with a layer of chocolate. We call them s'mores. Ever heard of s'mores?"

"Sure I have. Used to make 'em myself, years ago when I was a Boy Scout. Where do you get the fixings from?"

"From the grocery store, of course. You don't know nofing, do you?"

"And how do you get them without having any money? Stand about and beg?"

"'Course we don't. Can't tell you how, though."

"Sure you can. I won't tell anyone your secrets."

"Promise?"

"I promise," Duffy affirmed.

"Well..."

Mindy looked around, satisfying herself no one else was within ear-shot, raised herself on her knees, leaned over and held her head up for a moment to Duffy's ears and whispered.

"We take the stuff when the lady in charge of the store ain't looking! Jimmy shoves it under his shirt."

Mindy lowered herself, sat back and began to giggle.

"It's funny," she said. "It makes him look like a stuffed Teddy Bear."

Duffy joined in with the laughter, even though he did not consider it to be funny. He believed children who started off life pilfering would come to no good, meeting up later on with big problems, perhaps ending up in prison—or even worse. The best thing for them to do would be to get a job of some kind to take care of their needs.

"You won't tell no one, will you? You promised!"

He shook his head, no. A promise is a promise and whenever he made one, being gored by wild boars would not force him to break his vow. He did not tell the little tot of his viewpoint, however. Not being their parent, or a teacher, or any other person of authority, he was not in a position to point out the consequences of their behavior, making them feel guilty and ashamed.

As far as he knew, all of the stories they told him were false, anyway. He had heard of fabulously wealthy people, housed in extravagant man-sions and living splendid lives of opulent comfort, enjoying the magnifi-cence such wealth could provide. They were known to prowl the streets from to time to time, just for fun, seeking out and mingling with the less af-fluent and often destitute people they met, later telling tales to their friends of the complete devastation and squalor in which 'those people' lived. For all Duffy knew, the three children were the offspring of prosperous parents who lived a life of affluence and, when he saw them, they were slumming just for fun, just as other children spend their leisure hours playing baseball, or engaging in some other endeavor.

"There they are," exclaimed Mindy suddenly after a spell of silence, pointing to the park entrance.

"Hi, folks," called out Duffy, as Lucinda and Jimmy came toward them, quickening their steps as they saw the two on the park bench. Duffy noticed them slipping something they had been holding into their pockets, but he made no mention of his observation and they were soon standing before them.

"Hi, ya, Mister," said Jimmy in greeting, a salutation immediately echoed by Lucinda.

"Haven't seen you around here for a while," he added.

"What cha up to?" asked Lucinda.

"Oh, just sitting and gabbing with Mindy."

"Yeah? What's she been telling you about us, Mr. Duffy?" Lucinda asked, but directing her inquiry at her younger sibling.

"Nothing, Lucy," Mindy retorted. "I ain't been telling him our secrets."

"I'm glad to hear you haven't," said Lucinda, a frown deepening the lines of her face. "You know much better than to tell, don't you?"

"Course, I do."

"You shouldn't even tell people we *have* secrets to hide," Jimmy said, his voice tense and a bit cross. "They might imagine all sorts of things."

"But I didn't tell him about … about, you know what," she insisted.

"Shhh," cautioned Lucinda. "The nice man isn't interested in our secrets, anyway. Are you, sir?"

"Wee..ell…" returned Duffy slowly, enjoying the banter and drawing out the word much longer than was necessary. "Actually, I *do* like secrets and I'm good at keeping them, too."

"Shall we tell him, Sis?" asked Jimmy, glancing at Lucinda with a look of perplexity.

"Of course, not," she returned instantly. "For all we know, Mr. Duffy might be a policeman."

"Oh, yeah," agreed Jimmy, "We do have to be careful about what we tell people."

Duffy smiled at him gently, all the while wondering what strange enigmas they did not want others to know about. Their conversation had gone in a direction he had never imagined it would take, forcing the young people to adopt an unexpectedly defensive demeanor.

"She's right, Jimmy," he assured him. "You *should* be careful about what you tell people. I don't have to know your secrets, especially if they're against the law. But, as a matter of fact, I'm not in law enforcement. I work for a company selling and installing carpeting."

Duffy decided he was being a nosey ninny, showing too much interest in their behavior, and said no more.

"We're not breaking the law, Mister Duffy," said Lucinda, drawing a deep breath. "We ain't doing nothing…like…like…that ain't legal."

"No, siree," jumped in Jimmy.

"We don't never stay up late at night to watch *them*," stated Mindy, with conviction.

"To watch whom?" asked Duffy, seemingly unconcerned, but wondering what the little girl was talking about. It seemed to him there was too much denial going on and the children were protesting far more than they should.

"You stop!" demanded Lucinda, addressing her sister crossly, "or I'll give you a good poke."

"I won't tell anyone," insisted the little one, realizing she had crossed the line. She jumped off the bench and cowered back a few steps. Apparently, for some reason, Lucinda's jab was one she had some reason to fear.

"What's this all about?" asked Duffy innocently. "Have you youngsters been drinking too much Kool-Aid lately and seeing pink elephants climbing up the trees?"

"No, no," said Jimmy quickly, but giggling at the absurd picture popping into his mind. Mindy joined in the merriment, but Lucinda remained as silent and as still as a puppet severed from its strings; amusement failed to brighten her face.

"Shut up!" she cried, totally unladylike and completely out of character.

"I won't say no more!" promised Jimmy and drew a straight line across his lips with a finger, as though he was zipping them closed.

"Me neither," promised the littlest one. "Besides, Basil wouldn't want them to know, either."

"That does it!" exclaimed Lucinda. She stamped her foot in unexpected anger, turned around and stalked off in a direction taking her deeper into the park.

"Uh, oh," said Jimmy. "Sis's *really* mad now!"

"Sure is," agreed Mindy. "She's in a real snit!"

"Who's Basil?" asked Duffy, forgetting his resolve to ask no further questions.

The two children burst out giggling again, but Duffy could see nothing to be laughing about. He looked suspiciously at them.

"Basil is a friend of ours," stated Jimmy, forgetting the vow of silence made to his older sister moments ago. "One of the gang."

"He's real nice," said Mindy.

"He is *not*," disagreed Jimmy. "Sometimes he's *real* mean to people… or other creatures he doesn't like—and, sometimes, even to his friends."

"Yeah," agreed Mindy, changing her mind. "He does have an awfully, wicked dispo… dispo… dispo…"

"Disposition?" suggested Duffy.

"Yeah. Disposition. So, we go out of our way to be extra nice when we're around him, and he's good to us, too," she finished.

"'Specially at night," Jimmy continued on, "when the whole flock is sitting around the bonfire."

Mindy finished her ice-cream cone and licked her fingers before wiping them on her dress.

"Probably making s'more?" Duffy suggested.

"Naw," disagreed Jimmy. "Chimeras don't eat s'mores."

"Neither do dragons or gargoyles," stated Mindy emphatically.

"Whoa…" said Duffy. "What is a chimera?"

"It's a creature with a goat's body and a lion's head," said Jimmy, matter-of-factly.

"And it has a snake's tail," added Mindy.

"How did dragons and gargoyles and…and…chimeras get into this?"

"No reason," said Jimmy. "Mindy is just talking silliness."

"Am not!" Mindy declared. "Chimeras eat imps and baby griffins, dragons eat mostly big animals, like lions, and gargoyles eat anything they can dig their claws into."

"Really?" asked Duffy. He knew next to nothing about such fantastic beings. "The creatures you've named are fictitious—make believe, you know?"

"That's what most people think," said Mindy, meaningfully. "But Boris is one. We've seen lots of them singing and dancing while we're sitting around the bon fires. Just at night, though," she added.

"Yeah, way past midnight," Jimmy added.

"I know a riddle, Mikey," said Mindy. "What has to gargle to clear its throat?"

"I give up. What?"

"A gasping gargoyle! Get it?"

Duffy got it, but did not think it was at all funny.

Duffy gave zero credence to what the children were saying. It sounded like a kind of make believe game they were playing, or maybe they were repeating parts of fairy tales told to them at an earlier age. More than likely, however, they were only feeding him a pack of falsehoods. Jimmy was noted for telling them, he remembered, but now even Mindy was willing to make up her own. But their words did arouse his curiosity and he was interested in hearing how the stories ended.

"How many have you seen?" he asked, harmlessly.

"Oh, lots and lots of them," Mindy told him.

"Maybe three dozen of 'em, or more," Jimmy estimated. "Whenever we have our meeting."

"So many fairy tale creatures?" said Duffy. "They must be extremely scary."

"Naw, not a bit," Jimmy disagreed. "They don't frighten me at all."

"Just don't bother them when they're feeding or having fun," cautioned Mindy.

"Sometimes I fall asleep just watching them," said Jimmy.

"Me, too," said his smaller sister, making sure she was an essential part of the conversation. "Sometimes, Lucy has to wake us up when it's nearly dawn and it's time to go home."

"You know, I don't believe I've ever seen a chimera, or any of these other improbable creatures—especially not dozens of them. They're not at all real," insisted Duffy.

"Are so," asserted the little tot. "As a matter of fact, we're…"

"Now you stop that, Mindy!" burst a sharp voice from behind. Lucinda, who had quietly returned to hear what her siblings were saying, was greatly upset. "This good man isn't interested in your nonsense talk!"

"Awe, alright, Lucy. But he's probably seen them on the streets, lots of times, walking around in their human form. The imps, too. Probably talked with them, and had lunch with them, maybe."

"I don't remember meeting any of them. What do the imps look like?"

The two youngsters began to snicker again and it was not until they were able to control themselves Mindy said, "They're very funny looking."

"And they're real small," said Jimmy.

"Smaller than me, even," said Mindy. "It would take five of them standing on each other's shoulders to touch the top of my head."

"You'll be sorry you talk so much," admonished Lucinda, angry her brother and sister did not guard their tongues no matter how many warnings they were given. In a sulk, she left them and made her way out of the park.

"Not very tall, at all," was Duffy's comment.

"No, it ain't." Jimmy bent down and held his hand less than a foot off of the ground. "This's how big they are," he demonstrated.

"Oh, my," voiced Duffy. "Are they really that tiny, Mindy?"

The little girl nodded her head in agreement with her brother.

"They must be as small as little dollies," Duffy guessed, delighted with the imagination expressed by his fledgling friends.

The three chattered for a while longer until Duffy glanced at his watch and realized he had stayed far longer than he had intended. The time allotted to him by his boss had passed and he still had not eaten his lunch. He decided he would have to forfeit it this one time and stood up to leave when Mindy spoke up.

"Would you like to see some of our friends?" she asked, in invitation.

Duffy, who was just about to say goodbye, halted in his tracks.

"What? You want me to come and see the imps sing and dance?"

"Them and the dragons and gargoyles, too. The whole gang is fun to be with. It's like a circus. They have their festival once a month, late at night when the moon is full."

"Lucy might not like for him to come," Jimmy cautioned her.

"So what?" she returned, defiantly. "We just won't tell her."

Duffy neither agreed to attend, nor did he disagree, but was confident he'd rather not waste his time deep in the woods, late at night, for what was almost certainly a wild, pretend adventure at best, or a mischievous children's prank at worst, but he stayed a minute longer to tell the kids how to reach him if they ever wanted to get in contact with him; in turn, they explained briefly, but not quite clearly, how to reach the grove of trees where the festival was to take place, as it always did on the first night of the full moon.

He was noncommittal when he left them, but was quite certain he would not continue to play their game much longer, unable to escape the certainty they found enjoyment with their playful antics. He would not mind seeing and conversing with them again; in fact, he would look forward to it, but under more normal and structured situations, believing he would be rewarded with a degree of fun and amusement while chatting with them. Even so, as far as he was concerned, he would rather they played their childish pranks on someone else.

Duffy happily executed the routine tasks of his position at his brother's shop, and one day, while looking at his desk calendar, he noted the appearance of the full moon would occur this very night.

He had not seen the children recently and had almost forgotten their invitation. For a moment he considered looking for them to find out more about the festival being held, but his decision was already made. What a gigantic waste of time it would surely be and he had much better things to occupy his hours at the YMCA where he was still renting a room, prior to finding more ideal quarters for himself.

But did he really have better things to do?

Duffy knew this night would be one more in a series of lonely evenings when he would settle himself in the large lobby of the Y to watch television, or go upstairs, curl up by himself on the bed in his tiny room, and read a book. This had been his customary routine since stepping onto the streets of Birmingham. He had not seen the children for more than a week now and found himself wondering how they were spending their time. Perhaps sharing a few minutes with them would provide a little variety to the sameness of his life. Not for a moment did he believe in their mythical bestiary or that a gathering would actually take place tonight at the park, but if it did, perhaps a concert or a carnival, it might be of some interest to him.

Attending such an event, however, was doubtful, he thought, glancing at the wall clock as its hands reached to touch the five o'clock hour and quitting time. He did not know where the children were, only that they lived high, high up in an apartment building. He was not at all certain how to contact them, nor did he know of the particulars of where in the park the entertainment would be. He straightened his desk, putting odds and ends away until they would be needed the following day.

"G'night, Max," he called to his brother, looking in at the next cubicle as he passed by.

Max looked up, waved and responded with, "G'night, Mike. See you tomorrow."

Duffy told him to have a pleasant evening and left the building.

Outside, he walked to the corner, looking both ways before crossing the street, when he heard a wee voice coming from behind.

"Hey, Mikey, wait for us. We're not wearing Nikes, you know!"

Turning, he saw rapidly closing the distance, the three friends with whom he had taken such a liking.

"Say, hey, what are you people doing here?" he asked, as Mindy, Lucinda and Jimmy skidded to a stop before him.

"You told us where you work," asserted the boy. "Remember?"

Duffy did not recall doing so, but figured he must have at some point during their conversations.

"We guessed you'd be leaving around five o'clock—when lots of workers do—and you did," explained Lucinda.

"Yeah," contributed Jimmy, "and we wanted to remind you the jubilee is tonight."

"Well…I'm…err…haven't really thought about it very much. So, tonight's the big night, is it?"

"Yeah," said Jimmy, "and we're hoping you'd come."

"I don't think so, but thanks for inviting me."

"Awe, c'mon, Mikey. You'll have lots of fun."

"We've been hoping you'd join us," said Lucinda. "Lots of strange and fantastic creatures will be there."

"You mean the mythological ones, of course."

"They ain't myth..log…cal at all," attempted Mindy. "They're for *real*."

"Yeah," said Lucinda. "The imps and dragons and gargoyles will be there and others. They always are."

"The chimeras, too?"

"Yeah, them, too. But it ain't all," said Mindy, with intense enthusiasm. "Sometimes we get a satyr and once in a while a unicorn shows up…"

"Sounds as though all the beasties come to these assemblies," jested Duffy.

"…and don't be surprised if you see a cyclops or two!"

"We expect a big crowd, Mikey!" said Mindy. "Will you join us?"

"Well, I wasn't planning to…"

"C'mon, Mister Duffy. It'll be tons of fun."

"Well, okay. I'll join you for a little while. Where's it at?"

"In the park, of course. Just meet us at the entrance; we'll be there waiting for you and take you to it."

"Around nine o'clock," advised Mindy, grabbing his hand and pulling on it, childishly.

"Well, okay. I'll try it, just this once."

"That's great, Mikey," she said, joyously.

"We'll see you later on this evening, then," said Lucinda.

Duffy took a step in the street and then stopped. "Oh, I forgot to ask. Do they have concession stands? Sell food there?"

"No," answered Lucinda. "Most of them eat before they go, or after they leave."

"Some of 'em bring their own food with them," said Jimmy, which seemed to strike the others as amusing, for they all began to laugh.

It might be a grand evening, after all, thought Duffy, strolling down the street after darkness had fallen. He had dined moderately and had taken a short nap, expecting to be out later than usual. He reached the park, only to find no one was there but himself. He had expected to find a large, possibly rowdy, partying group, out for a good time in the cool of the evening. But even the children were not at the entrance waiting for him. Perhaps they had not arrived yet, he reasoned, or maybe they had come earlier and decided to go to the clearing without him.

The sky had been washed clean of cloud formations, and a multitude of stars poked out of the heavens in twinkling splendor. The moon smiled down at him as friendly as he had ever seen it before, providing amble light as he stood there shifting from one foot to the other. He wondered how long he should wait before going back to his room.

Fortunately, he did not have long to linger before he spied Jimmy coming up the street, hurriedly.

"Hi, Mister," the lad called, stopping before him. "My sisters have gone inside to find good seats and I've been walking around, waiting to take you to the festival clearing when you got here."

Duffy thanked him and followed him through the entrance and down a winding trail, passing picnic tables and benches and a small pond with water glittering in the moonlight. Their trek along the wooded pathway had hardly begun, when Duffy began to experience unexpected and inexplicable distortions, slowly at first and then more rapidly, as they advanced into the deeper shadows and forested environs. The park, he discovered, was much larger than the two or three block rectangle he had envisioned and he was unable to explain how it had expanded in size so considerably, creating a curious, inexplicable modification in spatial proportions.

An alteration in time was also noticeable. The stroll, which should not have taken more than ten minutes, had already lasted nearly half an hour and perhaps much, much longer. Duffy found he had lost all notion of time and they had still not reached the further border of the arboreal local. It almost seemed to him as though an enchantment had been cast over him, or he had been captured within an unfathomable illusion taking place.

Was he was experiencing a rent in the fabric of reality—a shattering of the space-time continuum itself? How else could such revisions be explained? Either that, or they had not been walking nearly as long or as far as it seemed. He did not believe in such notions, however and finally concluded the distortions were only in his mind. The alternative, and this was far more likely, was they had simply been walking in circles for the last half hour.

Was it possible? He thought not and it did not help for him to realize with each step they took they seemed to be blundering along an alien landscape, an ephemeral area of dreamland, perhaps, and one he had never visited before. His surmise was rapidly turning into a conviction, becoming stronger as his sense of reality grew denser, more disarrayed, more indistinct.

"What is this place? Where are we?" Duffy wanted to ask of his small companion as they continued along the pathway. Somehow, he was unable to get the words out.

A tingling sensation of unexpected fear began to crawl along his spine.

The minutes passed, their footsteps continued, as Duffy fought against the impression they had stepped from one dimension into another and they were moving in a slower motion along a warp in time and space itself.

Everything seemed to be so…so…surreal!

Eventually, they saw a flickering of light through the trees ahead and shortly reached a large, treeless glade in the shape of an amphitheater. They entered and found they were not the first to arrive. Shadowy, obscure creatures, large and small, walked about or sat on boulders and logs, chattering, joking and laughing with each other. Duffy could distinguish some of the garbled words, but many of the noises uttered were curious grunts and whistling or clicking sounds with strange, alien intonations. A sizeable fire burned brightly in the middle of the clearing and a strange-looking form stood before it, feeding twigs and sticks into the blaze.

Not everyone or everything there was human.

Duffy's confused senses became fixed upon a quivering in the atmosphere as a purplish coloration of the air and landscape pulsed as though something alive. A visible, unaccountable vibration did nothing to free him from the anxiety building in his mind with every passing second. He stepped back a pace, frightened nearly to the very core of his being.

"There they are," cried Jimmy, pointing off to a large tree trunk being dragged closer to the conflagration. On it, their backs turned to them, were two forms; judging by their respective sizes, Duffy thought they might well be Lucinda and Mindy, the smaller one talking animatedly to the larger.

Jimmy led the way over to them pulling Duffy along by the hand and they stood behind them, unnoticed, listening to Mindy's excited voice, energized by her enthusiastic observations.

"Look over there, Lucy," she was saying, pointing to a yawning dragon on the other side of the fire circle. "Who is it?"

"It's Simon," responded the thirteen-year old, "one of the dragons from France where so many of them were exiled."

"Ooh! I haven't met Simon yet," said Mindy. "Is he a good one or a bad one?"

"I've only met him once and when I did, I didn't form a good impression of him. He snorts too loudly and many of his scales are mutilated or missing, as though he's been through dozens of skirmishes. I've heard he's a mean one, but you might enjoy talking with his girlfriend, sitting next to him. I'm told she's quite gentle, for a full sized flamethrower, and has some very funny stories to tell."

"What's her name?"

"Skelly. If you'd like, I'll take you over later and introduce you to her."

"No thanks, Sis. It'd rather meet Simon."

"Suit yourself, but I wouldn't go anywhere near him. At least, not in his present form."

Everyone there, human and nonhuman, were casual, relaxed and conversational, and seemed to be having a good time. Duffy, however, was in a state of perplexed distress, becoming more and more uncomfortable as the bewitching enchantment held him enthralled, persisting unbroken, and the cloudiness festering in his mind caused his sense of reality to become even more obscured.

He had seen and heard enough—more than enough—and believed

leaving sooner rather than later would be best for him to do. He was about to insist the young boy take him back to the park entrance, when Jimmy spoke.

"Hey, you two," he said, announcing their presence, "everyone here yet?"

"Not yet," said Lucinda, as the girls turned to greet them. "Most of our friends are late."

At that moment, a tiny *something* stepped out of the shadows, looking for a place to sit, and walked toward an unoccupied boulder. Carelessly, he got too close to Simon, who opened his long, scaly muzzle and torched him as he might a wayward frankfurter.

"It's just an imp!" exclaimed Jimmy to Duffy, who was now sitting next to him.

"It *was* an imp," corrected Mindy, as the dragon, not yet satisfied, opened its maw even wider, reached out with its long neck and snatched the little creature off the ground. With masticating swiftness, the massive creature gobbled it down.

"There're so many of them just one won't never be missed," Mindy observed.

"My, my," said Duffy, nearly petrified by what he had seen. "That was…was… *gross*!"

"Not really," observed the lad sitting next him. "It was a small urchin; barely a mouthful for a large dragon."

"I can hardly wait for snack time," said Mindy enthusiastically, leaning closer to the fire.

"S'mores?" asked Duffy, nervously.

"Mmmm! Yummy!"

At that moment an enormous *thing,* bat-like at first glance, swept out of the darkness beyond the fire. It settled on a small log just a few feet away from the foursome.

To his horror, Duffy realized it was *not* a huge chiropteran, although it had webbed wings folded up neatly behind its back. Its horned head swiveled to glance curiously at the four with a rocky face appearing to have been sculpted out of granite. Its facial construction, with furrowed, grey skin, unblinking eyes and puffy lips, was unbelievable. When opened, scimitar-like teeth were revealed. Its hunched back was curved and enormous talons clung tenaciously to the log upon which it perched.

"Nice evening," mouthed the creature, with a gritty intonation, looking at Duffy and his companions. Its voice sounded like a small avalanche and its grunting mouth moved so slowly it appeared to grind away in slow motion.

"Good grief!" Duffy exclaimed, edging away from it as far as he could.

"What's *that*?"

"That's a goyle," Jimmy answered.

"What in the world is a goyle?"

"A goyle," Jimmy repeated. "A gargoyle."

"Oooh," Duffy sputtered and then stuttered, "o-one of those things? But wa-what's it doing here, si-sitting on a l-log? Doesn't it belong on the r-roof of a ca-cathedral?"

"Of course, it does, but not all the time."

"Sometimes they get tired during the day, sitting up there like statues of solid rock," explained Lucinda, "and they transform themselves into their people persona you see walking the streets from time to time, not knowing what they really are."

"And during the night," added Jimmy, "they fly around as much as they like. I recognize this one just fine. He's a nice guy; I've seen him around here lots of times."

Duffy began to snicker, approaching a state boarding on total hysteria, unable to acknowledge the reality of the scenario evolving before him and rapidly losing total control of himself.

"Would you like to get closer and pet him?" asked Mindy.

Duffy was quivering now, one baby step away from insanity, he believed, and feeling much as Alice did as she tumbled down the rabbit's hole.

"I wouldn't do it if I were you," advised Jimmy. "Lots of 'em bite. The goyle might take a large chunk out of you if it's hungry."

"All of them bite," Lucinda elaborated. "The smaller ones can take huge hunks out of you, but the bigger goyles can eat you whole in one mouthful."

"The imps and fairies who show up are afraid of them," said Mindy, knowingly. "They disappear in one big swallow if they get too close."

"The big brutes are usually hungry and some of them bring their own meals with them," said Lucinda. "You don't have to worry about *them.*"

"Then I'll b-be careful to stay away f-from the goyles," stated Duffy with a childish giggle, adding to what he hoped was playful banter.

"Look over there," said the teenager to her brother, pointing to another animal nearby, perched on a tree branch. "You can just make out its form. It's Estelle, isn't it?"

"I think so," he said, agreeing with her.

"Estelle is a goblin," explained Mindy. "So few of them are left they're on an endangered species list."

"How un-unfortunate," giggled Duffy, dryly, unable to comprehend and accept the existence of the fantastic brutes around them. He studied the animated form a few seconds and then shifted his gaze to four tiny beings entering the fire circle, leaping and gyrating as though they danced to the strains of unheard music. One of them grabbed a backpack another had been carrying, set it on the ground and opened it. Another one snatched from inside a box of graham crackers, and the last one withdrew a stack of candy bars. They broke off pieces of chocolate, placed each between graham crackers, added a blackened marshmallow from the fire, and began to eat.

"How did I ever get involved with this?" Duffy wondered. "All I wanted was to be friendly and helpful."

"What're they da-doing?" he asked, unable to clearly follow their rapid movements.

"They're making s'mores," explained Jimmy. "If you'd like to have one, just raise your hand and they'll bring one over to you."

Duffy thought this was so silly he could not restrain the snicker chortling from his mouth.

"No th-thank you; I'm not hu-hungry. But you th-three go ahead and eat some."

"We don't have to," said Mindy. "We brought our snack with us."

"You did? I don't see any food here for you."

Then it was Mindy's turn to giggle with a tone sounding far more ominous than Duffy wished.

"You don't understand yet, do you, Mikey? It's because you've only seen us in our human form."

"*You're* our food!" said Jimmy, calmly.

"Whaaaa…?"

"Snack time," Lucinda announced to her brother and sister.

Adroitly, Mindy slipped to the ground and as she did so the structure of her body underwent an unexpected transformation. Duffy watched speechlessly as as her lips bent and twisted and her other facial features and body reassembled itself, shifting and contorting into a form nothing at all like a little girl. Her small shoulders began to broaden and harden; her flesh loosened, then tightened again, its texture becoming leathery and wrinkled before hardening into its new shape. Within seconds, she assumed the features of something chiseled out of granite.

At the same time, Jimmy's body was also altering in size and contour. His head swelled enormously; tiny horns appeared above his forehead; and a smug, self-satisfied grin appeared on his face giving him the grotesque appearance of a leering reptile. The last change to take place were rudimentary wings springing from his shoulder blades and folding back into place.

Duffy stared, his mouth agape, unable to understand the weird conversions. He had no notion of what was happening until Mindy grabbed his leg in her expanded mouth and clamped her grinders together. The pain was excruciating—unbearable—and then he felt the same agony in his arm. Turning, he saw it grasped in Jimmy's cavernous maw, his own alteration now complete. Mindy bit into his leg again, crunching and shearing through bone and causing such pain as might be felt by the ripsaw at a lumber mill.

Barely conscious, blood spurting everywhere as each young goyle quietly fed, Duffy remembered the time when Jimmy pointed to the top of the apartment building to show where they lived and he realized now the boy had not been indicating the top floor, but rather the roof—the place where figureheads of stone congregated and spent their leisure hours.

Duffy lifted his head to see Lucinda mid-way through *her* renovation. The soft contours of her face lost its suppleness as it solidified into a pasty gray, her entire body stiffening and hardening, her mouth slightly open to reveal fangs of stone growing harder and larger as she assumed the structure of a gargantuan goyle.

The final atrocity occurred when Lucinda completed her conversion, pitching him into a paroxysm of horror as bouldered wings fluttered and she lurched at him with craggy jaws opened wide enough to snatch off his head.

✗

EMPRESS OF VAMPIRES

K.A. Opperman

She wears the moonlight for her maquillage,
And darkest kohl to shroud her olive eyes;
She almost seems to shimmer, a mirage
Amid the slumbrous blossoms' balmy sighs;
Her fanning ruff, a gemmy camouflage
Round chestnut tresses, is an orchid-bloom
Of ivory lace occulting mauvy skies.

Her slender fingers grasp a pale pink rose
Adorned with blood-drops spilt from parted lips;
Her enigmatic gaze, her pensive pose—
Beneath a crescent moon so near eclipse—
Suggest the weight of more-than-mortal woes;
While her black dress, the vestment of the tomb,
Curves out to veil her cold and childless hips.

✗

GODLIKE
Edward Morris and Konstantine Paradias

A drop of water falls, falls, onto the still gray surface of a flat mirror, sprays across the static shape, repeats.

Repeats.

Repeats.

Until the glass itself impossibly ripples back, reflects again. A breath of wind dances through this most profound of all prisons, blowing from nowhere to know where in this wild darkness with nothing between the wind and the stars.

A rage for flesh. A riot of gathering scream that falls back and grows, falls back and grows. An eternity to slowly stew and simmer in Conscience.

I can think. Remember. I can remember who put me here. Who tied up my body and put me here in my head. Had my brother given me a choice, I would have elected Death, and bent my neck for him gladly.

Oh, there is so much work to do. I must break free, must...

Must not give into the magic that is in Anger, and numbers and clocks. That is my brother's evil, and the slavery he taught these native beings first. I taught them to sing, to paint pictures and keep stories in their heads, the way we do. The way we learn to. The way I have to keep doing now, just to keep my very soul alive.

There were seven of us who made the first attempt. A few others followed later. This is the account of that journey, in the fourth year of the Twin Duelling Moons on Noh Ek (whose home star comes ahead of Earth's sun in the darkness just before the dawn.)

I had my own reasons for leaving Home. But they were slightly more moral. I wanted to find a world where I could write without interruption, without everything that my caste have to do to earn our food. Where I could sing as loudly as the sky, and teach a whole species to do the same, with no Elder standing over me and picking apart my technique. I confess that. And I confess that I'd do it again and again. Only because none of us have yet come back.

The humans dedicated festivals to me, and only deaths to him, and behold which brother is now entombed! The one who taught their law-givers to forbid sacrificing their own kind! Entombed! I—

I must remember where my own power first lies. In breath. Words. Smoke across a mirror.

Breath. So I encrypt and record all, while my body lies yet in chains. So I tell you all these things now and prepare to sing them Home, to propagate the truth among our folk.

So I record. So it was:

* * * *

There was no sound, no motion, in the silence where we hung on our journey, surrounded by light in the sky-sea of outer space. All was silent and still in mist and myth when we broke the last chains of Home. Sound returned, the rushing wind, the bright fire. We danced down off the Sideways Band and the engines cut right on cue, and let this planet's lesser gravity do all the work.

Out of the black, and into the blue. The green. The swift green, the boom and smoke and black again, then light. Light and air we learned we could breathe. Native species swiftly gathered around the smoking rim of the vast crater where our vessel *Xiquiripat* made her planetfall.

Brother Hurakàn rose first to meet them, and ate the ones that raised up stone axes and slings, bows and *maquahitl* war-clubs against him. Terrible was the wind of my brother's wrath, as it was at home when the Elders cited him for perversion of Science and our natural bodies, and Brother raged against them, and fell.

Brother fell to Earth, as did the rest of us. Brother fell to eating his fill of humans because they attacked him first. Surprisingly, this act opened several arcs of negotiation.

* * * *.

So began the first inning of a long, long game atop limestone thrones looking out over vast herds of those my older brother called lesser beasts. So began Gumarcaah, and this pantheon of waste and shame. No excuse. No reason. No rime. He taught them every horrid thing the Elders ever banned at home, and used the new environment to increase his own invention.

If you hear, if the wind of my words crosses the mirror of your understanding, oh my Folk, you cannot imagine the barbarism that emerged in him. We do not even treat animals created in the laboratory for experiments the way he treats these beings.

Have clemency on us. On all of our crew. We were barely more than larvae when we left Noh Ek. This does not excuse our actions. But if you would come and put me to death, do it quickly and honorably for the things I record and tell you now. I will go to my death with a sigh of relief for having uttered them.

I tried to tell the rest of our crew these things, and the humans, too.

The way Ix Chel showed me. The way Chel did…does…on hi/r own, out in the field. The way s/he respects every rat and capy, all creatures tiny and sprawling. All unpoisoned ecospheres, left to flame and flourish endless forms. All evolution.

My muse, mentor, priest and priestess, left *Xiquiripat* with me. We struck out, down the pyramid where we landed what felt like one full home-epoch ago. The centipedes that Brother enlarged and trained were everywhere. By the time the scolopendrid troops caught up to us in the highland passes, most of our work was done.

But not all. All is not done. We're not done.

Damn it, we. Are not done.

Damn it.

Damn it.. Those strange swarms of Little People that came out of the forest toward the end got Chel. I think. I'm pretty sure. I took a nasty knock on the head in that last firefight, and my memory isn't what it should be in many respects.

The minute we parted, those dwarven primates, no taller than two human hands, were all I saw blotting out the forest floor, up into the canopy, in the place where the one who called me starblood had recently stood. Like those piranha-fish in some of the rivers taking down some beef creature that waded through the wrong branch. Or so I remember.

Bad end to a long bad spell of work in the jungle that was supposed to end in putting down roots somehow, somewhere. Close quarters and few resources put us at each other's throats, and Ix Chel snarled and snarked about living with another as much as s/he did about mating with just one. (Before I advanced one opinion on the matter, you understand, but that's another tale.)

Chel studied everything. Every species. The humans were a constant delight, but every bird and butterfly, every blind worm and cave fish, were too. The dancing webs of my best friend's hands that made rainbows on the Earth-lit air when s/he worked, steadying one with the other, classifying, regrowing. Changing. Going native.

Native. Chel would have waded in and found my body, and if the love I think I see sometimes is there, eaten it the way we do on any field of battle. If I have that right. (If not, I have little to lose in my current predicament, doped and roped with chains of seething flesh…Better the memory of a kind of love that might or might not have changed form as we all did, and do, into something like what I wished.)

But I couldn't wade in and find Chel's. That honor was denied me. Beautiful, noble, silly, warrior Chel, who threw my brother from the Sun Pyramid at Itzamàl during the final firefight, while Death rained down from the sky and the 'pedes ate the brains of half our human war-party. Ix Chel, my starblood, who I lost in the jungle.

I saw Chel drop into the swarm of littlefolk when crippled Hurakàn shot back from the forest floor. I almost waded in and found Chel's body. I tried. I have to remember.

I turned, and dipped, and ducked to do that very thing, to dive into the swarm. But no more did I begin to move than the blow-dart was sticking out of my blue-green robe, near the small of the human back I wore like a constricting girdle. With my last breath, I called a swarm of dragonflies to search for Ix Chel's life-signs for one Earth year.

Then my brother tore himself upright on the one leg Chel left him with, and dragged me back to our ship. Beneath its pyramid where we landed, the natives call the fused glass and burning-ground Hell. Xibalba.

"Brother, spare my life," I croaked. He sneered down at me with a human face and a cold black beak, two halves of two of all tomorrow's bodies thrown on in mid-debauch.

"Sure," was all he said. "I'll spare your life." Then he got down to work, and caustic was the steam from that splicing. Brother set snakes in the arms of my human-skin, up and down, fangs-deep, and then began to work the *Puz Naul Haleb*, the grafting of any living tissue to any living tissue that the Elders called 'ungodly,' and 'forbidden.'

Brother also grew a vast, fleshy mat of growth-medium for their food, then folded it into this stone tomb. Even in my dreams, the growth-medium stinks like nothing I could ever describe.

He grew the snakes into my skin, the poison into my veins. The mamba. The viper. The cocktail of toxins that, when stirred, put me all the way to sleep. As long as all those snakes are fed.

Now you see. Now I have told the first circle of this calendar. I know there will be—

* * * *

Oh, what is this? With no further fuss or fanfare, the wide and merciless sky belongs to my peeled, chilly eyes that fill with real rain.

Nowhere is the stinking mat, nowhere the snakes, as if they had never been. My arms don't look like mine now, skinny and pasty and full of holes. But the fingers move when I think about it.

No horn. No annunciation. The world is a wet vacuum of wind and noise. Too fast. Too fast. I vomit strings of gritty black dirt. I can distinguish the sky, but the things on the ground are taking a while. So I try not to look down. Not yet.

I am lying flat on stone, covered in various ick, naked in battered humanskin raw as the throbbing nerve of a tooth knocked clean out in a fight. (Amazing, the way the human thinking stays.)

Raw-tooth-nerve me is strangely fine with just lying here for the moment. Until I begin to move toes, and eyelids, bits many and various. Taking stock.

I know Suicide-Girl's smell before I even sense her human shape, the one she uses to go out among the cities and taunt the natives. The pretty one, with the flat head and long black braid, the filed emerald teeth. One of Brother's sick half-human offspring from the last roeing.

Black stone gargoyles stretch the lobes of Ixtab's ears with their tails. Around her neck is a noose tied in thirteen knots. Her chiton looks like another human skin, one peeled from an actual human and pounded into a garment. (Perhaps it is.)

Ixtab grew up fast. Her voice in my ears is all woman. Unnerving.

"Pick up the knife." The strangling-cords whicker out from the flesh of her human arms with soft gutty sounds, wrapping around my tattered self, yanking me upright. I see my old robe and boots on the cold stone floor with little surprise, and make myself move to reach for them, croaking something else:

"Why?" I know what the knife is for. A simple courtesy. That's not my question. "Why any of this? Why"

This irritates my 'niece.' "Look up. I haven't got all night to play guessing-games. You know what week it is?"

I've had no way of reckoning time for a while, but I don't like the look of those clouds. "Ouayeb,"

I mutter. My voice is like a hoe on wet rocks. "Duel Week. He… he let me out during Duel Week? What kind of *coca* is he smoking?"

Ixtab rolls her black eyes. "He wants a public execution. He sent me to lure you out to where the sun rises. At the main gate to Xibalba."

Ixtab blows bloody droplets from her own hand. My right eye comes all the way back on. Standing up is still making me see colors unbeheld by god or demon. "Listen, is there any way I could find something to eat? I—"
I sit down right there, in the rain, as if the ground were a straw mattress. Every joint of this body screams in the cold.

"You've waited six Earthyears." My spiteful niece spits her *chicle* on the stones. The cords retreat back into her forearms. "Plenty of time for that on the road. Just listen for a moment. He wants a show trial. You're to duel him directly, be killed and eaten."

Ixtab spreads those funny hands expansively, looking at me with something like compassion. The effect is chilling. "Blood of my blood, life is always a war. Find some armor for it in a hurry, or every arrow will find its mark in your wounded pride." Her inhuman eyes bore through me, and I understand everything when I peer into them all the way as she continues. "Kulkulcán. Uncle. We are tired of him. We want more voice. Give us air."

Kulkulcán. I try to say it back, but at first I can't pronounce my own name. I burp very loudly, but there's nothing left to cough up. Ixtab waits again.

"You shall be the first to arise. Your name shall not be lost. So it shall be!"

More blood comes up in my throat in a clot. I spit it out, and speak again. "But with you, dear heart, there are always strings attached. What strings this time?"

Ixtab turns away, brooding. "This is more than me. He wants to...he wants to sacrifice whole cities at a time. I've seen the plans. So I..." Whatever she swallows sounds like a mountain in her throat. "So I came here."

The golden herons of her hands carve failure from the gigantic raindrops. "He's planning on turning whole continents against each other. Religious mercenaries, I don't know what all. He wants to take over the whole planet. When he found out that the monkeys weren't just in this hemisphere—"

I feel like killing something and eating it. "I was there when your Dad lost his leg. This isn't my first time at the ball-court."

But I pick up the stone knife when I'm done sliding on my boots. With it, I try to finish removing the snake-tissue from my arms, and get most of that. "You did the right thing," I tell her, but my eyes are full of the sky after this long and I can't keep from singing.

I taste ozone in my throat, and croon the song far down in my belly. Just a test. At the first notes, the stones come back to listen, and form a roof, slowly, making many wet sparks.

The storm has crept into my back and made my loins shake. Ixtab looks all around, fearful. Those nasty things from her arms shoot everywhere, forming a sphere all about her. No stone touches her flesh.

"We haven't got all day. Dad's main Vuc satellite will be making another pass over this region in..." She closes her eyes. "Ninety minutes and counting. I can walk you as far as the Culecha, then I have to travel fast..."

I wait. My human face reflected in her eyes looks kind and unhappy. There's a trephination scar high in the middle of my forehead.My left eye is blue, the right one green. "I almost forgot. What of the Executioners?" Fishing in the pouch at the waist of my cloak as I ask, I fill a cornshuck with *marihuana* and try to remember the noun for fire. Ixtab sneers but says nothing.

"He exiled them up here. They've been agitators ever since. Dad just doesn't want to deal with them, and they're hard to catch. No tactical advantage in eliminating them. So he says. If only he knew..."

And on. For hours of family gossip. The cornshuck rolls over into life and sweet blue smoke. We share it. Great shall be the wisdom of enterprises that begin at first light.

* * * *

When the storm finally breaks, sleepy, strung-out Ixtab walks me down to the Great Red Road, the Culecha, in the low mutter of life and the smell of hot chocolate. Earth spreads cool and dry before us. We set out through the dawn, over a trail in the lush volcanic forest.

My senses make everything leap out. Part of me thinks I'm still dreaming. It's just after the dry season. The black smoke of Burning Time in the fields slowly leaves the atmosphere after a month of new growth. Their babies can breathe again.

On the road, we pass *marihuana* growers pulling carts to market, women walking with baskets of *tzitzé* and corn and beans atop their heads, or carring trussed-up chickens.

Long-haired farmers stir in doorways, lugging mattocks and hand-axes and gourds full of steaming corn mush. Inside a few places we pass, I hear the creaking shuttle-songs of looms. Monkeys howl and brachiate in the vines.Birds sing the sun out from behind the hill.

We come to a crossroads, surrounded by maize fields stretching away to the burned edges of the jungle. I only notice Ixtab fading when she's fully gone, having slid out of sight in that irritating way she loves. You forget she's there until she isn't at all.

This crossroads rises crookedly from sorrowful fields that terrace up and away to a foggy height. Close to the road, a big honey badger is nosing in the sheaves. The badger's green. It's crying.

It looks like a toad when I blink again, only then realizing that I've smoked my big cornshuck right down to the dog-end and I feel that, but I haven't seen a cane toad that big above ground since memory permits. Then, all of a sudden, the toad just decides to stand up on two legs, and change again.

I shudder, but wait, sensing friendly forces in the area. A little green jade man covered in moss hobbles up from the field on stumpy legs my Brother once broke repeatedly with the two-handed maul which Kac U Pakat now wears at his wide belt. He smells like chiles and beer. His ears don't stop wiggling.

"Did you summon this?" He gestures with his hammer, skyward toward the gathering stormfront that hasn't yet broken. The clouds burst apart at the hammer's faint light, slowly…

To reveal the Vuc satellite, too close for my liking, down from the upper atmosphere. The sharp-winged silhouette hangs behind the cruel red light it flicks down, feeling and smelling through the canopy.

"We gotta migrate." Kac U Pakat barks a spell: "*Nu zivan cul*!!"

The red light in my eyes goes purple. Then white.

* * * *

I open them again way, way down in a limestone cave, on the bank of a glowing stream.

"Good to see you again, too, cousin," I manage, vomiting the last clot of black earth. A worm slithers out of it, appearing quite confused. I deeply sympathize.

"We should go." The sweat turns to cold wax on my skin. "To Gumarcaah, and find what we must burn before him."

Kac snickers. "You're high. I've been running arms to the rebels. Just came to walk you around a little, get you back on your feet, see that ya don't hurt yourself. Much. You can't fight him," here I almost make some rejoinder, "But you can sneak in and cut out his hamstrings."

I see the sense of that, and nod slowly. Axolotls and blind dragon fish swim by us in the stream. Kac catches a fresh, slimy grub out of the dirt and gnashes it down.

"Anyway, you realize we're just outside Gumarcaah in the first place? Time to play ball, Kulkulcán. You weren't set free to make things worse. Things are real broken up there, real bad, but you're awake."

He sees the light touch my eyes, and grins. "We don't have long. We've already been made." When he barks the spell again, backward, I steel myself for the lurch and the light.

* * * *

Kac and I go vertical, out onto the red clay of the Culecha that knits the thirteen Mayan countries of Vucamag-Tecpán. The sun's all but up now. Creatures wake on the riverbanks, in the ravines, and on the mountaintops, to turn their faces to the sky and roar. Queletzú the bird of paradise conducts the orchestra out in there: the scree of eagles, the yarkings of macaws, the hiss of white vulture wings far above…

An hour down the road, the storm us worsens. The birds in the canopy start going nuts. Kac drags me back into the undergrowth. "Ssssh," he bids.

The slowly-pinkening sky's clear of metal hawks. There's nothing. Red clay, red stones. The knife's out of my belt before I even know I made the move.

The fields still stretch out around us in all directions, but this far down the maize has given way to *tzité*, shushing in the wind. Just up the road, the armed column of *Xtuzl* march in slow lock step, legs and legs and legs scuttering and squealing on the stones.

The centipedes' stink is tremendous. Their voices chill my blood. Dark are their many red eyes, their skins corroded brass. Their helms are long, greased heads, as of spiked phalli. In every one of their clutching claws is a cruel *maqahitl*. In every other, a pulse-cane for long-range whacking.

The alpha of their unit holds up one claw flat. The column halts, red eyes flickering and stuttering, forcipules and mandibles chattering.

Only one thing left to do. I begin to whistle.Kac's hammer is in his hand. "Good to have you back. Now let's play."

Holding the knife overhead, I call the fog from the hot mirror of the road, and make it poisonous. But not to us.

* * * *

Brother's centipedes meet us halfway. They come in waves, a black chittering carpet of clicking mandibles and restless feet. Kac smashes the heads of the alphas into pulp but we are outnumbered, overpowered. We fight like wounded jaguars, but even at the height of our diminished state, we cannot hope to best their infinite numbers.

Then the centipedes scream and chitter. When my fog hits them, they begin summarily tearing each other apart with very loud, wet noises and a great deal of debris. Their blood smells like sweet roast stingray. Sometimes there are sparks.

Up in the vines, close to the canopy, I see massive, growing swarms of those strange tiny humans hopping and leaping through the shadows, chattering to each other, swinging their own tiny clubs. "They're Xulú!" Kac bellows over from where his hammer whirls at its work. "Not a threat! They—Oh."

Then every one of them are simply gone, faster than a school of minnows disappearing under a rock. The centipedes continue dying, with many grunts and screams and unbelievable sounds. A few stragglers are still on their 'feet.' Kac stops helping them along after a while and returns to where I stand, clean of the pulpy 'pede blood that covers him from head to mossy foot.

"And a very good morning to you, too." Kac bows low, still trying to flick various bits of battle from his clothes. A rustling comes, far out in the low, shushing sheaves of *tzitzé*.

Two streaks between the rows pop up like capybaras just long enough to PHUTT… PHUTT…

The blowguns the black blurs carry are mighty, with heliographs on the ends to catch the sun and make a target right between the eyes.

A squawk from a dying 'pede answers every PHUTT, yellow blood and silicate brains spraying in smooth black bursts out the backs of their upthrust heads. The road empties more. The entire unit twitches, discombobulated in its own slime, on the red stones of the Culecha.

Hurakán's twin half-human sons Hunchevén and Hunahau hush-hush-hush up out of the field, dressed in the black belts and greaves and head-bands of a day at the ballcourt. Other than Hunchevén's green eyes and

Hunahau's blue ones, I can't tell them apart.

"Or did Hunahau have green eyes…" I ask aloud. The blue-eyed one wears the head of the jaguar Balam as his helmet. He's left-handed. I can tell because he uses that one first to pick Kac up and spins him around like a toy.

"We got tired of waiting and we came," he tells him. Kac slaps him on the back, climbs down and hands him up the new, smoldering marihuana cornshuck he has produced from somewhere.

"Who are they that are making so much noise? Go call them, you two. Here will we take them down, since their respect is no more and they go over our heads."

The right-handed one's helm is the Coh, the puma. I frown at the contrasting colors of their ball-court armor. *Opposing teams?* There is much here that makes no sense.

Did I invent that, the bloodless war, the ball game? I might have, once, but it became co-opted in a hurry. Inside, I weep for the future. Puma-helm, the green-eyed one, surveys me in turn.

"We shall only change their nature, their appearance, and thus our word be fulfilled, "he boasts back to Kac, "They wanted us to die, and be lost. For that… we should teach them a lesson. And we shall."

His hooded young eyes survey us all. Like his father's, they glow a little red. The jungle shadows gather around our group. His brother squints up the road, and smiles.

"Death walks with us into Gumarcaah, my bretheren. Right hand and left. Behold."

I see the two newcomers approaching on foot from a long way off, but walking too fast to be all human. Far down the red road, they stride over the soft shoulder, smoking and talking, not exactly hurrying.

Humwawa wears a pale straw hat and a black poncho. He looks like a withered scarecrow or a sinister old woman, gesturing with a shepherd's crook of carven white bone. "Now, they're going to put the highway over *heeere…*"

At his right, Ah Pook dwarfs him, smoking a giant cigar, Night to Humwawa's Day. His eyes are as jet-black as his own tall hat. His cane is a human skull and spine in crystal, with a golden gravedigger's spade for a foot. "I still don't think they'd be that stupid," he says back in a voice that vibrates my feet. "I…Oh, hello."

Humwawa regards me. In his undreaming insect eyes is no emotion I can identify. The twins move together, standing at the edge of the underbrush with blowguns up.

"Hail!" I cry back, letting my voice carry a bit too much. The Lord Executioners of Xibalba pause.

"Kulculkán," Humwawa drawls wearily. "Going our way?" He already knows. Humwawa never says all he knows. The twins stand down. "What way do you walk, elders?" Puma-helm asks him. Both twins touch their fists to their foreheads in obeisance. He nods imperially.

"Through us, the way to the City of Refuge," Ah Pook rumbles gently, drawing up beside us. On his own breath are blood and rum. Then he breaks character, blowing rich cigar smoke and chuckling. "We're gonna to rob the King for a lark and wreck his little stage execution he's planning. You all can watch. There is no need for fear." Here he regards me heavily. "Lift up your hearts from sorrow, oh kindred. For we stand at your shoulders."

Ah Pook makes a gesture. Kac U Pakat climbs up onto his back. My astonishment trails us all out onto the road.

* * * *

As we walk, we cover our heads and hands with earth, and smear our faces. The twins lead the way for ten miles through the blistering heat that saps the salt and spirit from any body and leaves the nerves in a melted pool. The dirt changes with that sweat, giving us the old faces, miserable countenances and ragged clothes of itinerant pilgrims seeking indentured day-labor.

I hope it's enough. Gumarcaah has become a ghetto, by the look, one big peasant ghetto full of all manner of crippling poverty and insensate vice. Even when I was in charge here and there was righteous government among the humans, the decay and pestilence lay in wait. The first war happened here.

Now the mossy ruins breed shantytowns.Thinking bleak thoughts about every building I pass, I bow low before the squat human soldier who bids us halt at the vast stone gates which stretch further above us than I can comfortably crane even my long, birdlike neck.

I abase myself before the cross-eyed, snaggle-toothed buck sergeant. His brow is singular, one long one like a caterpillar. The stud through the bridge of his nose is shiny copper. Staring at it has apparently made him crosseyed, after the fashion of the nobility.

Behind me, my untouchable entourage clears throats and digs toes in the dirt. "We have no names," I tell the soldier, "We are nothing more than hunters on the mountains. We are poor, and we have nothing. *Xa qo qu'il caquiyc.*"

He's skeptical. "Where do you come from?"

I pretend to look dumber than he is.

"I don't know! Sir! I do not know the faces of my mother and father. I was small when they died."

He considers this. "What do you want?"

"We do not want anything," Humwawa wheedles. "But really we are very much afraid. Did we miss the baaall maaatch—"

The sergeant winces, putting his hands to his ears for a moment. Then he motions the archers to lower their bows and slings."Shut up, slave. Let me think. We must take you there between us." His companions ring us as we are granted access through the gates. "And with all haste. There are criminals everywhere. We can't be bothered with you…"

And on, through the gates. Our hearts are calm. We give ourselves up to be overcome, and take the black road up the high pass, the mountain gate down into Gumarcaah. Xibalba. Hell.

The sky is on fire with the green light of day. The top of Mount Chi-Pixab is cleared of trees. Death-bats flutter far overhead. Below us, vast ravines surround the temple-city. Bones litter the landscape.

This part of town was once a burning-ground, a place of sacrifice to Ixtab. The crowd has been on their feet for hours in the dripping heat of the jungle, most of the unmarried men smeared with body-paint as well.

We pass with the swirling fiesta crowd over a river of sewage, and another one of bloody runoff.

Further down the hill, the tourist-trap districtof Carchah booms and roars with an influx of more Maya than I've ever seen in my life.

They trickle over the mountain, a tide of hungry ants under a magnifying-lens, bathing in Death. They all got the day off work. The poorest villager and the haughtiest litter-borne princess jostle up through that black gate as one.

The soldiers turn our little band loose into the crowd, where blind leprous idiot pipers with humpbacks and goiters hop and spasm and tootle on bone nose-flutes. The tide of humans is vast. The smell is indescribable.

Up the stairway to the temple, the drunken Lords of the High Council sit in their skybox seats with tamales and earthen mugs of warm beer, looking out over the pilgrimage to this hastily-called Feast of the Gods. We gaze up past them, to the base of the enormous red-white-and-blue pyramid, up the four stairways to the little stone house at the top, and the altar…

And the God-King Hurakàn standing there in human skin, a bare-faced leper messiah.

The feathers of his headdress are the same three colors as the pyramid. His head's small and round, like a calabash. His gray hair is cut short, not long like a real king's,oiled to his skull. His ears stick out like oarlocks, the lobes shot through with giant hoops of gold. His eyes are black stars. He grins with filed emerald-inlaid teeth.

His eyes roll. He's flying on the *coca*, waving a two-headed crocodile scepter as he tosses out the first red rubber ball of the death-match poised to begin in the court far below, that vast whitewashed pool where the twins have crept onto the opposing teams.

Blue and green flash back at me when I look at the ball court. Then I finally get it. The twins are going to throw the game. With one of them on a side, no one wins. So the ritual has already been perverted.

The kingly mouth of the human skin standing up there falls open, and lo does the hot air pour forth unto the Maya. Beside me, Humwawa makes retching noises, pretending to shove one spindly gray finger down his throat.

"Oh daylight beauty, great flood, Hurakán, rage, thou, blow! Thou, Heart of Heaven and of Earth, giver of richness! Turn upon us your power, grant life! Let us not meet disgrace! Let not the Deceiver come behind or before! Let us not fall, or be wounded on the descent or on the ascent of the obstacle. Let there be but peace in Thy mouth, in Thy presence!"

Brother looses his own inhumanly long tongue, and jabs the stingray blade down once. A rope runs through the new and bloody hole. The droplets smoke upon the fire before him. The crowd gasps as one.

"Behold, I am great above all beings created and formed! I am the sun, the light, the moon. Because of me, men conquer. My eye is bright silver, a precious ruby, my teeth shine like perfect emeralds, my beak like the moon, my throne of purest jade. Listen! I am the sun who made the earth, who shook the heavens and the hells!"

I look around the higher steps of the pyramid, where more centipedes occupy corner sniping positions, up and down at staggered intervals to monitor the enemies of their imagined happy life. Many tribes are also there, full of sorrow, to come and pay tribute.

The storm rolls in, quenching their fires. The people roar. The storm roars louder. The lowlands are beginning to flood, clearly visible from on high.

"The invaders are coming down from the north! Our enemies are on all sides! All the tribes are turning away from us, all those who worship gods other than Hurakán! The Yaquí, the Olmeca, even the Xicalanca to the south, turn against Him! Are you with us or them? We will root out the dissenters in our midst! Their kings will be made prisoners! They will be obliged to surrender their gods! Surely they are finished! Already are their shoulder-bones broken, and they have eaten their own entrails!"

Out of the blood-smoke of his offering, a one-legged white vulture stretches its one-eyed head to the sky, mouth and eyes one organ snapping with green teeth. The crowd erupts in wild cheers, no longer able to understand each other clearly.

The faces of the war-party, inner circle in that crowd, are painted red, white and blue as well. Their eyes are full of mist, clouded like breath on a mirror, that they might only see and kill what is close and clear to them, and destroy all wisdom and knowledge of the beginning.

"PREPARE FOR WAR," Hurakàn rumbles, his voice suddenly ten octaves deeper than Ah Pook's.

Then a blowgun pellet hits Brother in the side of the head, and his face goes wavery and strange.

The crowd is horrified. Humwawa cranes his neck to see who shot first, pushing closer through the herd toward the base and the ballcourt, following Pook and Kac, approaching the steps.

Jaguar-Twin fills the silence nicely from the other side of the court, shouting up, "Your gods aren't even gods! We know! Even you will die! This temple will fall, and be the home of owls and wildcats!"

The ballcourt begins to split. Trees and vines crack the limestone floor. Unperturbed, the twins begin to climb the pyramid. Puma-Twin waves his blowgun.

"We, those whom you see here, are, then, the avengers of the torments and suffering of this planet, and all the evil you did here! No longer shall you seize men for sacrifice!"

But my brother's not even looking at his sons as he changes, splitting through his own pasteboard shape. I stare up into the ruby light of Hurakàn's thrice-lobed burning eye, feeling the blast of fouled meat breath from that beak.

His wings pull the mist up from the ground, rippling the clouds as the wind kicks up in turn, leveling trees. His one-legged form gets hard to see.

"KULCULCÁN COMES TO DIE" that voice says down at me through the mist, ignoring everything else, "Accept your destiny. You shall be torn to pieces."

Around me, the crowd bolts. Battle sounds echo through the fog and filthy air. Close by, I see the Xulù gathering, swarming along the sides of buildings, creeping up from the cracks, chittering…

"What's this?!" I shriek. "This isn't your fight, little ones! Why—" I look all around. I am at nines. I am going to die. I am I am I am…

The little people rally, swooping down upon Xibalba like starving maggots hatching out into dead flesh. Royalty and guard and 'pede alike begin slapping at their necks and falling face-first into the mud.

These troubled little creatures of the woods pay me no heed, nor offer any explanation. They wear untanned skins, and fight their way through centipede and war-party alike with the strength of tiny men, surrounding the pyramid, whooping and beating drums, swinging clubs and swords.

The sun's trying to come out again. Over the center of the ballcourt, a double…

Rainbow. Now the song in my throat catches a different chord, a louder one when I cough it up like a dog coughing up a soup-bone. On the opposite mountaintop comes a waterfall of light, slowly resolving into

In two. Then one. A golden-gray field of beautiful wrath. A human skin. Red hair, tied back, squirming as though every lock were alive. Toltec armor. Backwoods. Reinforced with chainmail in dazzling hues. Every. Dazzling. Rainbow. Hue. Claws, the whole way up both arms, grown from the skin, insectile as those bright multifaceted eyes that blaze and burn…

Damn it. The shape of the armor conforms to a third sound. A dual sex. Ix Chel.

Damn it. It's like watching a comet, or a forest fire. The blaze of invention skips and hops, pent-up no more. Free.

Free in wrath, and howling harmony to my own scream. I stop where I am, looking up, throw away Ixtab's stupid knife, and approach the pyramid. Whistling

Whistling through that graveyard, that abbatoir, louder, louder. This time, the stormfront hides no satellite, and the lightning heeds my call like a pack of trained dogs. When I look again from the carnage my hands are weaving, Humwawa and Ah Pook are down in the center of the ballcourt, making beautiful music, playing covering fire.

Bone flutes crunch in their teeth in unison, and centipedes pop, spraying pus. Our song forms a wall of mist, welling a great flood up, darkening the face of Earth with tears for all we'd undone and unmade.

Roaring, roaring up out of Time, I sing stones up at Hurakàn's head. Meanwhile, the desperate people climb to the tops of the houses. The houses fall, and throw them to the ground, and the trees cast them far away, and the caverns of Xibalba fill and pop them back to the surface.

Slowly, the earth is dried by the glowing mirror of the sun. The ground breathes smoke. The Executioners of Xibalba unmask, Kac scuttering at their heels, spattered in blood from head to toe, hammer in his jade fist.

"We're out!" I scream, "Abandoning ship! Abandoning Earth! We are going, going away, you who came from our distant country. We begin our return.Give them your death-shroud to place behind their altars!"

Then Ix Chel de-cloaks quietly behind mighty Hurakàn, and his head whistles into the mist.

A little while later, the holy dove sings.

* * * *

By a miracle did we vanquish Hurakán, the arrogant one, whose history I tell now. We told the humans not to weep, and left them the signs of fate.

Ix Chel and the Executioners and I played one more song. One that leveled the walls of Gumarcaah, so that the vines and trees, the wood-watchers and mountain-guards would make their nests and give praise to the true creators in the true tongues of their kinds, *chi be quih, chi be zac*, as long as the sun walks, as long as there is light.

This recording will be transmitted without a mouth to tell it in flesh. Our remaining crew decided not to return home immediately. There are better worlds to learn.

* * * *

"Will it be good?" I asked, at the end. Ix Chel looked at me long-sufferingly.

"It already is."

We rose instantly through the mist, the dawn, with the whole arch of Space and the face of Earth lit brightly before our eyes.

Then we passed upward, and were changed into stars in the sky.

For Lucius Shepard and David Brockie.

✗

DARK RIFT

Ann K.Schwader

Clawed through the milky minefield of those stars
we know as home, a greater midnight veils
some wound within. Once, dust obscured that scar
from mundane sight; & ignorance prevailed
in safety, as it must for us. To fail
temptation's test is fatal, yet to know
is all we're born for. Caught like moths impaled
on mystery, we mutate vision—go
X-ray or infrared, whichever shows
the most of what we mustn't yet suspect
has quickened in that fertile dark. Aglow
too late with apprehension, we detect
Their natal stirrings: wrongness turning right
against our species & its failing light.

✗

RONKONKOMA
Glynn Owen Barrass

They had a history, Cassey and the house, although it was many years since she had last seen it. It had waited however, biding its time, an event marked on her timeline from the moment of her birth. As she drove down the narrow road, the sides of which stood thick with evergreen cedars, the vision of a car crash, instigated by another vehicle shooting towards her, filled Cassey's mind.

This was how her parents had perished, twelve years earlier. Cassey mused that if she pulled up and searched around some, she would probably find evidence of that wreck. She shook her head and drove on. The road ended at a right turn, and as she steered into it, Cassey didn't bother indicating. There was no one around to see her infraction.

Beyond the right turn, a few hundred feet away, stood her former home. Before that, the road led to a pair of tall, wrought iron gates. After the gates the road, surrounded by open grass, ascended gently to the house. She released the gas pedal a little and lowered her gears: She wanted to fully absorb what lay ahead.

The house, constructed from brown sandstone bricks, stood three stories high. The roof, partially caved in at its centre, bore a black hole between the grey slate tiles and narrow chimney pots. Above that a blue sky, spattered with metallic, dirty-grey clouds, loomed over the house and its overgrown grounds.

Now nearing the gate, Cassey pulled up, set the parking brake, and left the engine running as she opened the door.

Cold air filled her nostrils, bearing a hint of salt from nearby Lake Ronkonkoma. She hugged herself as she headed to the gates, took the bars of the left one and pulled. It creaked shrilly, but opened easily despite its size. Cassey examined the house again as she stepped to the other gate. There were two cars parked outside: a small red compact, and a silver Cherokee jeep. The latter she recognised—it was her friend Abe's car. The sight filled her with relief—she wouldn't be alone.

"Dependable Abe," Cassey said, and after pulling the gate back, returned to her car. She climbed in and soon after was driving up the slope.

A circle of Eastern Red cedars, part of the primeval forest covering the lands hereabouts, surrounded the house's grounds. As a little girl, Cassey had played on the grass with a long dead family dog. The woods, she had always avoided.

The road became gravelled, crunching under the tyres as she approached. A small lump formed in her belly.

The house really was quite innocent looking.

Four windows lined the first floor with a large double door between them. The second and third floors had five windows, sharing the centre window above the front doors. A few windows were broken, with curtains dangling limply outside.

Cassey frowned at the disrepair. If she had known the house was still in the family, not sold off like her uncle had said years earlier, she would have had it looked after. *No scrap that,* she thought with cynicism: her stepbrothers would have sold it already.

Her car completed the ascent and reached the wide gravel space facing the house. Cassey veered left, parking beside Abe's car.

The cars were empty, and Cassey stared at them with a puzzled look as she turned off her engine. She had the keys, and the deeds to the house, in her glove compartment. The former should have certainly been necessary for Abe and Ronson to enter.

She undid her seatbelt and leaned over, opening the glove compartment to remove a heavy brown envelope. She caught sight of her 9mm Colt Defender, something she never kept far from her, and considered taking it.

"I know I'm afraid of the house but still…" she scolded herself, and slammed the glove compartment shut.

Cassey left her car, and pausing, stared at the other vehicles. She scowled and turned towards the house, walking across the crunching gravel with slow, deliberate steps.

The front doors looked rotted. Swollen with damp, the orange paint had peeled off on the lower parts, the bare wood decayed to leave deep, diseased-looking gouges. The wood there had chunks missing, leaving small dark holes—miniature entrances for all kinds of horrible vermin.

The doors opened, and Cassey froze.

To her relief, Abe stepped out. Dressed in a white shirt and black slacks, his Japanese face smiled as he barrelled down the steps towards her. Behind him came a much shorter man, large, bald headed with a huge grey handlebar moustache. Ronson, she guessed, and the man behind Abe, dressed in a long, green wax windbreaker, bustled forward and held out his hand.

"Hey Cassey! said Abe.

"Miss Bane a pleasure to finally meet you," Ronson said, in a Southern accent quite unlike her friend's broad New Yorker tones.

Still flustered after her fright, Cassey pulled herself together and reached out to shake hands.

"Mister Ronson?" she said. "I have the house deeds and the keys right here. She held the envelope out with the other hand.

"Oh call me George, please," Ronson replied, and releasing her hand, reached out and accepted the envelope.

"Found the door unlocked, so we took a look," Abe said. "Hope you didn't mind. I know you wanted me to get here first, didn't want to be alone."

Ronson opened the envelope and retrieved the keys, which he brandished with a smirk. "If the other doors match the fine example behind us, these may be surplus to requirement!"

He spoke in jest, but from what Cassey had seen already, the old homestead was in a terrible state of affairs.

"You wanna come take a look, before we leave?" Abe questioned. The expression on his face was one of concern.

Cassey, appreciating this, nodded and said, "Let's take a look."

To her chagrin, the two men, probably wanting to appear gentlemanly, let her go first.

Might as well get this over with, she thought, and going up the steps, passed the open doors and entered the place of her birth.

Her feet stepped upon cracked, dirty tiles, the stink of mould filled her nostrils. The large lobby had panelled wooden walls, a cracked tile floor littered with debris. The light filtering in from the doorway and window revealed the ceiling had collapsed on the eastern side. That area was thick with broken wood and rubble. Before her, between the entrance and the staircase, a ceiling chandelier has fallen to the floor.

She cringed at the mess, then felt relief that it was no longer her responsibility.

Footsteps sounded behind her, light in the case of Abe, loud from his companion.

"Work, work, work!" Ronson said eagerly, and walking past Cassey, paused near the fallen chandelier. "Louis the Fourteenth, this chandelier *was*," he continued, turning to her. "Sadly now, it's nothing."

Cassey had the sudden fear that Ronson might want to back out. No that was impossible, the documents were signed and sealed. Abe, a lawyer himself, had dealt with it.

"You staying here then, Mister Ronson?" Abe asked from behind her.

"Oh yes, I'll be camping here until I sort something more permanent," Ronson replied with enthusiasm.

Cassey considered having to spend one single night here, and shivered.

A few minutes later, she and Abe said their goodbyes to Ronson and left the house. Outside they made some small talk, then Abe squeezed her shoulder and the pair departed. Cassey assumed... hoped, this was the last she would ever see of the place.

* * * *

A month passed, and Cassey put the house and its memories behind her. Concentrating on work, she had new and old cases alike to deal with. Of the former, there was plenty to do. She was driving home from her latest case, tracking down a client's stolen property, when her phone, tucked in her inside jacket pocket, began to vibrate.

Cassey sighed and found a parking spot near her apartment building. Her client, a wealthy woman named Mrs. Atworthy, had hired her to retrieve some stolen family heirlooms. She had recovered *most* of them. From her previous dealings with Atworthy, most was probably not good enough, and after speaking to the woman's secretary an hour earlier, she expected this to be Atworthy herself, calling to complain.

She pulled up behind a neighbour's van, undid her seatbelt and took the phone from her pocket.

A swipe of the screen illuminated it, revealing the caller was Abe. Did they have plans she had forgotten about? A tap later and she put the phone to her ear.

"Hey Abe."

"Hi Cassey," Abe replied, "I tried earlier but you were engaged. Uh... you remember the guy you sold the old house to, Ronson?"

A cold wave rushed down her spine; her mouth turned suddenly dry.

"Go on," she said, trying to keep her voice even.

"Well we got a call at the office today," Abe explained, "a niece of Ronson's. She's been trying to contact him for a few days now, with no reply either on his cellphone or his home number. She wondered if we had an alternate number for him, which I at least, don't have."

Cassey closed her eyes. *That damned house.*

"You alright, Cassey?"

"Oh yeah... sorry Abe," she replied, opening her eyes. "I have the same numbers you have. He could just be having trouble with the electricity up there though. We've had some stormy nights this week."

Abe was silent on his end. She knew what was coming, moments before he spoke.

"Think we should go up there, check on him?" Abe said and paused. He knew what he was asking, knew how much she despised the place.

"I'll meet you there tonight," Cassey replied, the words leaving her mouth of their own volition. She blinked, surprised at herself.

"Can do, Cassey," Abe said. "I'm over near Long Island way anyway."

After a hesitant silence, she continued, "Alright Abe, see you soon."

Cassey broke the connection and stared down at her cellphone. *What was I thinking? What am I doing?* The screen went blank, and she returned the phone to her pocket.

* * * *

From her previous trip Cassey knew the journey would take around an hour. The time seemed to stretch though, and as she drove, she theorized on what might be stopping Ronson answering his phone. When she left Brooklyn, she speculated he had perhaps fallen through some rotted floorboards. After leaving Queens and entering Long Island proper, she imagined the whole house had collapsed on top of him, the crumbled ruins forming the old man's grave, House of Usher style.

Doubtful, Cassey thought, but the knot in her stomach insisted something bad awaited her. It was a familiar, intimate feeling, one she experienced all too often. Usually though, it didn't concern something so... closely connected to her.

Full night had recently fallen, and a sudden onslaught of rain sullied her mood further.

It was a straight drive after Queens, down tree-lined, drizzle-darkened service roads. The I-495 followed, and she managed some speed despite the weather. Cassey left the Interstate forty-five minutes into her journey, and approached the unmarked turnoff she dreaded following.

An urge she had been fighting for a while, that of turning back and heading for home, grew suddenly stronger.

Instead, she bit her lower lip, indicated and turned the corner.

Here again, Cassey thought, driving slowly because the rain and wind were playing havoc on visibility. Her headlights, switched to full beam, illuminated the drenched tarmac, the edges of the wind-racked forest. She saw all this through windshield wipers that battled vainly against the downpour.

The hesitance, the fear she felt over returning, was far worse than last time. Her hopes of never seeing the place again had been tempting fate, obviously.

She reached the right turn and indicated, taking it slow. The wide-open gates wobbled dangerously, and as she approached, Cassey worried they might suddenly slide towards her car. They shuddered, but did not attack. She released a held in breath and started up the slippery gravel towards the house. A monstrous mass of rain clouds hovered over it, the damaged roof and broken chimney pots stood in stark relief against the sky.

No lights were visible and it looked empty, abandoned. The area around the house was alive with movements however, the wind furrowing the grass, the surrounding trees swaying drunkenly.

Her headlight beams, illuminating the slimy-looking gravel leading to the house, brought two cars into view: Ronson's and Abe's.

The latter was a welcome sight, and Cassey felt a flood of relief. It dissipated when a bulbous shape detached itself from the house's shadows. *What the?* A moment later, she realized it was Abe, holding a large black umbrella in his hands. He struggled with it as he approached, the wind doing its hardest to steal it from him.

Cassey pulled up, prepared to leave the car as Abe rushed towards the driver's side door. She opened it, getting wet and cold as the wind tried ripping her hair from her ponytail. Next, she was linking arms with Abe and rushing towards the house.

Damn, left my gun, she thought, considered going back for it, but instead continued on.

They reached the doors and paused, Cassey releasing Abe's arm to look up at him.

Abe yelled through the wind, "Doors are locked Cassey. There another way in?"

Cassey wiped her wet face, hugged herself and thought for a moment.

"One of the windows," she shouted back. "This way."

Turning on her heels and stepping left, she kept close to the house with Abe fast behind her.

The first window she reached was broken, but someone, probably Ronson, had placed a sheet of cloth, damp and sagging from the elements, on the inside. Cassey reached over and found the window hasp, slick and cold in her hand. A form loomed behind her, and she found herself suddenly protected from the storm. Upon examining the lower section of frame, she found two sections devoid of broken glass, and pulled upwards. The wood complained then reciprocated. Raising it a fraction, she managed to get her hands under to pull it up further. Disturbed glass fell from the window as she raised the frame, but soon she had it high enough for ingress. The next moment, Cassey was clambering through, pulling the sodden sheet down as she entered the house.

Her shoes touched damp carpet. Everywhere around her was dark with shadows.

Apart from the wetness on her back, she had managed to avoid much of the deluge. Noises informed her Abe was coming through the window. Cassey turned, backed up a little, and watched him climbing through, sans umbrella. His white shirt was soaked, his hair slick from the rain.

"Christ! Dammit!" he said. He used his hands to drag some of the water from his hair.

Cassey considered retrieving the cloth, re-covering the window, but the rain wasn't coming in too heavily. Seeing a pile of folded sheets to her right, she knelt down and retrieved one, passing it to Abe.

"Thanks Cassey," he said, accepting the sheet. "Damned dark in here isn't it."

"Oh… hold on," she replied, and reached into her jacket.

As she went to remove her cellphone, a beam of light fell across her: Abe had a small but powerful LED flashlight in his hand.

"Nice one Abe." She smiled as he approached. The sheet, which she now saw was pink, hung draped over his shoulders.

"Which way?" he asked, and shining the flashlight around the walls, illuminated peeling red wallpaper, the double doors to the dining room.

"The lobby is the best start," Cassey said, and headed towards the door on the west wall. She paused there, trying the light switches. The clicks didn't do anything, making her wonder if Ronson even had the house connected up yet.

The door creaked outwards into the darkened lobby, the only light that which shone through the tall window. Abe fixed this with his flashlight, and shone it around as Cassey stepped into the room. Her footsteps were slow, hesitant. With rotten floorboards on her mind, she felt like she was walking through a minefield. It all looked innocent enough however, exactly the same as when they were last here.

Cassey halted near the staircase and the collapsed chandelier and said, "Hello, Mister Ronson?"

Her words echoed through the room.

Abe stopped beside her. "Did some looking into Ronson, seems he was studying Long Island myths for a book he was working on."

A folklorist yeah, she recalled Ronson mentioning that when she first spoke to him.

"Plenty of that to go around in Long Island," she said absently, and stared up the large wooden staircase, its ornate banisters leading to the second floor balcony.

He'd better not be up there. I'm not going up there.

"Hey look Cassey." Abe aimed his flashlight at the wood-panelled wall beyond the staircase. There were two doors there. A narrow beam of light lined the base of the door on the right.

He started towards it and Cassey followed suit.

"My mom's old library," she said, keeping stride with him.

He waited while she knocked.

"Hello, Mister Ronson?" Cassey said and tried the door. The knob turned, and a moment later, a memory resurfaced: her mother, sat at a table near the centre of the library. She recalled the heady musk of ancient books accompanied by the subtler odor of lilac perfume.

The door opened to a reek of damp: a strong, mildewy stink. This quashed the happy memory quickly, the sight and smells replaced by things decayed.

The table was still there, bearing books and the illuminated storm lamp that had led them here. The wall beyond it held a window. Boarded up badly, cold wind whispered through the gaps. The bookshelves that once brimmed with books were now sagging, spotted with patches of rot.

"Hey?" Abe's touched her shoulder, making her flinch.

"Sorry Cassey," he continued.

She reached up, patted his hand. "Just, it's…" leaving the sentence unfinished, Cassey stepped into the room, examining it more thoroughly as she did. The carpet, light blue once but now dark with dirt, was covered in brown stains. To her right, between empty shelves, stood the door to the kitchen. Beneath it were two large rucksacks, one blue the other red. A rolled up green sleeping bag stood balanced atop them. She paused at the table and found the majority of its surface covered by a large map. One of the two chairs flanking the table held the green wax windbreaker Ronson had been wearing a month earlier.

"I guess the old guy set up some kind of camp here." Abe said, pausing on the opposite side of the table.

Cassey nodded and leant forward to examine the map more closely. It was a large topographical map of the Long Island area. Slightly yellowed from age, there were coffee rings on the areas designating the ocean. What drew her attention however, were the lines and circles drawn in red marker pen.

"Kings Park Psychiatric Center, Kings Park," she read aloud, and tapped the red circle, "That's west of here, below Smithtown Bay. I've heard rumours about the place—it's meant to be a haunted hellhole."

As she continued to examine the map, she noticed Abe looking through the papers and books.

"Oh… Hah! The Amityville house, a hundred and eight, Ocean Avenue." She grinned at this notation. Her smile fell as she traced her finger east, towards their current location. The red line ended at a circle surrounding Lake Ronkonkoma, which lay northeast of the house.

"He's following myths and urban legends it looks like." Abe said. "Here, listen to this: 'There is a tale of an Algonquian maiden, sacrificed in the lake's waters to a god that lived under the lake. This tale is sometimes confused or mixed with another Algonquian myth, of the Lady of the Lake, where a princess, due to marry a member of her tribe, was raped and murdered by a settler on the eve of their wedding. Thrown in the lake, her body was never recovered.'"

"That from a book Abe?" Cassey looked up, saw him reading from a pile of A4 sheets.

"Ronson's own notes it looks like," Abe replied. "'The legend goes that she returns each and every year, haunting the shore of Lake Ronkonkoma in search of victims to appease her tortured soul.'"

"The Phantom Princess. Yeah I've heard of that. My mom had a thing about the folklore hereabouts." *More than that, it consumed her*, Cassey thought. "When I was a kid, she didn't like me going near the lake alone, but that was probably just parental concern." She didn't know if she believed the latter: her mother had always been very superstitious.

Abe put the papers down, scanned the table. "Oh look there's the phone." He reached over and retrieved an old, battered-looking Nokia. "Dead," he continued after tapping a few buttons. "That explains it."

Does it though, she thought, and watched Abe return the phone to the table. *He's an old man, and could have gone out there, fallen in the woods, slipped near the lake.*

Abe began searching through the remainder of the table's contents, old hardcover books on folklore for the most part, with some newer ones with glossy covers.

"Abe," she said, and returned her gaze to the map and the circled area of Lake Ronkonkoma. "I think we need to go search for him."

* * * *

Abe was against the idea, at first, but Cassey talked him round under the condition they wait out the weather. She didn't think it *would* improve, but after half an hour of waiting, the rain eased off. The pair left through the kitchen's back entrance, heading across the soft, overgrown lawn towards the woods surrounding the house.

Apart from the tramping of their feet and the sighing of the trees, it was quiet outside. Abe, now wearing Ronson's windbreaker, had his flashlight aimed forward, a cone of light illuminating the wild grass and weeds leading to the woods.

"You know Cassey, all good intentions aside, this may be us looking for a needle in a haystack."

This wasn't the first time Abe had expressed concern since she brought up her plan, and she certainly couldn't argue the logic of it.

"I know Abe, I just want to scout the area, call for him and see if he responds. Visibility will be better once we reach the lake anyway." *Decent, logical words*, she thought, though they did nothing to ease the fact her own misgivings had evolved into a nebulous but frightening sense of impending doom.

As the woods grew nearer, Cassey decided to get something off her chest.

"This place... even before my parents died, there was something about it. Perhaps that explains the route my life has gone, these encounters I've had with outré things."

They walked in silence for a minute or so, then Abe cleared his throat.

"I know what you mean Cassey, I really do. Brought up in an area so steeped in myths and legends, maybe you've developed a compass for this kinda thing."

Or they have a compass for me, she thought but didn't say.

The woods were in reach now, the tall evergreens swaying like spectres in the wind.

Abe raised the flashlight beam, illuminating thick, ancient tree trunks spotted with burls. The woods' nearly impenetrable darkness fought against the light, and feeling suddenly colder, Cassey braced herself before stepping into the forest proper.

Wet mulch squelched underfoot and she heard rustling around her. Higher up, the tops of the trees sang in the wind. Abe caught up with her, adding his footsteps to her own. Droplets of water, from high up in the trees, hit her as she walked. Cassey found her footing unsteady as mud sucked at her shoes and plant matter tried tripping her up.

She cupped her hands around her mouth. "Mister Ronson? Hey you here?"

There was no reply other than the sounds of the forest. Beyond the flashlight's illumination, the darkness, near complete, appeared filled with movement. Cassey pictured the tree trunks slimy, squirming with abominable life, the burrs puckered orifices, spewing filth and—

"Cassey look."

The interruption dispelled her morbid thoughts.

"Just over there," Abe continued, and aimed the flashlight beam to their left. Cassey stepped in that direction and saw a dark grey bundle, heavily stained and wet from the elements. It appeared too small to be a person, but still she felt a shiver as she reached it. The fabric was damp, coated in dirt. Cassey gripped it one-handed, felt her heart throbbing in her mouth, and pulled.

Beneath was muddy earth, wriggling worms, and nothing else.

"A coat," Abe said, "could be Ronson's?"

She shook the coat, letting muck and droplets of water fall from it. Checking the pockets and finding them empty, she tossed the coat to the ground and wiped her hands on her pants.

She shouted, "Mister Ronson?"

"Hey... you around?" Abe added.

"Let's carry on to the lake," Cassey said, and stepped over the coat to continue the way they were headed.

The visibility soon grew better, indicating they were nearing the end of the woods.

Cassey smelled brackish water on the wind, and passing the last of the trees, saw a sandy shore ahead.

"End of the line," Abe said behind her.

Past the shore, the lake, shimmering a cobalt blue, stood illuminated by a star-littered night sky. Beyond the rippling surface, the far-away silhouettes of trees and buildings lined the horizon. Distant lights were visible, stationary and moving, the latter she attributed to vehicles on the road surrounding the lake.

Her shoes touched wet sand, gritty and cloying underfoot. She looked left and right but saw nothing, no evidence of the missing man.

The lake could have taken him, Cassey thought, and shuddered. This place intimidated her, always had when she was a child, even as a teenager. Her mother said monsters lurked here, and feeling suddenly alone, she took a step back towards the woods.

A light from behind sent her shadow lurching upon the sand. Then Abe appeared, a welcome relief.

"North or south? Which way Abe?"

He stepped beside her, paused, and took a long look left, then right.

"I see something that way," he said.

Cassey turned, squinted, and replied, "Oh yeah, I think there is a shape down there."

The pair headed across the sand, the flashlight illuminating tiny, shining particles as they trudged south.

As they progressed, the shape grew clearer. Cassey was expecting a corpse, but still she felt a fluttering in her chest, a little light-headed as they approached.

At first she thought it was a sand statue. It *was* Ronson however, his head and clothes pitted in a thick coating of sand.

He was crouched with his head down, facing the direction of the lake. Stones were embedded deep in the sand around him, different sized but arranged in an odd but purposeful way. Just beyond him lay a rucksack. Smothered in sand, it had papers poking from its open top.

Cassey took a few tentative steps forward, then went to her knees before Ronson.

"Shit how long has he been out here?" Abe asked in horror.

She reached over, went to feel a hand embedded in the sand. The moment she touched it, the hand flinched, as did she.

"Christ!" she scooted back as the man they thought dead trembled all over.

Ronson's eyes blinked open and his lips parted.

"Alive? He's Alive?" Abe said in surprise, and Cassey hurriedly shushed him.

Ronson was mumbling, his cracked lips mouthing words she couldn't quite catch. Then, bloody drool poured from his mouth.

She leaned forward, her palms pressing down on the wet sand.

"Na-hull-lo ta-sim-bo see-ya." The words came quietly from Ronson's raw, ruined lips.

"Mister Ronson, can you hear me?" Cassey said gently.

Showing no sign of hearing her, he repeated the chant.

Abe knelt beside her. "We should pick him up, get him back to the house."

It seemed a good idea. Cassey went to reply when Ronson's head snapped upwards violently.

"NA-HULL-LO. TA-SIM-BO SEE-YA," he roared, his eyes bulging in their sockets.

A bright illumination appeared from her left. For a confused moment Cassey thought it was Abe's flashlight, but how could that be? It came from the direction of the lake.

Everything turned white. Cassey closed her eyes against the light's intensity and stood. It was bright even beneath the protection of her eyelids. A sound followed: a cacophonous, watery roar.

A pair of hands gripped her shoulders and she heard Abe's voice through the din. "Something coming, we need to leave!"

Cassey let the hands take her, but a few seconds later she found herself released. Raising a hand to her eyes, she risked squeezing them open. The intense light issued from a nearby section of lake, a huge white orb that hovered just inches above the water.

A shape lurked within its depths, a dark, humanoid silhouette. *The princess?* Cassey wondered, recalling the legend. Through the gap in her fingers, she searched round for her friend. She shouted, "Abe!" but the roars absorbed the word.

"Abe!" she cried louder, then saw movement, the indistinct shape of a man stepping towards the glowing ball.

Whatever was in there, raised its arms in welcome.

Oh dear God don't let it be Abe, she thought, went to rush forward, and slipping on a rock, fell to the sand.

The light flashed with painfully bright intensity, then disappeared, as did the noise.

For terrible seconds, Cassey thought she was blind. Her vision soon cleared however, but the orb's afterimages remained.

She climbed to her feet. A sound of quiet sobbing turned her gaze right, and she saw Ronson there, crouched on the sand.

And that means—

Abe! She rushed towards the lake, saw footprints on the sand that terminated at the water's edge.

No. No! He was nowhere to be seen. She stepped into the lake, the cold water reaching her ankles, and cupped her hands around her mouth.

"Abe! Abe! Where are you?"

The waters shifted sluggishly around her, impervious, ignorant to her pleas.

Lake Ronkonkoma would not surrender its secrets so easily.

Epilogue

Cassey sat arms folded, her elbows pressed against the lacquered, grey stone surface of her office desk. Her laptop stood open to her left, the computer in screensaver mode and displaying faux television static.

Before her lay two piles of papers: on the left side, a neat stack of printed sheets, the right: a scrunched, water-damaged pile.

The latter she had retrieved from the dirty rucksack near Ronson, back at Lake Ronkonkoma.

That night... Cassey sighed, shook her head.

The police divers searched the lake for hours, but found nothing. She hadn't expected them to. Ronson, taken away by paramedics, died two weeks later of pneumonia. His niece got the house, and as far as she knew, was still in possession of it.

The other papers, taken from the house, contained the first draft of the book Ronson had been working on. The title, and she leaned forward to read the small print, read:

The Lady of the Lake, and other Long Island Mysteries
by George R. Ronson

Cassey lifted the pile, rolled it up, and turning, dropped it into the waste paper basket behind her desk. Suddenly feeling contaminated, she brushed her hands together vigorously. Then she turned her attention to the other papers. The half-ruined pages held notes about the ghostly Indian princess legend, diagrams, and calendar dates.

The dates were of especial interest. Not only did they cover the time two months earlier when Ronson had tried contacting the princess, but three further dates were marked.

Ten months away, over three consecutive nights, Ronson's studies claimed the princess would reappear.

If she could challenge the apparition, communicate with it even, perhaps she could secure Abe's return.

It was the best, the only plan Cassey had.

KING'S PYRE
W.D. Clifton

The frost was on the headland,
The wind did smell of fire,
As men looked on
With reverent awe
At the old king's funeral pyre.

He was laid in repose on a warship
With treasures of which he'd been fond.
His sword and his shield
Were placed by his side
For the journey into the beyond.

His wealth was laid about him,
though it all would burn or sink;
Yet his deeds would live on
In word and in song
When his folk shared their meat and drink.

Known for his bold adventures,
He was fair and good to all;
The giver of rings
Whose noble life
Would live on in the hall.

He had braved the darksome moors,
As in later days it was told,
To the fen-trolls' lair
Where no other would dare
And returned heavy-laden with gold.

In the deepest depths of the earth,
In caverns as cold as a tomb,
The foul beasts met their match
On the king's red blade;
The steel-clad bringer of doom.

He stood firm on the field of battle,
Always he fought in the fore;
The leader of men

Who laughed in the midst
Of the red-handed madness of war.

Ever so fond of the front lines
When arrows fell out of the blue;
Death came to him,
As it must come to all,
When, at last, an arrow struck true.

And so, upon a lonely headland,
Gathered folk in their mourning to stand
Looking down on their king,
The great giver of rings,
As, burning, he sailed from the land.

THE DRAGON'S GOLD
Ngo Binh Anh Khoa

"I'll journey to the Mountain Old,
The Peak from ages past,
And seize the ancient Dragon's Gold,
The treasure ocean-vast.
To aid my people, poor and frail,
I speak this solemn vow:
Bright wall-bound gems lit up the ground,
Bewitching sparkles gleamed.

I'll claim that Gold, I shall not fail;
Creations, mark me now!

Great Heavens' King, O Boundless One,
Please guide me on this quest,
This oath I give beneath your Sun,
And beg thee, have me blessed."

With single sword and shield and steed,
All bearing mystic runes,
Galvaria would then proceed
To leave his native dunes.

The Sun, the glaring eye of yore,
With every blinking Star,
Would watch his steps to Fortune's Door
In treacherous lands afar.

Through biting blizzards, searing storms,
Sharp gales and battering rains,
Through forests plagued with toxic swarms,
Dank swamps and lifeless plains,

Through realms whose mountains pierced the sky,
And valleys split the ground,
Where shadows snatched all who'd come nigh,
And those in secrets bound.

Lone man and horse through dangers rode,
Enchanted arms in hand
Long soaked with blood from beasts untold,
In search of fabled land.

Bright suns, pale moons would oft trade place,
Six autumns swiftly flew,
Now frost adorned his hair and face,
Draped scenes in somber blue.

Till lastly, he, alone and worn,
Had reached the Mountain Old,
Where dwelled the mutant Dragon-born,
Whose sight none did behold.

The pitch-black entrance of the cave
Appeared an open maw,
But still, the knight, gait steady, brave,
Stepped in that beastly jaw.

There, streams of lava ran around,
Like blood veins they all seemed;

And narrower, and narrower
The way ahead would grow.
But suddenly, the earth would stir;
He'd spot a radiant glow.

A spacious chamber made of stone
With endless boons spread out,
On which the Worm, as bleak as bone,
Crawled zealously about.

Its massive, ivory serpent frame
Loomed o'er the treasure pile;
Twelve fiendish wings, six eyes aflame,
Each boasting vicious wile.

It slithered through the blinding heap;
Sharp teeth glowed in the air;
A spiky tail around would sweep,
Abyssal maw aglare.

The Bastard of unhallowed birth—
The Dragon-kind's dark stain—
Had robbed their gold and fled to Earth,
Into this exiled reign.

So madly it would guard its prize;
Wings beat, eyes flared, teeth flashed;
Out came its shrill, discordant cries,
And frenziedly it thrashed.

The chamber quaked, the Mountain boomed,
And sweltering flames burnt hot,
Old Death (he knew) in shadows loomed,
His faithful scythe he'd brought.

Galvaria, still tall and proud,
Raised high his shield and sword,
"Your gold is mine," he'd shout aloud,
And offer no more word.

One man, one beast, one blazing stage,
Thus fiercely both sides fought,
For neither could escape this cage
Till fatal end was wrought.

By instinct moved, the Worm unleashed
Its hellish, fearsome might.
Dark flames erupted from the beast
To smite the daring knight.

A rapid fiery torrent came
As it took to the air,
And all below was drowned in flame,
But not the cursed gold there.

The agile knight, with sharpened wits,
Leapt on that treasure pile;
His blessed shield hid him from the blitz
Of fires impure and vile.

The battle reached a stalemate then,
For none could forward move,
But cunningness of mortal men
The knight would strive to prove.

Against the Fiend long vexed by Greed,
A scheme he'd fast devise
To lure it down, to make it bleed,
To claim his lordly prize.

With sword now sheathed and shield still raised,
He'd pick an item up.
And to the Worm he'd show, unfazed,
A stolen gem-decked cup.

Exploded then, infernal hot,
Its wild, volcanic wrath.
The airborne frame was earthward brought
Unto the blazing bath.

Long seconds passed, still came no sound,
Save that of sizzling sea.
Then, its large form in fires drowned,
Launched forward forcefully.

And thus the Worm of monstrous size
Would open its mouth wide,
A raging pit that'd brought demise
To all souls trapped inside.

But he with feet as light as air
Escaped that rancid maw;
His foe was briefly stranded there;
An opening he saw.

With movements swift as lightning strikes,
Roars fierce as thunderclap,
Blade once more drawn, he'd pass its spikes;
Unto its flesh he'd stab.

The mystic symbols would ignite,
And pierce through Time-honed scales,
Broadsword imbued with cleansing might
There forced out anguished wails.

Laboriously went the blade
Into unholy skin,
The more the struck Fiend thrashed and swayed,
The deeper it sank in.

He twisted his enchanted steel,
And ran along its length;
The Worm could not as swiftly heal,
And slowly lost its strength.

The knight then reached its spiteful eyes,
Demonic orbs aflame,
And with a string of booming cries,
Slashes on slashes came.

Thus one by one, each eye was robbed
Of vision once acute,
Loud howls of pain though never stopped,
To callous ears were mute.

Upon its bulbous head, he'd stand,
His form majestic, proud.
Then down came his broadsword in hand,
Strained howls rang clear and loud.

Then, desperation fueled its mind;
It'd harshly jerk its head.
And he by bloodlust urged would find,
Below, a pit of red.

A spiral, bottomless abyss
With rings of yellowed teeth.
Corrosive mist spread with each hiss
And every breath it'd breathe.

The knight feared he would meet end,
By poison or by flame.
Still, he'd hold up his shield, defend
Against all things that came.

'Twas like a comet falling fast
Toward the chasm dark.
In haste, a risky spell he'd cast,
"I shan't die here!" he'd bark.

The rune-inscribed blade burnt with light,
A glimmer in the storm.
And like an arrow blazing, bright,
It'd fly toward the Worm.

Into the depth it'd disappear,
A quickly fading dot.
Each moment seemed a painful year
When no effect was wrought.

The pained man further fearful grew
At what lied underneath,
As every second closer drew
Him to the waiting teeth.

He'd close his eyes, awaiting Death
To take that which he owed.
His lungs ached with each labored breath;
His heart with dread turned cold.

As though the gods had heard his prayer,
Great mercy they'd then show.
From deep within the pit down there
Burst forth a dazzling glow.

The creature tossed and turned around,
While roaring bloody cries.
As he fell on the gold-filled ground;
Relief filled blurry eyes.

He'd dodge the blindly writhing Worm
And grab a nearby spear,
Then fast toward its squirming form,
With heavy steps come near.

The Greedy One, now magic-bound,
Collapsed; its outrage stilled.
Where it went down, the gold around
Was stained by dark blood spilled.

He'd close in on the fallen beast
And wear a vicious grin.
All fading strength the man unleashed
To thrust the gold spear in.

Repeatedly, repeatedly,
He'd stab into its brain.
Till from each gaping injury,
Black blood down poured like rain.

With one last strike, the end was spelled,
No more noise from it came.
The Last of Dragon-kind was felled,
The gold was his to claim.

The panting man, imbued with pride,
Let loose triumphant cries.
Beside the ravaged carcass's side,

He'd laugh with foggy eyes.

His quest was done, the prize was his,
His dream at last came true.
No other joys could rival this
Beneath the heaven blue.

How he had crossed o'er countless lands
And slain the Worm of old.
Thus, with a pair of trembling hands,
He'd touch the tainted gold.

No further independent thought
His once sharp mind conceived.
By that for which he'd fiercely fought
His reason was bereaved.

The Dragon's Gold must guarded be
By one with Dragon's blood,
Which had long dyed each injury
And in his veins now gushed.

That ancient law must be obeyed,
A guardian must rise.
The new Protector there thus stayed,
Renounced all earthly ties.

His foe he'd slain, the gold he'd claimed,
All at a heavy cost.
By dark blood chained, he was condemned
To live with freedom lost.

Upon that chamber's shattered throne
Within the timeless keep,
The Deathless King now sits alone
Entrapped in endless sleep.

Yet, if one looks upon his face,
He'll lift his arms and rise.
And in that ring with flames ablaze,
They'll battle till one dies.

Hence, those who wish to seize the gold,
Its King they must defeat.
And should one win the Treasure Old,
They'll thenceforth take his seat.

THE FURY OF ANGELS
Adrian Cole

"You sure you want to see this?"

Krale studied the mine. "I drove two hundred miles to get here. I'm not on holiday."

"It's not pretty."

"Never is." Krale watched several men emerge, carrying tool bags. Others had their hands shoved deep in pockets. All wore looks of suppressed horror.

Manning, the local detective running the investigation, took a deep, uncomfortable breath. "Okay. Shall we go in?"

Krale nodded. He looked around at the steep side of the tor and the mine's restored wheel house, its tapering chimney. His gaze took in the stunted woodland, and the valley's isolated village, where he'd already seen outraged locals. The press had been there, of course, but sensibly Manning had had the entire area cordoned off and warned everyone to keep away or risk arrest.

The mine was unexpectedly warm, the air thick and dusty. Its tunnel was barely above head height, the walls strengthened with planks and thick beams. Krale hated anything underground. They'd told him going down was safe. He'd just have to ignore his churning gut.

Further along, the smell hit him. Beside him, Manning already had a handkerchief across his mouth. Krale was familiar with the reek of death—he'd seen enough corpses to last him several lifetimes, some of them pretty nasty. These came with a sharp, pungent stench. Flesh and bone, guts and innards, exposed and roasted.

A claustrophobic cage dropped deep to levels where the miners still toiled for minerals. Here, copper. After a long fight to revive the mine, the owning company was working it again, sure it would pay. This disaster could wreck that plan, Krale knew, although mining's history was littered with fatal accidents that had never stopped its inexorable progress.

At the bottom levels, the smell was worse. Krale put his own handkerchief around his face: it hardly reduced the appalling fetor. Several of Manning's men were waiting, eyes filled with outrage.

Along the tunnel, Manning stopped. Lamps had been strung out along the ceiling, casting a dull glow over stone and earth, walls and spoil.

Everything gleamed, the walls leaking and dripping.

Krale swore softly. Blood! The stone had been basted in it, as if a madman had carelessly thrown paint everywhere. Krale identified jutting spars of bone, charred and broken. A closer look at the discarded heaps of thick bags revealed they were flesh, corpses reduced to scorched leather, seared and boiled down to the size of children. The miners.

Krale's superior had told him the official line was an explosion. In the outside world, people, relatives, were waiting for reports, anticipating news of collapsed workings, a mine choked with consequential debris. A head count of the missing. All likely dead.

Krale didn't envy the forensic people their job in this hell. "This wasn't an explosion," he said.

"No. The shafts and tunnels are strongly built, but they'd not have survived a blast. A few pockets, maybe. Possibly survivors. Not this."

"I've seen the results of explosions," said Krale. "In labs, some in battlefields. This is something else." Freakish, he thought. Intense heat. What would have generated it?

"Some of the surface miners felt a surge of heat," said Manning. "Took their breath away. They were the only survivors."

"Where are they?"

"Isolated in a temporary hut. Families told they're okay, otherwise no communicating. Until you give the word. My orders from London." Manning almost made it sound like he didn't mind, didn't resent it.

Krale nodded. "It's unfortunate, but we don't want to start a panic. Okay, take me to them."

* * * *

Krale chewed on a sandwich from the pile Manning's people had ordered from a local pub, along with a mug of strong tea. Manning had briefed him about the five miners. All were in shock, some reduced to tears, unable to say much. The medics attended them, but Krale asked for a word with them all in private, much to Manning's irritation.

One, Jed Rouse, a hardened man from a long line of miners, sat stiffly, his anger barely concealed. "Some bastard is going to pay for this."

Krale ignored the comment. "What do you think happened?"

"You a superstitious man?"

It was a challenge, unexpected but interesting. Krale shrugged. "In my job you explore every avenue."

"The mines thrive on myths and legends."

"This mine? Wheel Rose?"

"Sure. The company knew. Laughed at it, likely. Who wouldn't these days?"

"You're not laughing."

Rouse glared at him, then looked away. "No."

"I've got nothing, so far. No clues, no hint of what happened. What I saw makes no sense. No normal explosion, no collapses, no gas escapes. Intense heat, that's all."

Krale saw the words strike something in Rouse.

"Before the men died, did they send a message?"

"Didn't make sense."

"Try me."

"Anders, the foreman, spoke on the phone. They'd disturbed something. Drilled through to a fresh cavern. It was very hot down there. And brilliant, white light, he said. Nothing else."

Krale sat back. "You reckon they released a pocket of high octane gas? Caught fire, burned everything to a crisp?"

"Could be." Rouse looked suddenly evasive.

"Why did you mention legends?"

"Some might say they were responsible."

"Any in particular?"

Rouse looked uneasy, as if he'd said something dumb. "Fire demon."

* * * *

Krale retired to his hotel room early and soaked in his *en suite* bath. He toweled down, dressed and put on the TV. There was nothing fresh in the news broadcasts, nationally or locally. The explosion theory was holding up. Relatives, reporters, so-called experts, geological and the rest, all had their say. Krale grunted at some of the explanations people came up with. Always highly plausibly, no matter how ludicrous.

Fire. As a kid, it had terrified him, more than water, or snakes, or heights. A school mate had set a fire in an old building—died when it collapsed. *Fire*. He'd seen a couple of blazes in London, his job to investigate, to mingle with the panic and pain of those involved. Listening to the firemen describing the horrors of multiple deaths. *Fire*. A weapon to some. Pyromania. He'd encountered it. Madness, a lust for the blaze, the conflagration. Raising the demon. It had a life of its own, brief, ferocious, and yes, demonic.

He studied himself in the mirror, the reflection a fifty year old. Overweight, medium height, slightly sloping shoulders. Thinning hair, though it had never mattered to him. Pop music and its fashions had inspired a lot of his friends, but had passed him by. His face was pasty, too many lines. He preferred city life to the outdoor one. Even as a kid, family trips to the seaside had been no more than okay, something to be endured, not enjoyed. He'd never learned to swim. Or take up any sport for that matter. It seemed trivial, transient.

Testing his brain, solving puzzles, was much more satisfying. He'd always wanted to be a detective. He was a natural, although at The Yard there were colleagues who joked about his intensity. Some of them settled for quick answers, convenient truths, the easy route to success. Notch up the cases solved, move on, and up. He was more dogged. Was that what he saw in his mirrored face now, that ponderous determination to be certain of his facts? Had it aged him?

Fire. The word licked at him, a taunting flame, a prompting reminder why he was here. Gorrell, his superior at the Yard, had called him in a few days ago.

"To be honest, Krale, they don't know what the fuck caused it. Looks like an explosion. Their man down there doesn't think so, nor do the miners. You've had some experience with this sort of thing."

There it was, that inevitable reference. Two years ago. He'd been responsible for bringing in a basket-case called Moran. A nutter who'd set himself up as a gang leader, gathering disaffected youths to his 'cause.' Never hard to find such kids in the slums, eager for excitement. Nothing stirred them up like fire. Moran became their high priest. He started small, but Krale knew his real target was to take down a mosque or two. When Moran was cornered, he told Krale he was a fire-worshiper. "I can summon fire demons," he'd boasted.

Moran got a long sentence, his leading gang members incarcerated, the rest scattered, forgotten. Krale was praised for his part in the affair. Arson. No more than that, though it was bad enough. No demons. Gorrell and his masters only wanted the simple, cold facts on file. Moran's rantings about demons were bollocks. Krale kept his views to himself, but occasionally, in the blurred atmosphere of a pub, someone would grin and mention the case. Krale never rose to the bait.

He contacted Manning on his cell phone.

"Where's the nearest library? They have a local history section? Old newspapers, archives?"

* * * *

Jed Rouse settled in his private spot beside the river, concealed by ferns and trees. His shadow fell behind him, not across the running water, where it would have alerted the fat salmon he was trying to catch. It was close to midday: for the first time since the recent disaster, he was able to shut out its horrors. The Company had called a halt to operations, sympathetically giving everyone time off. The police were still busy, though their efforts were fruitless. The guy from London, Krale, seemed open-minded, but not the rest. Media buzzing around impotently. No one spoke to them, stoic in their agreed silence.

Across the river, beyond steep woods, the sun reached its zenith, burning hot in a cloudless day. Rouse screened his eyes, gently reeling in his fly. He re-cast it, deftly flicking it into calm water.

Sunlight flared, amplified. The massed trees shrank behind its glare. Rouse grimaced, dropping his rod, turning away. The opposite bank was a mirror, reflecting and magnifying the light. Heat boiled off it. Rouse felt the temperature soar, like he'd stepped inside a huge oven. It became unbearable: he stumbled from the bank. Around him the trees and plants burst into flame, trapping him.

In desperation he looked to escape, but he was ringed by fire, the sunlight intolerable. Crying out in agony, he leaped into the river, ducking down, immersing himself. He flung himself upwards immediately—the water was boiling. He clawed himself back to the bank, slipping awkwardly. His clothes were burning, sloughing away like spent skin. In moments it was his skin he was shedding as the heat reached his spine, incinerating it. He felt his eyes melt and would have screamed, but his lips had liquefied.

* * * *

Krale studied the river bank, now fenced off, like the mine. Manning and his men moved up and down the river, trying to find something revealing other than the obvious. A man had been fried alive—*melted*. All that remained was a mess of liquid flesh and bone, barely recognizable. A dog-walker had found the stinking traces and the buckled fishing rod.

On the river, a small boat slid up and back, more of Manning's men studying the water. Manning stepped across scorched, blackened bracken, the ground an ash carpet.

"A conflagration. Hell of a way to die."

"Any ID?" Krale asked.

"Private stretch of river. Reserved for fishermen. See that rod? We're checking, but it's probably Jed Rouse."

Coincidence? Krale asked himself. Rouse, the one man who'd given him anything, albeit a crazy idea. "What else?"

"Opposite bank. More traces of fire."

Manning had them row over. In the cool of the forest they followed a vague trail, signs of fire, leading upwards.

"What's up there?" asked Krale.

"More forest, a few disused mines. Fenced off. Dangerous. You wouldn't go down without specialized equipment. Even then it'd be risky. What do you think we're looking for?" Manning was clearly angry. He didn't like being made a fool of; this whole business had him baffled.

"Unlikely any equipment was used. You'd expect it, to generate fire that intense. We'd have found traces of fuel. On the other hand, there's such a thing as spontaneous combustion, weird as it sounds."

"It's connected to the fire at the mine, surely."

"Probably."

"Pyromaniac? Someone with a grudge against the mine? There was a lot of opposition to it re-opening."

Krale nodded. "Yes, I've been reading up back issues of the local papers."

"Find much?"

"No. I just feel it's going to happen again."

"You don't know that," said Manning, but his eyes betrayed an absolute fear that Krale was right.

* * * *

Krale had persuaded the librarian to let him borrow a few reference books not usually allowed off the premises. His status had won her over; he didn't pretend to have any natural charm with women. His one serious relationship had ended in chaos. He blamed himself and his own inadequacies, not Molly. His friends told him otherwise, but he guessed they were being diplomatic.

He went through the eclectic writings. One was an account of regional mining, with a section on Wheel Rose in its heyday. Others were on local legends, both detailed textbooks and small press pamphlets. According to the material, this countryside was saturated with various mythic creatures. That and witches, sorcerers, demonologists. Krale grinned wryly.

Much of the research was attributable to a man named Augustus Trevannion, who'd published numerous articles and pamphlets, some recently. Which suggested he was still alive. Krale contacted Manning.

"He's a basket case," said Manning. "About two hundred years old. Full of bullshit theories." Nevertheless he gave Krale an address. Krale sensed his irritation, but let it wash over him. He read more until his eyelids drooped and he went to sleep, dreaming of demons dancing and fire scourging the land.

* * * *

After an early breakfast, he rang Trevannion's number. The voice on the line was elderly and fragile, but happy to co-operate.

Trevannion's house was a large building set back from the road in spacious grounds, typical of this area. A quietly spoken housekeeper took Krale to a huge drawing room with a stunning view of grounds and forest. Trevannion sat in an armchair, his frail body curled up. He studied Krale through spectacles that exaggerated the size of his eyes.

"Welcome, inspector."

"It's superintendent, sir," said Krale gently.

"Ah. How can I help?"

"Perhaps you've heard about events at Wheel Rose mine. The explosion."

"Is that what it was?" Trevannion looked skeptical.

"As far as we know, sir. I've read some of your articles. You were quite strongly opposed to the mine being reopened."

Trevannion smiled, though his face looked sour. "Tactfully put, superintendent. I warned against it. I was afraid of something like this. No one heeded me. How many died? Do they even know?"

"You've suggested there was something hostile in the mine. Not to be disturbed at any cost."

"I met with typical modern scorn and derision. Are you a practical man? Why pay any attention to the writings of an old charlatan like me?"

Krale grinned. "I'm not passing judgment, sir. Your theory interests me."

"Know anything about Zoroastrianism? It flourished a long time ago, almost wiped out by the Muslims. Its adherents fled across the world: you'd be surprised where it still resurfaces. Its gods were at war, typifying their nature. Ahura Mazda was the strongest. His divine warriors were given the task of eliminating the *daevas*, the terrible destroyers, the demons of his rival. Many were killed, but some were imprisoned. Deep under the earth, as far away from sunlight as possible, chained in perpetual darkness."

"In places like Wheel Rose?"

"Rather a fanciful notion, isn't it? I've been following the recent news. The media is clueless. I'll tell you what I think you really found."

Krale nodded, his face blank as he listened to the old man describe the scene precisely as it had been found, as if Trevannion had visited it and studied its details. Not possible, he knew.

"The destroyers are angels of light, superintendent. Intense heat, beyond anything we'd normally encounter. Light so strong it'd turn stone molten and flesh—well, it would simply dissolve. I know what you're thinking, but I assure you, what those miners have unwittingly released is an incredibly dangerous source of energy. It's sentient, all-powerful and merciless. It'll undoubtedly strike again, absorbing the energy of those it kills. And it *will* kill."

Krale's mask of feigned indifference slipped.

Trevannion saw it at once. "Dear God, has it has already done so?"

Krale described Jed Rouse's death.

Trevannion sagged back, his eyes haunted. "Now it's fed, it'll begin a terrible campaign. You must evacuate the town. It won't be welcome.

Find an excuse. Warn of more explosions, anything to get people away." Trevannion looked almost hysterical, his convictions absolute.

"No one will believe you, Mr Trevannion. It's too preposterous."

"Not when that thing starts slaughtering people wholesale."

"If we can temporarily move people away—then what? How do we deal with the problem?"

Trevannion's wasted form shuddered as he gathered himself. "It has to be revoked, re-chained in its ancient prison. The mine *must be sealed*."

What did he mean? Revoked? How could that be done? A ritual? Krale rubbed his tired eyes. Christ, he'd be a laughing stock. Who the hell would swallow any of this? Maybe they didn't have to. Maybe he could take Trevannion to the mine and have him do what he thought necessary without involving Manning or anyone else. No one need know. If it worked, fine.

"You can do this?" he asked.

"There's no one else. It has to be me. Some years ago, before the mine was reopened, I visited it with two colleagues. We found an Arabic inscription, a warning. We reported it to the Museum authorities. They were prevented from acting. Silenced."

"Who by?"

"The Government. It gave substantial grants to the project and had a vested interest in the mine's reopening. Our findings were hushed up. My colleagues died a few years ago. I'm a lone voice. But I can show you photographs of the inscription. The real thing was destroyed. Stopped anyone getting too nosy."

* * * *

Krale drove them along narrow lanes to the edge of the moorland. Overhead, clouds piled together ominously, presaging a summer deluge. Beyond the horizon a low grumble of thunder rolled across the high lands like an incoming flood tide. Beside Krale, the old man shrank back into his seat, little more than skin and bones.

His eyes grew even wider behind his spectacles as a flicker of lightning daubed the empty land in its eerie, pale hue.

"Being on high ground is inadvisable," said Krale, turning and aiming the car back towards shelter.

"It's no ordinary storm."

Krale knew the Moors suffered freakish weather, sudden cloud banks lowering like milk, vivid sunlight blotted by abrupt squalls. Trevannion's expression suggested something deeper.

"The *daeva* thrives in light and hides at night. We must get under cover. As the storm breaks, the *daeva* will swirl within it. It has conjured it."

Krale tried to reconcile his acceptance that something abnormal was at work with Trevannion's anthropomorphization of the power. It was a vision too far. As he focused on the road, a white light speared down from the heavens and struck the ground close to the car. Earth and stone erupted as if a mine had exploded; the sound and shock wave hit the car like an angry fist. Krale fought to control it.

"You think that was by chance?" said Trevannion.

The idea that the storm was deliberately singling them out was still too much for Krale. Admittedly they were exposed. Lightning often hit anything even a few feet above ground level. He accelerated as another bolt crashed into the roadside ahead, churning up more earth and riven granite. The car roared past, reaching the first trees of a small copse before swinging into a narrow side road with high banks. Further on it dropped into a steep valley with taller, thicker trees. Krale pulled in to a turning place, the woods forming a canopy. Rain thumped down on the roof, the sound blunting conversation. Lightning flickered brilliantly beyond the screen of foliage.

"The *daeva* will kill to devour knowledge," said Trevannion. "Initially it'll select a handful of people, learning everything it needs. Once it has enough, it'll turn on the town. Hopefully not for a few days. Time to warn people."

As suddenly as it had started, the rain ceased. The clouds dissipated, blown into the distance by a strong wind that disappeared with them. Krale's chest heaved, his knuckles white on the steering wheel.

"Jesus," he breathed. "Any further out on the Moor, we'd have been incinerated."

"Others won't have been so fortunate."

Driving back up the side road, they passed an open gateway, leading into a field. Trevannion gasped, looking across its fallow grasses. A tractor and an old van were parked, abandoned. Both looked like wrecks, smoke gently bubbling from flaking metal.

Krale parked and got out, watching the skies. They were azure, cloudless to the horizons. Beyond the gate, he and Trevannion made their uneasy way through knee-high grass to the vehicles. They knew what had happened. There had been a small group of people here, probably the farmer and some of his workers. The ground around the damaged vehicles was blackened ash. Bodies—their remains—were strewn about like smashed, charred scarecrows.

"They had no chance," said Trevannion. "Such easy targets. We owe them our lives. The *daeva* took them instead of us."

Krale didn't want to think about that. He studied the stinking human debris, appalled at the total destruction. Four of them.

"It may buy us another day," said Trevannion. "The *daeva* will be sat-ed for now. We'll never find it by day—it could be in any patch of sunlight. Tonight it'll hide itself. It hates darkness but needs its cloak. So it'll go underground. Another mine, a tunnel, anywhere deep, where its light cannot be seen."

Krale took in the carnage. If this was not the grim result of a random lightning strike, instead something intelligent and merciless, it must not happen again. And not to an entire *town*.

"Can you stop it?" he asked Trevannion.

"If we can find it tonight, I'll do what I can. It'll be easier to locate. I've been naive. Hunting it in daylight, when it was hunting us."

* * * *

Krale went back to Manning and reported the four deaths. Manning arranged an immediate investigation: the reports that came back were prompt and predictable. Lightning strike. Krale said nothing about his own narrow escape.

"Forecast for tomorrow is crap," said Manning. He shared a hastily prepared sandwich and coffee with Krale. "Heavy rain. Probably thunderstorms. Makes this job a nightmare. Get much out of Augustus Trevannion? His mind's gone. He was brilliant once. Worked with the Government for a while. Some scandal. Trevannion was discredited. It was hushed up."

Krale chewed with difficulty. If Trevannion's prediction about the so-called *daeva* was right, all hell was going to break loose.

* * * *

Night on the Moor was uniquely silent. The clear sky was star-lit, the sliver of moon adding to the gentle light. Krale sat behind the wheel of the car, waiting while Trevannion fussed about in the boot, organizing his various bits of paraphernalia.

Am I really doing this? Krale thought. Demon hunting on the Moor near midnight. What would Molly have thought? I mocked her obsession with the supernatural. No, that's not fair. It wasn't an obsession, just something that intrigued her. I was too arrogant to let it pass. I paid for it, though. Mocked her to the point of anger. I was too stubborn to back down. Told her it was all bollocks and she should grow up. Kind, patient Molly, blazing with unfamiliar rage, driven away. Long gone. Never replaced.

Maybe tonight was for her. My open-mindedness would have amazed her.

"I'm ready," said Trevannion.

Krale got out, locking the car. There was a path through the heather and jutting knobs of granite, winding towards the tors. Lower down the hillside, a few miles away, a village was a darker stain against the night landscape, speckled with lights, deeply silent. Krale turned, holding the flashlight's beam steady, keeping it angled down so it wouldn't spear outwards and alert anyone, any*thing* watching.

Trevannion had a small bag. He walked more easily, his movements less hampered by age and illness, as though, ironically, this hunt had brought back some of the vigor of younger days.

They said nothing, walking on for a distance, high up on the Moor now, completely isolated, in a soundless vacuum. A huge black mass of rocks loomed, its presence impenetrable. Heaped up like the sculpture of a giant, the stack as it was called locally, made Krale start, as if shifting in its bed. Men who had farmed these lands before history began had venerated such places.

"Watch the moorlands," said Trevannion, approaching a flattish grass area at the base of the rocks. He opened his bag. Krale watched him take small implements from it. The old man pressed something into the earth, on his knees. He reached out with both hands, putting his palms flat against the stone and began muttering. Krale caught the name, Ahura Mazda.

Krale turned away. *I have to go through with this now, no matter how bizarre.* The surrounding view was spectacular, even in this quasi-light. He studied the near horizon, the dip of land. Had he felt something underground? A gentle vibration, as if a heavy vehicle had passed. It came again. Christ, had Trevannion disturbed something?

He looked harder at the landscape. Again he felt a reverberation, a minor tremor. Trevannion's head was bowed, hands still on the stone. The stack's grotesque shape was blurred in shadows, softly humming like a generator.

Lower down, where a small stream cut incisively into deep folds of heather, a nimbus flared, a white light, fierce and unwavering. Krale shielded his eyes, afraid the light would sear his eyeballs. There was movement beside him. Trevannion had exchanged his usual glasses for a wide pair of sunglasses.

He handed Krale another pair and he put them on. At once the night closed in, except for the area around the nimbus. He knew what it must be.

"Come to the stones. Their power will protect us."

They set their backs to the base of the stack. Trevannion continued his ritual, when a second light appeared further along the curve of moor. Krale spun round to see a third light, slightly above them, and then, God help them, a fourth.

He swore crudely.

Trevannion's face was a white mask, his frame somehow shriveled, diminished even more by his fear of what was to come.

Krale watched the lights growing in intensity. The earth trembled more perceptibly, a minor quake. It almost shook him to his knees. Beside him, Trevannion was murmuring, words tumbling out of him, foreign sounds, an archaic prayer maybe. Nothing checked the progress of the lights. They were closing in. There was nowhere to run, no way of escaping their tightening trap. Krale pictured the scorched corpses he'd seen, the melted bones and swathes of blood. He forced himself to shut the visions out.

Light rose up from a dip yards away, a writhing cloud, thickening, its form churning until it twisted itself into a barely recognizable shape, a hunched, gnarled thing, with elongated arms and bludgeon-like hands. There was a smear of dreadful face, the teeth brilliant white light. Intensifying luminescence flooded from the thing, a rain of tiny arrows. Krale felt their stinging heat. *I'm going to die here.*

"*Daeva,*" cried Trevannion. "Look away! It's pulling images from your mind." Light reflected from his sunglasses, making his face alien, a contorted mask of terror. His body shrank, a husk, hands flapping uselessly.

Krale had no weapon with which to fight the fiery nightmare. The blazing heat increased, the *daeva* becoming a column of light revolving at speed, the creature's face blurred as the *daeva* fused with the ground, a gathering wave of boiling rock and soil, burrowing forward, eager to engulf the men. Krale felt the ground writhing, swelling like the sea, its temperature rising dangerously. Inevitably the *daeva* would rise a last time and the two men would be engulfed in its molten power. Krale wanted to scream, but had no voice. The rocks at his back were cold to the touch, unaffected by the *daeva's* fires. He grabbed for the stone in desperation, as if he could scale it, mentally praying to the primeval gods of the past.

* * * *

It seemed that the mass of melting stone and soil would burst over them, metamorphosing them, turning liquid flesh to lava. Around the two men the air pulsed and then shook to a combined detonation as more light erupted from the ground, too intense to look at. The *daeva* was wrapped in the dazzling glare, thrust further underground. Krale squinted and saw the wall of light blasting its way downward, no more than yards away, and yet, somehow, the heat faded. The earth appeared to suck the light into it, three swirling columns of it, until darkness abruptly swept over everything once more. Krale felt the ground immediately beneath him rock, and whatever powers churned it slipped with lightning speed even deeper. Krale looked around, searching for the other fire demons. Why had they not finished their murderous work?

"Where are they?" he said, his voice a dry rattle.

"Underground," Trevannion gasped, rising unsteadily to his feet. "The four of them. It's not us the others have come for."

The whole tor shook to another subterranean blast. Krale lurched and fell, Trevannion beside him. Faces close to the earth, they heard sounds below, amplified by the stone and packed soil. Sounds of destruction, collapsing walls of rock, an inner world thunder.

"The—car," Trevannion urged.

Krale helped him to his feet, but the old man could hardly move, energy sapped. Krale supported him, though Trevannion weighed no more than a child. They staggered back along the track, the ground still rippling. The grinding of stone sounded in some other, far-flung realm.

Krale got them to the car, bundling Trevannion into the passenger seat, where he slumped in darkness. The effort of all this had been too much for his heart, his life ebbing. He managed one word. "*Yazatas.*"

Krale realized Trevannion's sunglasses were welded to his face, fused to his flesh by the heat. Thin beads of blood trickled from beneath them.

"Why didn't they kill us? We were at their mercy."

There was no answer. Nothing more from Trevannion. His heart had given out.

Krale removed his own sunglasses and started the engine, moving off. Driving away, he recalled his conversations with Trevannion earlier, the old man talking so animatedly about Zoroastrianism. *Yazatas.* Servants of the god, Ahura Mazda. The *daeva's* original jailers, who'd incarcerated it, eons ago.

Maybe the power in the stone stack had amplified Trevannion's desperate call for help—or had it been a summoning? The old man had known what it would mean. It was the *daeva* the three *Yazatas* had come for, not the two men. To chain it anew, far down in the remotest guts of the earth. The huge tor and its piled boulders, etched against the spangled night, had become a silent, implacable tombstone.

KEISHA'S DINOSAUR
Nicole Givens Kurtz

A dinosaur!

Crouched behind a taco cart, Keisha Mabry knew better than to engage him in close quarters. Her spot by the Bob's Barbershop's trashcan counted as close. A faint trickle of water and the scampering of rats rushed out to greet her.

She tightened her grip on the thick strap of her backpack as she hoisted her head higher to monitor his movements. With her hoverboard in one hand, she released a tight breath. The moldy, stagnant stench of standing water came with the dinosaur. Around its left, rear ankle a brand read *ACH Corporation.*

Such a primitive way of labeling your pet, Keisha thought. Just insert a finder's chip and be done with it.

Keisha watched him, but didn't move from her hiding spot. It had to be a *him* because females didn't have the feathers. She'd learned in school that the male had to woo his potential mate, and often had more beautiful and more colorful feathers than the female in question. But if the female version of this was larger, as was common, then this one's mate must be huge! Bigger than any bus that rolled through Baltimore and definitively bigger than some of the buildings, the monster-sized reptile crawled out of the velvety ether. It creaked and moved in jerky movements. It erupted into the narrow alley-space between the dumpsters and the compost containers like The District's Striker, hitting the hole with ferocity, sprinting toward the goal.

Across the street, stepping a large foot out from the alley, the bright orange feathered beast peered out at the strange vehicles parked along the curb. Its head tilted to the side and it sniffed, nostrils enlarging as it smelled the aroma of gasoline and fire. It had teeth. Small beady eyes on either side of its head. Beneath the rows of feathers, along its spine, rows of slate-colored, bony plates shot through.

With a grimace, she remembered her momma's wisdom; a fire should be put out while it's still small. Despite the heat, Keisha shivered. Sweat gathered at the back of her neck.

Darn it! She'd waited too long to escape without risking the dinosaur seeing her.

A palpable buzz filled the sudden silence as people took their first eyeful of the monstrosity creeping from the alley. Keisha's stomach felt hollow. She hadn't meant to trigger the portal or whatever the hell happened to bring the blackness to life. It had simply hovered in the middle of the air, a tiny almost baseball-sized inky black glob.

She could see her reflection shining in the liquid ball, but when she poked it with a stick, it didn't burst. Instead it exploded, expanding faster than she could blink, sending her windmilling backwards into one of the dumpsters before fleeing outright to the safety behind the taco cart.

The screams ripped through her musings, snatching her with roughness back to the events unfolding in front of her. The dinosaur pushed further out into traffic, having found the car's fumes repulsive. It plowed on through people like a toddler stomping on ants. Screams, car horns, and crying rose up in a chaotic din on the cusp of exploding fully into panic. On all fours, it crawled through downtown traffic, both on the ground and in the air. Wauto, wind automobiles, and aerocycles zipped and scattered to avoid it. Blaring of horns and drivers shouting into the wind at the dinosaur only infuriated it more. The tension pushed tight and hard against Keisha, but she stood up to get a better view.

At that moment, a loud roar shattered above the din. Keisha put her hands over her ears, but didn't close her eyes. She needed awareness right now, not fear. Her neck felt hot with the shame of her actions and the heat flooded her face. Still, the magnificent creature was stunning in its grandeur. The dinosaur continued on its way, crushing anything and any*one* unlucky enough to find themselves in its path.

Heart thundering in her chest, Keisha stood up and slipped her hoverboard beneath her feet in one fluid moment. It levitated as she bent her knees, crouching slightly to get more height. Feeling steadier, she adjusted the weight of her left foot and shot off into the sky—away from the walking disaster. The acidic mix of fear and adrenaline made her nauseous, but no hurling on the board. That was Poppa's *numero uno* rule. No vomiting when hoverboarding. She didn't want folks thinking she couldn't handle her board.

Oh, but wait until Poppa got a load of this! The alley between Bob's Barbershop and the Thai restaurant hadn't produced anything like this—ever! This gave a whole other dimension to gentrification. She glanced over her shoulder to get a fix on where old fluffy had crashed. It roared as people ran, panic having finally burst over the area. The regulator sirens screamed and emergency horns blared as the area dissolved into complete and utter chaos. Debris and fiberglass rained down like a shower of diamonds.

She scrubbed a hand through her short afro. Keisha's blood pounded in her ears as it roared in fury. She could still make out the dino's rage and complete frustration at the surroundings. As she hurried toward the 134 train home, her heart pitched as the dinosaur roared again. It sounded sad and confused. Frustrated, like her little sister Melanie did when she couldn't clear the level on her VR gaming console. Keisha leaned forward a bit and the hoverboard slowed. A horn blared from behind her, spooking her so that she almost fell off her board. Her hands shot out to stabilize her.

"Move!" the driver shouted, sending spittle and a string of profanity as he streaked by.

Keisha gave her favorite hand signal in response, but she couldn't linger too long. The dinosaur's constant stomping shook the ground so hard that windows shattered and buildings crumbled. In all the rumbling, the dinosaur had spied her.

Its head had been turned to the side, but its oval, multi-lid eye locked on her. It started for her almost immediately. Had it gotten a good look at her in the alley? Or worse yet, a good scent? Groaning, Keisha slammed her left foot onto her hoverboard and took off into traffic. The roaring spooked her and she cringed. The pounding steps came after her as she looked back over her shoulder—it really was coming for her—pushed the acidic knot of terror higher into her throat. She imagined herself a bothersome fly, buzzing about like a black dot in front of the large dinosaur. If he managed to swat her down, she'd go *splat* for sure!

So she pushed on, bobbing and weaving through the panicked traffic. All hopes of folks obeying the elevated lanes' regulations were crushed as she clipped the bumper of a bright pink wauto who suddenly decided to stop short. Its scarlet brakes glared in her eyes, Keisha had to shut them to stop seeing red. The impact sent Keisha spinning into the other elevated lane, narrowly missing the front fender of stationary cargo craft. Her thigh shrieked in agony, and she knew there'd be a dark, angry purple bruise where she plowed into the wauto.

Once she'd stopped spinning, she found herself in the holding lane. Bright, flashing blue lights separate this section of sky from the lanes. An area for those who needed to fly out of traffic. Thankfully, no one had been hovering in the spot when she went careening into it. She wanted to sit down and check her thigh, but that was out of the question. Still, her head spun from the whirling around. Dizzy, she fought to keep her stomach from inching any further into her throat.

Waaaaah!

Keisha snatched her head up, and came face to face, well to nose, with the dinosaur. It blew out a deafening roar, perhaps in greeting, and then stayed still, peering at her from its left eye. She had to put her hands over her ears, but the noise shook through her, down to her bones. All around its feet, regulator cars and citizens attacked it, photographed it, and tried to get its attention. Nothing worked. Around its head, cargo crafts, aerocycles, and wautos zipped by, roaring their blasters in their wake as they fled.

The dinosaur ignored it all. It only had an eye for Keisha.

She swallowed but dared to move any other part of her body. Frozen to the spot, she forced herself to breathe. If she passed out here, she'd free fall to the pavement below. There wouldn't be time to erect a mat. *Splat.* She suppressed a shudder.

Suddenly, the dinosaur flinched.

Keisha looked at the metallic-colored wauto buzzing around the dinosaur's head. She could barely hear herself think over the roaring of its blasters. The passenger side door stood ajar as a person dressed in the sleek, black uniform of Baltimore's finest, leveled his laser-cannon and fired.

The electric blue sphere shot out of the cannon and plowed into the dinosaur's face, wrenching a scream from it. Its tail flailed and flipped, turning over vehicles and pedestrians on the ground, alike. It stomped people and possessions into wet liquid spots.

"Great, genius! Now, it's really mad!" Keisha shouted.

They couldn't hear her over the din and she knew it. Didn't they care about the lives of those on the ground, being crushed? Surely, there had to be another way to stop the unfurling pandemonium.

Across from her, in the wauto, the regulator readied for another shot. Keisha and the dinosaur's eyes met once more, but this time, she saw fear—and pain.

"This is my fault. This is all my fault." She ran a punishing hand through her afro.

And then, without thinking on it more, Keisha pushed off on her hoverboard into the elevated lanes, zipping through the screaming, crying, and in some instances, dead drivers lodged in their vehicles. She went right for the Baltimore Regulator wauto. Her adrenaline pumped harder, faster, as she got closer.

Once positioned between the wauto and the dinosaur, she threw her hands out and screamed, "Stop!"

The wauto's pilot waved her off.

"Stop shooting!" Keisha's voice sounded pitiful in the roar of the situation, but even if they couldn't hear her words, they saw her actions. "Don't shoot!"

Keisha bit her lip to keep it from trembling. Baltimore's regulators would most certainly shoot a young, black woman. They had proven, both historically and currently, that her life meant about as much, perhaps less, than the dinosaur behind her. She had to try. Misunderstood, the dinosaur had entered into a foreign place, and out of fear, confusion, and perhaps even a bit of anger, had caused a lot of carnage and destruction. That didn't mean it had to die for it.

"Citizen. Move!" The announcement blared from the regulator's loud-speaker.

"Please. It's afraid." Keisha pivoted on her board and she rose higher.

Now, she could see directly into the regulator's wauto. The heavily visored persons looked genderless, in their black uniforms and thick helmets. Gloved hands held the steering wheel, while the passenger crouched in the open doorway, laser-cannon shouldered on his right. The driver spoke into the loudspeaker again.

"Citizen. You are in the direct path of the dino…"

Just then a large, shadowy tail swept by Keisha, moving faster than she could blink.

"What the hell?"

Smack!

The regulator wauto shot across the air like a hot pink dart. The wauto bowled down through traffic, slamming into other vehicles, like bumper cars, briefly coming to a stop, before plummeting down to the earth.

Keisha swung around to find the dinosaur only a mere five feet from her. It breathed out a huff, as if saying *Take that!* to those regulators.

"Thank you." Keisha reached out a hand. Somehow, the dinosaur knew they both were in danger and acted. With her heart thundering and her palms sticky with sweat, she inched closer to the marvel.

Not monstrous. A marvel of science or magic, which depending on the day, were only two sides of the same coin. Keisha peered at the dinosaur. They'd been extinct since forever, but here one was, a mere few feet from her.

"Hi. I'm not gonna hurt you. Just a tiny touch of your feathers." Keisha cooed.

When her fingers brushed the soft, orange feathers, a sense of calm washed over her. This incredible creature settled her in a way that Keisha thought only her hoverboard could.

"You! Stop!" Blared another regulator issued loudspeaker.

Keisha turned around to see a group of regulator wautos, surrounding them.

"We've got to get out of here." Keisha shouted at the dinosaur.

The dinosaur didn't roar, but instead lowered her head.

"You can understand me?" Keisha couldn't believe it.

But she didn't have time to wait. She leapt from her hoverboard and onto the dinosaur's back, right against the first rocky plate that jutted out of its back.

With her hoverboard clutched beneath one arm, and her other arm partially wrapped around the plate, Keisha settled into the soft down of feathers. They felt strangely plush, but the stone-like plates were hard as they looked.

The dinosaur turned around, knocking into buildings, smashing into poles and people alike. *A bull in a China shop,* Keisha thought. Still, they had to get away from here. Far away.

"Let's go!" Keisha patted her.

The dinosaur agreed, heading back the way they'd come, toward the alley between Bob's Barbershop and the Thai restaurant. It seemed to instinctively know that pushing forward into the city would be a horrid idea. Did it pick up on that from her? Keisha didn't know.

She watched the world go sluggishly by as the four-legged dinosaur crawled back to the alley. It dawned on her that she was riding a dinosaur!

"Waaa-HOOOOOOO!" She laughed.

The regulators hadn't given up, as they chased them. Laser-cannon fire erupted around them. She'd spied a television crew's cargo craft. Now, they had an audience. With a citizen sitting on its back, she doubted the regulators would try to kill it—or they might kill her. Or maybe they would.

At that moment, Keisha didn't care. Her curiosity had gotten them into this situation, and now, it could kill her. But the dinosaur shouldn't pay the price. That had never stopped innocents from dying for others' ideology and actions before. Still, she didn't want that on her conscience.

"Just a little bit more!" Keisha patted the dinosaur's back. "You can make it. *We* can make it."

The laser-cannon fire landed, and the dinosaur roared. Yet, it kept on crawling towards its destination. Keisha looked at the wounds the laser-cannon created. Sure enough, they burned through the feathers and singed the flesh below. Raw, reddish, and beginning to ooze a pink liquid, the dinosaur's injuries would need treatment. Too many more of those and the beast might be seriously hurt.

"You must be female. Only a female would be so determined." Keisha patted her again.

Another roar, this one softer, as if agreeing with Keisha. It held no hints of pain or agitation.

"A female then." Keisha saw the carnage and destructive path the dinosaur had made come back into view. In a few more steps, they'd be at the alley's entrance.

"Please let the portal still be there." Keisha prayed. "You don't belong in this when."

"Stop! Halt!" The regulators' familiar song sounded more like background noise at this point.

"Yes! You did it!" Keisha shouted as the dinosaur turned into the alley.

Sure enough, the velvet blackness sat hovering in the air. Rippling with blue electricity crackling every so often. Keisha sighed. The fun had ended.

She stood up, dropped her hoverboard, and stepped onto it. Sailing out of the dinosaur's feathers, and around to her right eyes, Keisha turned to face her.

"Thank you, girl for visiting my when. You can't stay here. I know you must miss your own family and your own when."

The dinosaur watched her intently, but did not respond.

"Okay, so go on then! Go home!" Keisha floated toward the big oval and gestured for the dinosaur to enter. "Come on. Go!"

A laser-cannon blast lit up the gloomy alleyway. The dinosaur growled.

"No! Don't worry about them. Go home!" Keisha hovered higher, above the dinosaur so she could see the regulators. A sea of them now blocked the exit back to the street. Flashing scarlet and blue lights atop metallic wautos arranged in a formation that limited one's ability to soar over them.

Then she saw it. Each passenger side door had risen. Dozens of laser-cannons trained on the dinosaur.

"Go!" Keisha screamed with every fiber of her being.

Perhaps the being heard the fear in her voice, or the panic, Keisha didn't know which, but the dinosaur crept toward the portal. She moved slowly, not used to having to hurry to do anything, Keisha would guess because of her size.

"They're going to fire." Keisha zoomed on her hoverboard, positioning herself in front of the regulators, but behind the dinosaur.

"She's going back. Please don't shoot!"

"Citizen. Lower yourself to the ground. You will be taken into custody for harboring a dangerous creature and engaging in illegal scientific experiments."

"It isn't my dinosaur!" Keisha couldn't believe it. She didn't create it. Someone called the ACH Corporation did.

"Down!" The regulator spat.

She took her time. As she sank closer to the ground, the dinosaur had all but disappeared back into the portal from which it had come. Only a tiny bit of its giant tail remained. An enormous slug inching into the blackness. She didn't get to say goodbye.

"Hands on your head!" The regulator shouted, pulling her back to her current predicament. He snatched her arms with rough hands, while another one secured her hoverboard.

"It isn't my dinosaur!" Keisha said, fear making her voice thin.

The regulator shrugged. "Weren't you riding it?"

Keisha nodded numbly.

"Well, it's your dinosaur now." ✗

WILL HOME REMEMBER ME?
Joseph S. Pulver, Sr.

for LC and John Clare

THEY changed the doorlocks at the Chelsea Hotel, (asylum for some of us) (sigh). Left my now-useless (worn) key in the sewergrate at the end of the block (sigh).

Skeletal remains of midnight; painwalkers; nightwolves; tattoos and slowmotion deadendings; ain't got got; avalanche of butchers on the streetcorner singing dress-rehearsal-rags between the barked hotrushes of the Devil's crazy truth (sigh). No playful naked moon, lighting blessed hours (sigh). Out of fire (sigh). (But I still have an idea left in me) (sigh). No curatives for my waltz in this disorder (sigh) or what passes for love… (after closing time) (sigh).

Grief (sigh)

Lunacy (sigh)

Missed out (sigh)

Shit out (sigh)

(Ain't done) cryin' (sigh)

Old Army jacket I've draped over my spent is not blue, is no raincoat, not even close (sigh).

Streetlevel, after midnight (is put back in its coffin) (sigh). Tawdry neon winking… wounded-sexmusicsirens (evicted from Vienna and other spice-boxes) still pretty as they cry in the ashes and sand (sigh). Poolhall afterlife (sigh)—Fresh off the ghost ship, girl (from a Raymond Chandler movie) fixed to ruin, without a map of the graveyard shift (sigh); Alpha predator with claws to catch, at its 6 a greasy grey-toady, reeling in the scraps (sigh); Spit (sigh); Sparks (sigh); Screamer (sigh); Fever (sigh). Looking passed the tribe sharing crazy-with-crazy… through the cracks in the chessboard/dancefloor… toward… home……………. (sigh).

I was a king—iron that didn't ask questions. I had flowers for every occasion and friends who collected golden stories to brighten any temporary gloom. Thought my lamps wouldn't let the world change.

My broom out of roses and chocolates, pushing little but sand and dust, I didn't notice I was gathering rust. Lost the feathers on my bicycle. Wound up a loser—beautiful behind me with the hymns of history and all the bales I lifted on the shores of the Mohawk.

Home... do they let sparrows (that wasted the waltz) return? (sigh)

Home... is it still Sweet, or does she still wear, "Damn you!"? (sigh)

Roll a smoke, light it with a bent paper-match (sigh). My feet, sore in Hank Williams shoes, begin allnight—(sigh)

Miles... (no angels) (sigh)... Can't remember how far, or how many rivers need to be crossed, but it's That Way>miles>scar>hill>encounter>andMOREAGAIN (sigh)

Gravel—Asphalt—Grassy path—(South behind me)—Morning miles morning aches (sigh)... Thirst to exhume what I hid in the tombstone yard (sigh)

...washed linens on a line; dress, trousers, underclothes

...tobacconist

...barbershop

postoffice

bookstore

silent as The Long Letter written but never mailed

* * * *

Black girl with a broom, sweeping up dead sparrows, not the brown ones, only the smaller greys. Her skin reflects my return. Her eyes are full of the symptoms "They" claim showed up on the day "They" checked me outOF the asylum. Or is it fear? Hard to tell who went mad and who was sacrificed.

That's why I'm here. Back (on the streets AGAIN). Just me (and nature) (and the journey). Hungry and thirsty are we three.

The black girl (from this angle/in this light) looks like Charlotte Rampling, a younger version, with dark skin, and fuller lips, of course. I would have slept with Charlotte Rampling (her eyes are sexy [they know waking up alone and April spring by heart and what the universe reveals when the widows are open] and are as complex and mysterious as ghosts, or the motives of the moon). (I don't know if she would have thought our merger magic or a mistake) BUT I NEVER HAD THE CHANCE. Seems a shame. We could have had a meaningful conversation after (maybe many—the more the lovelier, of that I'm certain); life... up/down/the fragments explained by emotion/the screen credits, pretending to behave, how daring she was, examined sexual tension and who hurt who, or just asked each other, what's on your mind? Yes, standing here waiting for the tram, seems a shame we didn't get the chance to discover who we were.

I first saw Charlotte Rampling when she appeared as Laura in Sidney Lumet's THE VERDICT. Fell hard for her; I'm sure a lot of filmgoers did.

Then, she played Dorrie in Stardust Memories, and Margaret Krusemark in Angel Heart. Hat trick. Everything I wanted was in her eyes…and her smile. She'd be able to know who I was and why, and together we could fix everything, big things, day-to-day dullness, (all the ticks and chipped artifacts that devalue my truth of SELF). She'd understand the possibilities and what you could create from them, how our human energy and desire to rise above damned and war and the terrain and turmoil of paralysis, and could sweep away the negative aspects of the human condition. That's why I began sending her postcards. Not from New York or L.A., or London. I sent her postcards from my island.

The black girl looked at me momentarily. I wonder if the black girl's smile means I could sleep with her. Probably not. Probably means, hi, I don't bite.

But so many things do.

[mirror factory—the mirror didn't show your face, but the phrase that summed you up. {yes, I remember mine.} MUST you keep repeating it?]

[reliving it—the incarceration (in the room where the cobwebs droned on and on…) of the QUESTIONS. Where the bluE 7thEaster-rabbit went? (shameyour hands areso small when you need them to hold on to things youlove.) When and how you lost the/one-eyed/BEAR? Yet, you still have the monkey that sat with you the whole time you were in traction—sad, the plug fell out and you lost the penny for your dreams that was inside its hardplastic belly. How many times in your cell (they called it a room, but they also said you must always attempt to speak only the truth), strapped down to that bed, did you wonder what year that penny was minted?]

[the slow piano sounds like tears. the trumpeted, strangely-muted sounds that accompany it sound like the children of lonely wind. You're on rightbrain patrol, but you can't see the foggy shore where the players wait for you to catch up.]

Bicycle bell, comforting sound delightfully old school (like Mom's simple Westclock radio on the kitchen counter when you lived on 10th Avenue by the chemical plant), jars me from my rearward woolgathering. Funny, it's so easy to sleep/drift/lean into the viewing of an unexpected idea standing up. I look down to see if I'm wearing KEDS. I'm not. But there's a dime, face up. A whole dime. How much is it worth these days? Was a time (when I lived on Strong Street two doors from Rodken's tiny one-room store) it bought you 25 tar babies. 25 sweet, jelly tar babies… You were naked in the blue room with Gail, touching slowly—sailing, stroking her breast, kissing her, about TO, and as good as that was, and it was good—you were amazed and thankful and could have cried, it didn't quite live up to the taste of those tar babies. Shame. It was supposed to, that's what they all said. Everyone, plumbers and football players and poets even the ones with sad eyes and guitars, said it would be.) Girl, blonde Nordic-blonde, long hair, big smile, gentle big eyes—Nordic blue eyes summersky soft eyes, on a bicycle, rang her bell. I stepped back, out of her way. Thought to follow her.

But I've yet to decide what to do about the beautiful black girl. Can "Hi" hurt? Is it Okay now? Would "They" hurt me for asking? Have "They" fixed the fear and bigotry while I was away? Have I come far enough not to worry about what I've forgotten and the escape? I'm not sure it's a good idea to take out the memories and touch them; they always bit when they were annoyed. Might be better if they remained in those paintings of dust, where no dove language ever flew?

BUT… but

she's not smiling at the other people waiting for the tram. They don't even notice, she (I think her name must be Clare. She's bright enough, summersky soft enough, to be. Yes, Clare.) wears no shirt or shoes, just her black, Bojangles baggy pants and the black suspenders.

And she's so beautiful, elegant painting in a museum beautiful, model beautiful. And soft—it's a good look for her. Softer than the memories. Softer than the evidence "They" said was in my diaries.

(Is the diary I buried in the yard still there? "They" never said they found it. Never held it up and read from it, or yelled degradations.) {It's very possible "They" never discovered the map, which means "They" never unearthed that volume of my diary.} [I don't have a map. Dr. Clare did; said she did. Talked about re-forgetting and pre-remembered, about how they shape the map. I've done both, or so Dr. Clare told me.] (Have I decided the black girl's name is Clare due to my continuing feelings for Dr. Clare? Seems like the kind of thing I'd do. They both have soft dark eyes, soft dark hair, short hair. Both of their bodies are long and curvy, too. Clare, Dr. Clare, was always quick to smile—it felt like a lover's hand—it felt like a lover's tender kiss. I wonder if the black girl, this vibrant, delightful new Clare, would react in a similar fashion. It's easy to dream of my new Clare's kindness flying from her warm face directly to my heart.)

Curvy—womanly. Soft. Kind. Warm—afterglow warm, sweet as the afterschool cookies in Grandmother's cookie jar. Generous smile. Warm eyes that never catalog ill-weather bearing clouds, never invite ghosts to stretch into the space you have carved-out for dreaming. Soothing eyes you do not want to be free of. Big heart, one a vast chamber a garden of passions, one a hearth-warm endless chamber of serene. Nice hands, soft hands, loving hands—a fine summer morning you do not want to be free of, stimulating hands, nurturing hands—oasis, hands that do not interrogate a man's eccentricities—Oh Clare…

I could just dance right over to her. "Hi", one friendly word and we'd be talking, sharing, creating living from the aware-river of mind, and it would evolve significance to significance. Like a fairy tale, the princess and the lowly knight free of thorns (and chains and unsuccessful landscapes and nay and scorn) would rise, become pearl-colored stars ringing from the bell tower of grace. The dull dullbrown and drab-grey stage would become a canvas of roses, a panorama exhibiting the highest elevations of spring.

Hi is easy. "They" said it would be, over and over in the private sessions. Half the time I thought "They" were trying to convince themselves and not me. And I think I believe it might be easy. Starting to feel it might be.

The #7 tram that runs (mostly uphill) from the County Home for the Aged and the O. D. Driberg Developmental Center on upper Union Street to Downtown, has departed. The crowd here was bustle-to-I'm-late-quick to get on and sit, and whoosh, they've gone. They did not appear to be shoppers to me, but I'm told they come in all shapes and sizes, so they may have been. Just her and me here, now. Her, still sweeping, not spaced-out, but with purpose (though I could not discern it). Me, rolling Hi around in my mouth to see how it fits and wondering what it might do if it enters the Outer World. I've always had that problem, worrying what happens when I let it out. Will it behave; will it come out the way I hoped? "They" told me other people do the same thing, but they don't come with subtitles, so you can tell if that's what really going on behind their eyes.

Decipherability. I could go on for hours in regards to when and how and what, and WHY. Then there's the who-is-realy-in-there part, and the list of what ifs seems endless and fraught with numerous anxieties that rear up and compound themselves. Once that happens, you're smack-dab in the center of a new universe, and it's no funfair of WOW and appealing joys that are ready to embrace you like an old friend who has warmly invited you over for tea and easygoing pleasantries.

(Maybe that's why I like books so much. The writers, brilliant magi, decipher it for you. Line by line, the anchor, the crow's nest, every salt, old and greenhorn-manchild that has not been swept away on a Nantucket Sleighride. A to, after 400 pages of wonderment, FINI. All you need to do is be open and turn the page…and the poetry sings……………….)

I walk over. Keeping my gaze up, looking at her face, I say, hi, trying to make it sound summer;glad. And it is glad, all the parts that aren't nervous.

She smiles (apparently, summer;glad was shiny {hoped it would be; hard to tell, as I haven't had much time to practice it} and was received). Waits for my question.

Damn. My tongue is stoned, wants to say more, the right thing, but its search is all briared-up. Tips that way. Checks itself, steps back, leans right.

Having waited, the beautiful black woman looks at me like I'm a shy, lost puppy. "Can I help you?"

"I was—over there. Waiting. Not sure why; didn't need the tram. But I was there. And… like I said, was waiting. And I saw you. If I was walking, I would have stopped. Would have had too. If you were walking I would have had to follow, not in a dangerous manner, more like seeing a beautiful sailboat pass by and so admiring it you have to see its destination… Thought, maybe we could… do something? A drink or something?"

"You're very kind, but my schedule is crammed and today is overbooked. Sorry."

She sat sidesaddle on her broom and whisked off as strange bells began ringing.

I looked down at my feet. Looked up. Her alchemic venturousness gone. I left the tram stop and entered a park. Walked and walked. Goldenrod and hawks. Fields with butterflies and grasshoppers, voyaging from white flowers to yellow flowers. Trees, mushrooms, and moss. Light vanished. Spent my night in a shipwreck shack beyond the city's firedance.

The stars waltzed. Tortured, I watched. They have the life, glitter and shine, inspire poets and lovers. They don't need restaurants, or pleasant brought in to hold your hand. Whistled, never had, not in the dark. Wanted to see what it would do. Nothing. The dark stayed dark. Maybe dark is like weather and just is what it is?

Flitting bats was a nope. Not a one. No fox to see, or bark to hear. Owls delivering judgment in the night court, there were none.

Just night, installed. A site, not prison or village, near a river, waiting to be gutted by solarfire.

I dozed and waited with it.

Morning was green, no sin-voices in the flowers. Came with sparrows and meadowlarks winging. Some arced, as only morning-colored larks, gleaming sparkling futures, can. Bees, carrying their longterm goals, came out to mine the successful flowers.

I stopped sitting, rose and stretched. Strolled, lookin' to put something on my plate.

Found a path. It widened. Day and all its gates passed…no wine…no bankrobbery…met a turtle (in bloom), sat and talked. Said he came north with the ducks, thought the calm would help distance him from the nursery rhymes that didn't hold space and time for his moves. Wanted to meet Buddha and find a way to pay his bills, Devil showed up (offered him a job, but he couldn't fork up the dime to seal the promise), Buddha didn't. Turtle had idea where they might be servin' wine, never gave two-damns for the suff, soured his tastes. His stomach gurgled and without leaving a image of flight, or moonmad symbol, he rolled off to the pond, din-din on his mind.

I was glad I didn't meet Buddha, wouldn't have had the right words or questions, unfed as I am, never been much on sayin' grace and the end of time and when it might come prancin' down the road.

A hat on the ground. Plain hat. Light brown in color. One once-was-white-white feather in the slightly darker hatband. In the deepshade of high old pines, a woman-shape formed of greywhite mist appears over the hat, bends and picks it up. Offers it to me. "This is you, the part that was missing, fell when you fell. Please, take it."

On. Fits nicely. Feels familiar, as comfortable as the not uncomfortable part of me out strolling in the park on a pleasant evening where warm is just the right amount. Eyes closed, breathing, letting me, one of my lost voices, come back to me. Eyes open. The woman-shape gone. In her place, a coven of gypsies, they have coins and exotic jewelry, (devilish) red wine, and they follow me. Faces, that awake my warmest affections, under their magnified auroras of redhair (scented with honey and orange rinds and clove), sweetly smile, whisper to each other. They, having torn off their cloaks and colorful dresses and removed their slippers, dance away, flapping and swaying. I don't hear the music that guides them, but it must be angelic. Leaping and gliding along, the full-breasted and roundbottomed colorful swans, red and blue and yellow, and she's (the tallest by two heads) soft limegreen, flutter, ignoring the undressed scars and daylight-draining scarecrows that line the sides of the grey road.

And my desire, tied to a nest of strange and eager notions, follows the fruit of their play.

///magic gypsies. (trained in Old World ways on mother's knee, at mother's breast/schooled in the handwritten tomes passed down from the star-mad lips of crones for seven generations and crystal balls rooted in maps of fatedness) They know you, the whole picture, what you feel/ FELT/clawed to keep hold on, purposes/honesty/wounds/memories—the dangerous night prayers you orchestrated as the wind howled/the rot in your bricked-up temples, begging can't scrub out. tealeaves, cards—or bones, your eyes, the shapes and patterns in the curling incense smoke, by looking at your crotch {she told me about the porch in Louisville and the grave that still churns} {told me, in exacting detail, every word chosen for its color and weight so there could be no confusion, of the profit and loss of each name and the weather of its world}, they read it all, deeper than the animal you let your analyst skin, more than you confess (or DENY!) to your pastor. Know every facet. They sing—like happy-eyed angels, like basking demons playing with unholy fire (that crossed the bridge of the candle's flame)—don't blame them; it was you, you who brought the matches and cried FLAME ON. They dance, create hills filled with fire (in your valleys of rust), before your eyes/in your crotch. MAGIC! Beautiful.

Soft and tender, scented by the wings of the poet's dreams multiplying the space your mouth holds. Gypsies—Roma, hunted, persecuted, cast out, put down. Their pretty mouths are knives/hustles/other sides of the experience/truth or lies (of cowardness) (that never won a situation), depends on what you need and what you pay for. Some (if you pay enough) will allow your heat to dream within the paradise of their lower playgrounds. Some steal, what you, the FOOL, will let them take way—not their fault, you picked, you said YES, were quick to let it out, when you came BEGGING for pain management.///

When they stop, I don't know if we've traveled 2 blocks or two miles and ten. We're in a robust wildness acres-wide. Green and flowerfilled with midsummer cushions scented with the opposite of sorrow's migration. Broadleaf canopy above and a free-flowing stream beside us. Arcs of cheerfully-fat golden fish with heart-shaped red specks skip and hop, caper and dive in the clear water—their zigzag is a mosaic, a call to the breathing wings in the belly of the teahouse. [Most often, as the toy piano corrected everything, I had Darjeeling.]

Some of my new gypsy friends sit, regally. Some lie on the soft grass, their eyes say, this is as soft as any feather bed. Many are the smiles. Two, hand-in-hand as if they've never been distant, laugh. Their laughter is seamless and mossy, pleasing.

Sweetness is tossed my way. The puppy in me leans into it as it tussles my fur, gives rise to an urge to lie on the grass and roll and buck in the kindness. I could spin and spin and whirl in delight in thier kaleidoscope, never stop breathing this feathery happiness.

"Quixote, sound your horn. Offer us a tale—"

"Of love devoted to love and every flower it promises."

"Of natural love, of its sparks electric."

"Of a beautiful young woman, her body kissed by mystery and gentleness."

"Yes, she's escaped the war and hopelessness. Escaped the anvil of scorpions always at her heels."

"Fill this cricket orchard with a tale that will please the stars."

I reflected for a moment. What could I offer beauty? I've no soft tales. I had lived (many, many years) in the unforgiving black room across from the parish, thesedays, what did I know of pleasing to the welcoming ears of womanhood fair?

"A tale of love to refresh us. That is not too much to ask... is it?"

The heart follows feet. Feet go where heart pushes. Do I have it backwards? Which had They told me I should let steer me through any muddle of indecisiveness?

It came to me they were tall, so she, in my tale, would be short, and I had been away—far-away, and soldiers go away and do not always return, not wholly. And the road back from war, for the fighter (who blindly stands when the vultures land to feast and stumbles his way out) and the sufferer (contentedness raped, hearth and soul shattered), is long and inflexible and fraught with traps and nightmares, a maelstrom of puzzling briars.

"She was short and her nest had been trampled upon. He was low, had forgotten the magiks of sparkling dreams in the death-noise and lie-tall horrors of The War. Her road, stony, uphill. His path (from the cave of death) mud. The maid wanted a generous woodland of roses spread-fair. He sought to flush the bark of General Zeklag from his blood.

They met at a pocked crossroads where a weathered fingerpost stood. Faced each other for two minutes with no conversation or poetry between them. She eyed his scars. He noted her bent back. With a gesture of hand he offered her the road. She looked right—long and dusty. She looked left—longer, darker, the wind played there like an angry magus.

"Please," she said. "You may go first."

He, shocked to be met with kindness, with no shoes, had no direction in mind and fearing heavy weather, could not decide.

There was solid stand of trees to his right. From it the pulsing of crickets issued.

"I fear ill weather is aboard. I was going to camp within yonder wood; my bones would welcome the warmth of a fire. So, please, be on your way."

Foregoing foraging, breakfast, scenic reconnaissance, and copulation, silently steaming in, magpies and jays and (reason-curious) crows and a striking dotting of red cardinals had come (making no fuss), and polite and quiet as bookends warming treasure, wing-to-wing-to-wing-to-wing-to-stock-still-wing, filled the leafy branches above the wood. No free-for-one-and-all Saturday morning library reading of vibrantly-deployed Dr. Suess wonderments had ever been better attended. Also: nestled all about us, chipmunks and squirrels and red foxes and soft-coated bunny rabbits and deer and a lumbering bear with sleepy eyes and many sleek black weasels pressed their furry ears forward to listen.

The golden fish with heart-shaped red specks lined up at the bank to listen, too.

"I have no way. No nest of soft with a hearth of warmth and fairness. All I was anchored to was taken by the animosity."

"I, too, know that ocean of teeth. I was caught and only this very morning, with no guide or balance, have left its ferocious story. Surely, that wood and my fire, can accommodate two to curl around the glowing warmth my flint will animate? And I have a tin of beans I came upon earlier. Small fare, but it could be shared."

The woman straightened slightly. Reached in her cloth sack and withdrew a canteen. "I have fresh water and dove jerky I could contribute to the feast."

Though day's light was rapidly dimming, I thought she brightened a bit.

We crossed the road of littered rubble and braided ruins and made our way through the wounded yard of what had been (when it still, standing tall and shining, clutched generations in its philosophy) a church. Near the center of the ancient boles we made a small camp and I gave voice to fire. We dined. I watched her, watched the small smile bloom on her mouth as fear and weary weakened a notch.

Night. No sound of animals.

I looked at the assembly of intent furries, smiled. Almost winked before I returned to my little story.

She had removed her boots (a man's boots, perhaps taken from a corpse on the road) and was rubbing her feet, pushing them as close as she could to our small fire to warm them. I imagined her feet were sore (as were mine—watching my dinner companion made mine feel mightily so). No socks will do that, as the hard leather, stiffened and cracked by age and wear, rubs on soft pink flesh. From her cloth sack she removed a small tin that once held cookies. From it, she took out an old pipe and herb. "We used the herb to ease the suffering of the wounded, and our own pains as well… I was too young, only thirteen, to attend Woodstock, but I dreamed of being golden." She took a toke, held it long and deep, smiled, and offered me her pipe. She wiggled her toes. "It would be lovely to have a pair of socks."

I could have burst out laughing, but held it, and simply nodded in agreement.

Between tokes, softly, she hummed the chorus of "With A Little Help from My Friends". Thought I heard some hallalujahs in there somewhere.

I knew the words, yet, never one to sing, not with this unable-to-hold-a-tune croak of a voice, I did not join in, but I did enjoy her soothing tones. It had been a very long time since I last heard music.

There was wind and chill, but the rain I feared did not arrive.

I sat in my thick warcoat and offered her my blanket. Softened by warm and the embrace of herb, she slept. I watched her dream.

Morning. Sun. Cool. No wind.

We each chewed on a small piece of her jerky and sipped water from her canteen. The day was before us and we had yet to exchange a word. I wondered if we were to be traveling together, and to where, should we, we'd be headed.

12 days we traveled the road. Heard the souls of leaves bless freedom

with their poetry, saw a slave's loneliness embraced by mercy, saw the place where the moon goes to sleep, saw fruitful fields and ripe orchards the tiger's jaws can't find. Nights came, they were warm and calm.

On the 13th day we came to a river.

"I cannot swim."

She cupped my face in her hands and smiled. "I have a cure for that," she said, and called out across the water. On the far bank her sisters appeared with a canoe."

Yet my tale was not to be ferried across to garden days where love could spin gold for a beast with wolfeyes. The thunder of savage hooves and persecution's shouts clanged through the forest and fell upon our glade of repose. Old hatred, here to put out lives and remove tongues seeking joy, seated upon the crashing storm of great black war horses was everywhere. We ran, madly, leaping, stumbling. Ran from the granite curses of vipers, from the chops their swords barked. Ran from maps and budding dreams of spring blossoms and comforting skies. Ran until there was no strength of soil for our feet. Our backs were pressed to rough water, in terror, we were pushed into the wild current of a wide river's fist.

The delights of my gypsies made it across. I was swiftly pushed from the promises of their rooms, from promises of white lace and first nights joined to again and again.

Downstream...

muscles and thighs and fear

(and eyes shrieking)

lost—water risen'...

Landscapes later and surprisingly not drowned, I was stranded upon a bank of sand, a damp sliver of barren sand. There I sat for three days until the water receded and I was able to wade ashore.

Slower than a slow train I pressed on

the shapes of dusk-laden trees clinging to the cloudless sky/tall grass/ flat fields became a sea of seamless, borderless fog/a sign I don't understand/memoriesbulge/possible retracing its steps/slipping/vertigo/a cat that won't stop and share a story/reflections of the man I had been/doubt/without a word another masterpiece turned off/gravel/asphalt/rooftops/sewers/ dust/wearing tales with holes in them/drawn curtains/a tiring day/grief/ toad/flies/goat/a blind sundial/thunderstorm/when yes was on my feathers/ tree spirits with no crowns/rat/sitting alone with a broken clock/the brick-wall goodbye/birds, out of waltz, on a wire fence/avalanches/guilt, thick-ened with an incense cloud of despair/grave/avalanches/howl

sitting on a hardback chair in a darkened room, crying

* * * *

Pond with a girl beside it:

typewriter, weather and age have not crippled it, balanced, just so, on a small stump by a large pond. "It was mine. I did what I did. Left it behind, yet it follows me." She remembers every letter and tale written by it, the ones where her altitudes were snowed in and traces of what was sacrificed to the sky that October night, and the paths of the rivers beneath the surface of flowing current.

Sadsmile under sadeyes. My tender companion removes her hat and shoes, every stitch of clothing, and sits, begins to write. When she is done she folds her communication into a small paper boat and gently places it in my cupped hands. I carry it to the pond and send it off. No longer vexed, she rises and puts her clothes back on and we continue our journey.

The sun, his reasons remaining his own, has moved ahead and seems to hold no regard to us on the subject of catching up.

I enjoy her voice beside me as we walk. "It's like carrying a museum with me. There are doctors and painters, coyotes that know the scripts of the hills, and occulted-Barnum's to knit reasons for the scimitars and memoirs we come upon. Sorting mummies and their capsizing kin from the sea-wash, that's comforting, and helpful."

We have a small fire and a large blanket to share. We have food and water and my tender companion can sing magic little odes from the Old Country, and her laughter is the entrance to a warm rookery. I, like the fox and the owl and the rites of a thousand streets, have lives of tales to tell. I'm sure this is how nights were spent in the Old Days; two drowning in each other, sharing dreams that try to keep the fear away.

After unexpurgated, we, naked, fall asleep in each other's arm.

In the morning... I wake alone. No note of good-bye. Only the smell of her love on my fingers, hurting my heart.

I call out to her... again and again. Search. But I am alone.

* * * *

(slowfooted)...miles...moving leaves with my feet...
uphill, gasping...
...scarecrows and tombstones...
(weighted by poison from a courtroom I can barely remember)
a deadtown sunk by its own saints and desires—it could be a mirror...
(slower...until)
I sit on a wooden bench between a crow and a fox.
Crow: Why bother?
Fox: Because his psyche needs shit.
Crow: Another hope dashed. Another murder in the bedroom.
Fox: Look, kid, Desolation Row and Damnation Alley are for losers—

ain't no place for you. You're just like Dracula. You can't be nailed shut in that box. Not with all that hot sirenblood with your name on its lips. If you sit there on your ass there's no hope of winning the Love Lotto. Like the poet who put new skin in the old ceremony said, you want to kiss Rapunzel you have to climb and keep climbing, and maybe you find one licks the blue funk right out of you. Dig?

I stood. Said, thanks. Followed my lengthening shadow as it walked down the road.

Magus, Pimp, Steppenwolf, Spider, followed (thinking themselves careful—deceptively adept, and staying in the soundless shadows) my fantasies and I, as we, shooing away the-dream-is-over, moved one step closer to faraway. They, opportunists ready to deploy ill should a window open, did not EXIT as the next step forward became a part of history. If I leaned left the solitary harvesters tilted as well. When I stopped, and the fog (creeping like a thing—not undone by death—possessed with predatory hungers) hid me, they mirrored my pause. A prowl car, slow and straight— its destination to sting stupid with lightning, passes, but does not note the corruption of the soul stealers. How can it be unfazed by the metastasized bitterness of their desires, the street reeks of it? But its prowling was all I needed; an alley, an unlocked basement door, a door to another basement and a stairway to the roof and the adjoining tenements. Magus—wraped and cruel, Pimp—misshapen twisted, Steppenwolf—deformed perverted, Spider—depraved ruthless, prowl for my spore, but here among the alienated and the social-losers and the loneliness of fugitives and the dramas of as-yet-unsigned divorce papers, I do not stand out. My back pressed to the weathered-frame of an empty pigeon-coop I sit and smoke a cigarette. There are other actors, magnets of poverty and violence, in this dirty, lovelorn urban theater, they'll set upon another flavor soon and I'll continue on. One cigarette turns into two and I wish I had a pint of whiskey, or a soft spot to rest my head.

* * * *

Dusk soon to waken, soon to speak of Day's last. Stepped from the umbrella-canopy of a John Clare wood, no fairies or delights at my heels. No flowers capping summer hills.

Crickets (calling; courting; triumphal; aggressive) radiating.

View of the vaulted skyline: transmission lines and communication towers. A straight-line hardtrack of lattice, steel skeletons from my boot-tips to both horizons. Transmission lines and communication towers buzzing (a city of demons).

Tiger pancake octopus / Tiger pancake octopus / 2-0-5-2-0-5 / 0-0-2-9-3-0-0-2-9-3 / awf-awf-da-da / shopping-for-a-bathing-cap-shopping-for-a-bathing-cap-in-a-local-super-market / threat knowledge-A-2-6-1-3-9-2-threat knowledge-7-8-1-2-threat knowledge-3-8-7-4-2/Yankee foxtrot hotel / "I'm your man." / Bletchley-Margaret-Mavis-Jean-Clare-Rachel-Elisabeth / Bletchley-Margaret-Jean-Clare-Rachel / Bletchley-Clare-Rachel-Elisabeth / Enigma-Bonnie-Gail-Susan-Anita-Cheryl-Marsha/Enigma-Bonnie-Gail-Susan-Anita/Enigma-Bonnie-Gail-Susan

No cross, no decoder. No hardened heart.

rumor/a piece of monologue/testimony/TRUE-FALSE/facts/dreams/shreds/circumstances/factors/eventualities/message/communiqués/small talk/cheap talk/ghost stories from a vampire mouth/noise spit at tired/(soft lips)"I can't."/Hello hector I am swimming a b... c—cats d e f g swimming—flowering—arriving—no more... Hello hector I am swimming h—horses i j k l m no more/Tiger pancake octopus Tiger pancake octopus...

Unspooled clack and hum in my head, marching, mocking the November-skin of my sad-go-round.

argumentation

(desertland-heat murdering patience and grace)

explaining

(to the locustbringer at the temple gates)

no poetica

(she and I naked and sour in the shadowgrave,

our Eden-born starlings dissolving with our smiles)

My role (in this adharma for one) was Judas—henchman—prisoner.

By omission, I lied.

I was betrayed.

Saturday was a lizard.

Sunday a lion.

/Tiger pancake octopus Tiger pancake octopus.../"Heart? Try self-contained. Inner wilderness to inner wilderness, you lead yourself around on a noosed leash. There's no room for anything, or anyone, else."/Tiger pancake octopus Tiger pancake octopus.../Tiger pancake octopus Tiger pancake octopus...

Cloaked in the smells of a hunter, a large fox stepped on to the path and approached. Pricked his ears, cocked his head, listened momentarily. His unconcealed eyes took in my hit-down hide-to-stem, my bastard/beggarman/thief, trying to get back. Never having needed anyone, he chuckled. I failed to hold his attention long and he lopped away.

See also:

pitch

counterpoint

rate of speed (see Figure 3.17)

inhale <

exhale>

sequence duration—soft

　　　　—medium

　　　　—hard

/Loki star Loki grassman Nightshow raven Loki batwave Loki star Loki grassman Nightshow raven Loki batwave Loki star Loki grassman Nightshow raven Loki batwave Loki star Loki grassman Nightshow raven Loki batwave Loki star Loki grassman Nightshow raven Loki batwave/ Tiger pancake octopus/Tiger pancake octopus…

Full of dust and spider-lore, my lengthening shadow of November-skin leading me on, I walked on. No fairies or delights at my heels. No flowers capping summer hills.

Blameless, owing debt to no one, the air takes its time. It does not seek to find the man with the pen inside of me.

* * * *

A: I do not know how many days I have been without food or shelter.

A: She was not there.

A: I am… many things. Among them, the self-consumer of my woes.

A: Cocks and brooks and hills and vales and steeples and dangling leaves in the sun's warm beams and hay on harvest morning, far-off and near.

A: A bird on a barb-wire fence.

A: A chapel.

A: Some time tomorrow.

A: Last year's man.

A: The holes in your culture.

A: A grinning frog, sitting on top of a skull.

A: The future.

A: She has let her party-dress dress fall to her feet and I can now read her coding.

A: A tiger.

A: A pancake I had last week.

A: An octopus.

* * * *

She was sobbing. I noticed something in her eyes. Not sure if it was a ghost or a lie.

James Taylor would have been fitting, but a Jethro Tull song was playing.

The weather did not permit me to remain.

Selves. Bootstep by bootstep. Stopping to look. Turning to listen; a voice in need of a coat, another, in need of sleep, any break from the forest of delusion.

Branches and birdsong (awakened and scented with sweet mists), filtering light, that does not heed the doctor's drumsong. Leaves and layers that are not locked-up, not followed by deprivations.

Insects. Not vowels.

Unformed wind. Not mimes made unwell by the shackles of complex narratives.

All afternoon.

Twilight showing me the lane that did not fear distance, that takes no step back.

My pencil slept in a tunnel under the highway.

Morning.

I found a magazine thick with the shouts and disillusionments of crowded places; its trials, negatives, and rumors, all felt like suicide notes. Didn't read it. Returned the paper to the earth. Over it, I whispered, "Ashes to ashes."

Saw a flowering of pilgrims, a large bunny—introduced himself (to a young woman, out measuring miracles) as Harvey, an owl, a fox, many, many birds. None noticed my incandescence, or seemed to know my name. Not a one waved. The serpent and the lion within me could not keep up. I slowed my gravity to another tuning and came to another nightfall.

I in my escaping boots on an unwound path, pushing my imagination along; small hillock/limping creek/legends confessed on tombstones/the scents of earth from ages past/a puddle in a strange arrangement of rocks/ distance from birdsong to highways of fog/unscheduled drizzle shooing-away small fires.

No gusts.

No fairies.

Double-vision tired.

Pine. Maples and dense weeds and intense underbrush. Inching up a long slope, the leering moon above (ringed by circling stars), watching, breathing his cold down.

Long grass. A vast field (that has never had a name) (never been mown to fit boundaries, or been fit with transmission stones to evoke revelations) filled with the steady, wide-open chirping of swarmed crickets. In its sunken center, in the gathered darkness, a sole dweller, a great twisted oak.

Pieces of a shattered mirror hung (with thin strands of bloodred twine) from the branches of the immense dead tree. I touched a shard and the chirping (that sounded like my name being called by lonely messiahs) halted. Touched every piece, slowly. Looked into the narrative they exposed.

The nasturtiums are dead.

Booted outta Rehab Mansion after failin' the third degree / Former werewolf (no one will ever again call him, St.) (obsessed with limits), accused of peepin', accused of gettin' / Unstoppable interrogated the hanged man, found him ripe for last breath / All the letters (to and from) stopped when his neck was snapped by the lynchin' crowd's rules of the game / Hide tacked to the barn door / Speckled feathers pinned to the black ground / Now, shaped by silence, his tongue will never again test the unfurled brush of crazy moonlight coming ashore

* * * *

One short block from Government Lethal Chamber No. 7. Assortment of dive bars within stumbling distance of this cold park bench.

Pages of a fingertip-worn paperback, Helen Heck's 'monstrous elegance', The Neurastheniac, (night—sharing my pillow, and day, read and reread/day, flipped through in two directions, and night—sharing my pillow) (my pencil, filled with longing, has traveled through its moonless, autumnal hours), ripped out—the stars, the phantoms, what fell—crumbled in my fist. Tossed in the grass.

The fox, who jives with Clotho, Lachesis, and Atropos, watches my crisis of rain and chuckles. "So many stars. Which will you cast your pebble toward?"

"The brightest," I reply to his exiting tail. "Just wait, foul trickster, you'll see."

* * * *

The violin music of the old house had been silenced by fire. Our yard looked like it had been visited by war, patches of mud, piles of heat-savaged boards and insulation, nails and wiring, alien footprints everywhere. Half the crabapple tree (not twenty feet from the front door where we once hung welcoming holiday wreathes) black, charcoal. Beneath it, my diary jars, shattered, their pages saturated unreadable. From one, pages from a summer-gone-by still readable, in part. (I suspect there is as much dream and fancy, as fact, on the ruined paper.):

...shaped by:
> her face in my hands
> "Non Sum Qualis eram Bonae Sub Regno Cynarae"
> the drowsy kiss of the piano music
> the red wine
> "Let it be me."

leashed
(to the mindbook)
I follow
(no lantern of heroism)
memories
I cannot fight

a hazy border
without indulging in the facts
A chair
and a drought of apology
barred the door of the hut.
seeing it.
living it.
the creation stories.
the labyrinths.
the rows of unboxed days to and fro,
every joy in the bowl.
before the singer,
drunk on the face of the moon,
shouts destruct.
quit the street
and paris, and
made
frequent stops,
where I stood on the cliffs
with lonely messiahs
who could not
stop taking
about
their
angels of beauty
Once upon a time…
(without looking at the page number)
the smothering carelessness of a day past
unbuttoned
the memory I was trying to hold close
shedding tears,
unwillingly,
over you.
over
the poetry that couldn't avoid fear's jaws.

* * * *

She was robust, thick with insight and fact; I doubted she could mis-represent anything.

He, too thin, timid.

She was black, graceful, and proud. She would not be bent or turned, would not fall under the repeated and repeated lies and venomous malice they, the true subhumans, sought to saddle her people with.

She was mysterious, poetically so.

He was a grifter playing with fire.

She (before she found her heart) had spent her whole life at the shore-line, watching sails go by, afraid to dip her toes in the vast dark blue expanse. I recalled a letter from her saying if she'd been named Alice or Pippi she might have.

He mourned what had been banned and cast into the rivers of darkness.

She, in the loudest terms, made no bones about being terrified.

He had left the train of flesh-and-bone-humanity and was a tomb of ghosts. I found him shocking, and was uncomfortable with the comforts he gathered for pillow and dream-feast.

Tea in hand, I sat at the table with her and she told me of her art, detailed sightings I had not gleaned, and her sexual encounters and how she loved This Landscape and why she had come to this shore. She was dazzlingly intelligent, far more than I and naturally so, and lyrical, honest in ways men will not be. Witty danced from her tongue easily, and a time or two, blue. I wanted to hug her and tell her tomorrow would be better. I liked her strength and yearned to know more of her passion.

I rose to refill my tea cup and she, as suddenly as a wren having changed its mind about direction, returned to her place in the crowd.

Alone. Trapped (no voyage to ride), living the pain of the moment. Bent, stricken again (no answer to run to). I wandered, staring and not seeing; got caught out in the rain. I wanted a place to hide, to regroup, recharge. A CLOSED sign (nearly as loud as a wintery night of merciless disaster) beckoned.

In (through an unlatched read window). I now sat alone with my dis-obedience. Not my first spin with lawbreaker, not violent, never that. Bor-rower is how my desperation would describe it to you. Hungry wants fill-ing—nothing 5 Star, a sandwich of bread and cheese will quiet its protests, cold and wet wants dry. I've borrowed a few loaves and a dry room or two and this one is no different. My tenure inside its fine walls will be brief, I'll leave things clean and only take a little, things that can easily be replaced and should cause no harm and, I hope, not too much distress to its recurring company.

It was not the largest library I'd ever been in, but for two nights and a day it was mine. Old friends, and their many luxuries were about me. Moby-Dick said ah-hoy! Multiple copies of Fowles were on one shelf that brought back many sweet and astonishing reminiscences. I took Frankenstein from the shelf and admired the painting of Karloff, and again thanked Mary Shelly for her gift to 11-year-old-me. From another shelf I took Rechy's CITY OF NIGHT (seeing the courtyards of allnight neon and hearing the rock-n-roll-sexmusic) and reread the opening page, marveled at it grace and its fire. Lonely in a crowd of beautiful losers, I remember it too well, or is it just another anchor forged of mistakes I carry?

Cried as I held an old lover, as we tried to pardon each other, but, chained by things that could not be forgotten, we could not roll away the stone. Chains...

Puffy eyes. Emily Dickinson, The Poems of Emily Dickinson, ed. R. W. Franklin, (Cambridge, MA: Belknap Press of Harvard University Press, 1999).

Archeologist of morning—white rabbit—island—miracle—lance. The Collected Poems of Charles Olson, ed. George F. Butterick, (University of California Press, 1987). Chains...

pool
pedigree
an undressed cloud each morning
slept
too much
became
forget-me-not
loner / drawn by knots / not by choice
Fanny Howe
for Halloween fare
channel
cake
wrecking crew
of sorts
a hell of a woman / viewed from the train
after / flowers omitted
climb / what is real / less and less
endlessly / what did it mean
Monica Youn
expletive DELETED
Chains...

A world of spines, underneath their Look-At-This; hospitable eccentricities and funerals; sleepless angles; the clicking windmills of internal landscapes; poetry with its pants off and floods; apples for the chessmatch, coming through the cook's door; preludes and inquests; the dialogue between three modern (single) mothers, sharing a pack of cigarettes and a bottle of cheap wine while sitting on the stone frontporch steps one overly-warm Friday night; desperation in a Q & A of one; X marks the entrance of the rabbithole; she paints (deserts and skulls and flowers), he makes gestures at the TV; a shimmering soul on Moody Street, Pawtucketville, Lowell, Mass., with pencil and paper; "'Empty salons. Corridors. Salons. Doors. Doors. Salons. Empty chairs, deep armchairs, thick carpets. Heavy hangings. Stairs, steps. Steps, one after the other.'" Marienbad, her pact with X. ("Yes. I remember it well."); various ceremonies of bitterness and self-reform. And dark alleys full of fear and fragments (dear Jack O'Connell), wretches (poor David Goodis and James Loftus dead—gone), exhibitions (by madmen) and inventions (by sad men and sadder women) that didn't work. Chains…

There were many other hallucinatory pieces and I wanted to say hello to them all. Some were scary then, and I believe, would be as frightening today. Others were fine teachers and fingerposts, I thought, in my case, they'd performed ably. Adoring glances and comments, many beginning or ending with thank you, were offered (to the writers and editors, and to tons of fictional characters) by me as I explored.

It was blissfully dry inside the library. There was tea (and sugar and real milk) in the break room and a refrigerator that was rather well-stocked. I dined on a garden salad and peppercorn ranch dressing and roast beef from a brown paper bag marked STEPHEN by a pencil. The microwave did a fine job with the roast beef, and by my estimation, the (forgotten?) salad was a mere day old.

There was a private washroom and another private room behind a door in the head librarian's office. Behind the second door, was a cot (with a pillow and two blankets) and clean blue shirt and clean grey suit, hanging on a hook. The clothing, belonging to a tall man with a waist and shoulders broader than my own, was a size or two too large, but they allowed me to step out of my wet things and fully dry out. In the head librarian's desk I discovered a bottle of scotch (3/4 of it remained) and 2 fresh packs of cigarettes.

I took a cigarette out of the pack. Lit it.

Had a drink.

And another drink…

It was going to break my heart to leave this palace of abundance come Monday morning.

It was Monday. I was up and out early.

Left a THANK YOU note.

Miles…

dust and thirst…

four winds and a huff and a puff…

a cloud-portrait that's never had a name…

longitude colorful as spring real estate

and latitude in no mood to nick things…

Miles…

there are trees and streets, windows and clockwork scenes, but I am still far from the land between the Hudson River and Lake George…

…Wednesday. Coffee. After sadly and the earthquake that frightened the children. In an attic above, there's a chapter in a guidebook, it says, *I'll never forget you*, but it was written by a man who was newly-married and had not heard the whole of the opera.

More miles…

Night. (Why do they often feel like prisons?)

Friday. No eagles come out to play.

* * * *

Woke up…

alone,

unless you count my sorrows and the burdened kites they fly.

Fingerpost says PARTNERS LOST >

I walk…

Leagues (no ribbons of angels dancing) (sigh)… Can't remember how far or how many seas need to be crossed, but it's *that way* > Leagues > andMOREAGAIN (sigh)

The Fisherman's boat, fish stories caught and unloaded, under the nationsky. Little sail full of push. Tiller in a weathered hand, current-ready (I hope), steady (I hope). Home, port that won't be squashed by the sea's loneliness, in mind. Fingers crossed.

Raining.

Been all day. Tossed—no chariot ride. Crest a crest.

Gulls arcing, oboeing.

"Will home remember me?" I ask the sky.

Shoreline discloses—

scar

(of undead tormented fantasies fanned by sex and blasphemy)

hill

(of Self, hoarded parts and trinkets that offered no peace)

tombstone yard

(where I buried my lives)

Sodom's litter (sigh). Doves and kites tarred & tortured/mangled/split (sigh). Bars closed (sigh). Pictures taken down (sigh). Lanterns OFF (sigh). Lilies shorn (sigh). Gramophone without a needle (sigh). Scrapbooks and violins and wrist-ribbons left in the rain (I guess a million years was too long…) (sigh) One neon sign—*You're fucking cRaZY*—struggles (sigh)

["*Crazy.*" I look down into my dry, cracked hands. "Is that what the poison did to me?"] Compassion must have had a hell of a price to pay (sigh).

No children (sigh). No future (sigh). Landscape in ruins (sigh).

(In Hank Williams shoes) my sore feet on the stairs (AGAIN) (sigh). Don't need a key here, no door (sigh). No glass in the casements (sigh).

My empty room
in the Tower of Song.............................
Stagger in...
(sigh)
clock's wrecked
(sigh)
weathered partydress-curtains (canvas of *I no longer love you*) speak of piece-after-piece leaving—I wonder when the last time blue eyes that valued things in me were in this room
(sigh)
all the bottles are empty of laughter (can't even see traces of my dried contingency plans on the bottoms); didn't even leave me the EXIT of sleeping pills,
or the choice between accepting the cross of a deaf man or one blinded
(sigh)
no weapons...no traces of Manhattan...or Berlin...
(sigh)
all the words have leaked from my books of longing and mercy
(sigh)
(jaws clamped shut by frost) all my prayers are too sick to stand tall
(sigh)
Going home: I close my eyes. With them closed I look around: Gail's here. *In the warm sunlight. Barefoot, humming to the stuffed blue tiger I won for her at the carnival on Hungry Hill. Radiant. Soft—Aphrodite love—a ceremony of forest magic. She's at her easel in front of the living room window, painting her favorite stand of white birches on the bank of the Mohawk River. I'm on the sofa, lying on a quilt she made. She turned and came to me. There was a dot of river-blue paint on her cheek. My fingers began unbuttoning her soft blue blouse...*

In the rooms next to mine, I hear a man, who has moved through toomanystations and (long-ago) stopped comparing mythologies, coughing... and in another another clears his throat

(Leonard Cohen "Going Home", "Closing Time", "First We Take Manhattan", "Tower of Song", "Take This Waltz")

✗

YOU'RE GONNA LOVE THIS SONG

Michael S. Walker

"C'mon, let's show 'em," the Kid says. "Get your guitar and show 'em what we can do. Show 'em."

That's the Kid. Always impatient. Always manic. He is standing in the doorway to my bedroom, his bony hands clutching the doorjambs, swaying a little, never able to keep still for a second. His unruly brown hair curls around his ears. His blue eyes are bulging.

"C'mon... What are you waitin' for?"

"I will," I reply. I'm sitting on my bed drinking my third Miller High-Life. I need to get my courage up. What if we get rejected again? I don't think I could face that.

"Now," he says. He really is a kid. He can't wait for anything. I appraise him as I take another swig of my beer. He's wearing an old black leather jacket over a rumpled pink shirt. His blue jeans have holes at both knees and are stained and dirty.

In the kitchen, Troy X starts screaming again. You would think that, by now, he would be tired out, couldn't scream anymore. But each successive outburst gets a little more hysterical. He's beginning to sound like he does when he's on stage.

"You motherfucker!" he shouts. "Goddamnit, let me go! Let me go or I'm gonna punch your fuckin' lights out."

I almost have to laugh at this last threat. The Kid does laugh. We have Troy X tied up with nylon rope to one of the kitchen chairs. His hands are tied behind his back. His legs are tied to the legs of the chair. He's been that way for eight hours now. Ever since we abducted him from the bar. He's not going anywhere.

"Motherfucker!" he howls. Troy X can howl all he wants to. We are in Sullivan Township here. It's all farmland. Not another house for a mile or so.

Troy X., until recently, was the lead guitarist and singer for a heavy-metal group called Headload. Thought up the name myself, y'all," he had beamed from the dry ice-enshrouded stage while the rhythm guitarist fiddled with a broken string. "It's the amount of wood a person in

India can carry on their head. I dunno, I just liked the sound of it. Sounded kinda' cool."

The name of the bar that Headload had been playing in was La Rose Maison. It's a medium-sized club with an actual proscenium stage and a fairly decent sound system—a venue for bands that are either on their way up in the food chain or on their way down. Headload was definitely on their way up. They had just had a strong regional hit with a song called "Smack Me," and were touring a shitload of clubs just like the Maison to promote it. Four young guys with long hair, tight pants, and attitude. Always a bankable commodity.

Of course, the Kid and I had come to see Troy X. We knew right away, when we saw his picture in the weekend entertainment section of our local paper, that this was the one. He had had his hands poised like claws over the strings of his guitar, grimacing and sticking his tongue out for the camera.

"Look at him," the Kid had said, clapping his hands. "Look at him! Ain't he magnificent!"

Between sets at La Rose Maison, the Kid and I had followed Troy X. to the bar, where he stood swabbing his shiny forehead with a towel and waiting for a drink. He nodded at a few people who came up to talk to him, smiled at a couple of girls. Then, the Kid and I stepped forward.

"Hey, you guys got a good sound," I said.

"Thanks." He barely nodded in my direction.

I stepped a little closer.

"Yeah? What can I do for you?" he asked, suspiciously.

"Name's Bill Edwards," I said, smiling and sticking out my hand. "It's more what I can do for you."

"Whatta ya' mean?"

"Well… I got some dynamite blow, if you would care to partake."

That changed everything. Troy X started smiling like I was his long-lost best friend.

"You don't say. What did you say your name was? The shit we got backstage is pretty lame. Where is it?"

"It's out in my van. That is… If you've got a few minutes?"

Troy X looked at the clock over the bar. His beer had finally arrived and it sat there, foaming over, waiting for him to pick it up. He stood there for a second, staring at the glass.

"Sure, man. Why not? They ain't gonna start without me. I'm the whole damn show," he said, laughing.

"You sure are," I said.

The Kid nodded in agreement.

* * * *

And that was how we did it. Same as always. Same as the last four times. Troy X climbed into our van. I climbed up into the driver's seat and then I was on him in a second with the chloroform, the Kid yelling enthusiastically from the back while I subdued him. And then, we were off. And, wonder of wonder miracle of miracles, no one even saw us. Again. I had parked my van far away from the bar, in the parking lot of a restaurant that had already closed for the night.

And now, Troy X is here. And he is still screaming.

"C'mon," the Kid says. "That shit is really beginning to get on my last nerve."

"O.K.," I say, reluctantly. I still don't think I've had enough to drink yet. I still don't think I'm ready to "perform." Not just yet. But the Kid is so insistent. And that shouting is getting on my nerves too. Always does.

I go to the closet and get my guitar. It's a cheap Kay guitar with a blonde finish. The strings sit way up high on the neck and the action is terrible. But, if I end up having to smash it, it's no big loss.

"What are we gonna play?" the Kid asks, eagerly.

"I don't know," I reply.

"How 'bout 'Spanish Senorita'"? he says. "No, no. Forget that. Play 'em 'Ten Items or Less.' No. Gotta keep somethin' in reserve. Play 'em 'Parallel Parking.' Yeah! 'Parallel Parking'! That's the one!" He's grinning and jumping up and down now.

These are all songs that the Kid and I have written together. Well, actually, I wrote them—most of them more than twenty years ago when I looked a lot like the Kid and there was absolutely no question in my mind that I was going to be the next big thing in rock n' roll. But nobody was exactly beating down my door. If it weren't for the Kid, I would be done with this absurd dream.

Done… Done… Done.

"'Parallel Parking,'" he says, drooling at the thought. "Let's rock n' roll!"

The Kid leads the way and I follow him through the dark house to the kitchen. We can hear Troy X in there, muttering to himself over and over again, "Motherfucker, motherfucker, motherfucker," as if this phrase had suddenly become his personal mantra.

"This is it," the Kid says. He's reverentially touching all the glossy posters we have taped on the walls of the dining room—pictures of the Rolling Stones, the Beatles, Bob Dylan.

And there's Troy X in the kitchen, his face red and haggard. He's still wearing his stage clothes from the bar, of course—these skin-tight vermilion pants and a black tee-shirt with skeleton couples emblazoned all over it, enjoying all kinds of sexual positions. He doesn't look like much of a rock star right now. Just a little man wearing silly clothes whose body is going to paunch. And he smells bad too.

As soon as he sees the Kid and me, his eyes light up again with a murderous vengeance.

"Godamnit, you fuckin' creep!" he screams at me, pulling at his restraints.

"Tell 'em," the Kid says.

"Mr. X," I say, as calmly as I can. "I brought you here for a specific reason…"

"Yeah," he says. I suddenly notice that his eyes are full of fear.

"Yes. I want to play you a song. It's a song I wrote. I think… I think it's a good song and deserves to be heard by…somebody." This is the fifth time I've given this speech. I hope it will be the last. The Kid stands next to me, grinning stupidly and nodding his head as if he were listening to the music already.

"I don't want to hear no fuckin' song. I want you to let me go," Troy X says, his voice hoarse.

"I will," I say. "But I want you to listen to this song. I know you have connections in the record business and I know you could get me signed to record this. It's that good."

The Kid nods vigorously.

"So, if I listen to your fuckin' song, you'll let me go?" Strangely, he looks only at me. He doesn't even seem to see the Kid.

"Yes, I will," I say. "But you have to promise me you'll try to do something for my…career."

"How do you know I just won't get you turned over to the fuckin' cops?" he says.

"Oh, I don't think you will," I reply, softly. "You will like this song. You will love this song."

The fear is back in his eyes as he stares at me. Damnit, why doesn't he ever look at the Kid?

"You'll love this song," the Kid echoes.

Suddenly, I begin to play, the tinny sound of the guitar echoing in the cramped kitchen, the steel strings biting at my fingers.

> *"Goin' parallel parking/ Gonna pass my test*
> *Goin' parallel parking/ Gonna pass my test."*

I'm singing in my nasally baritone and the Kid's singing along with me, doing a high harmony.

> *"Goin' parallel parking/ Gonna pass my test*
> *Goin' parallel parking/ Gonna pass my test."*

I finish the song with a flourish and the Kid claps his hands and stomps his feet. I look at Troy X.

"Yeah, it's great," he says, slowly. "Genius. Listen, if you let me go right now, I'll call my fuckin' manager and we'll set you up with a deal… take you out on the road with us.

"Really?" I say. I look at the Kid. The Kid stares intently at Troy X and then he looks back at me, his face crestfallen.

"He's lying. Just like all the rest," the Kid says, shaking his head.

"You're lying," I say, turning to Troy X.

"No, really," he says. "It's a good song. A good song? It's a great fuckin' song. Look…untie me. We'll figure out something for you. You obviously have a lot of talent.

"Take 'em," the Kid says.

I raise the Kay guitar high over my head and bring it down like a bludgeon against Troy X's skull. As I do, the Kid begins to fade, becoming tiny pinpricks in my eyes…

"Just like all the rest…" the Kid sings, his voice like a dying wind in my parched throat.

THE PUMPKIN BOY ON SAMHAIN

Chad Hensley

autistically rocks back and forth
sitting cross-legged on top of a crooked, broken gravestone
barely able to contain his excitement
a wide, gnarled smile etched across his round and ribbed orange
     face.

Skeletal-like, persimmons-colored arms and bulbous, white-
     gloved hands
hold a small black cat perched in his seersucker-suited lap,
the kitten's glow-in-the-dark eyes ablaze above a slit-like mouth
filled with a hundred thousand tiny black fangs
that resemble sharp broken bits of rusted barbed wire.

He has decorated certain empty graves in the cemetery
with freshly cleaved jack-o-lantern handiworks;
cloven human heads, odd-shaped animal skulls of all sizes,
and multiple-eyed, tentacled masses—
the knife-sliced pumpkins quivering strangely,
wisps of steam rising from gourd carved caverns
plopped on angular patches of unturned tomb soil
in the sickly pale light of a sallow, sickle moon.

A ground fog of billowing ghosts
flows across the shallow graves
like a seething wave of soft candlelight.

Behind the cemetery,
a bright gangrenous glare
pours from an octagon-shaped, stained-glass window
on a grizzled, three-story house
in the center of the turret on the third-floor
like an enormous, bloodshot alien eye.

The great crumbling eaves of the slumped building
buckle with the weight of bloated, elephantine bats
with monstrous swollen claws and dagger-sized teeth.

They sway upside down and spread huge membranous wings.

Across the necropolis,
coffins pop out of the burial ground like a macabre sea of jack-
    in-the-boxes,
spilling crumbling bones of century-old skeletons
that spring together and dance slow motion in the anemic lunar
    light.

The pumpkin boy laughs in loud asthmatic wheezes,
points with a gangling, bony finger
at the Hallowe'en midnight antics
and disappears in a thick puff of carrot-colored smoke
that smells of burning leaves and cinnamon.

FROZEN TIME
by Rivka Jacobs

She squeezed the mug of hot cocoa between her palms, took a sip.

"Can we go over it one more time?" Bill McLoughlin asked, his tone nonthreatening. He sat directly across from her, leaning slightly forward. His hands formed a ball of white knuckles and locked fingers.

Hal Pintero, supervisor of McMurdo Station support staff, reclined beside him. "Nancy, Dr. Wenger, we just lost three people on the glacier. Your colleagues. My friends...."

"My friends too," she mumbled through stiff lips. "I'm sorry, I'm trying to remember...." She was angry—at them, at herself. She was an experienced glaciologist, a glaciospeliologist. Her team had worked together in Antarctica for a decade. "We were on the south flank of Mt. Erebus, about a kilometer upslope, on the saddle of the glacier proper. We had an excellent Pyne drilling tent, conditions were perfect. We completed a 200-meter bore. We were close to the igneous layers of the lower shield structure; I think the deepest layers of our core came from ice at least 200,000 years old. We were just cutting the core into samples, when there was a small quake...."

McLoughlin, a climatologist and NSF station manager, exhaled with a grunt and leaned back in his chair, lacing his hands behind his neck. "Okay, seismic monitors here didn't...."

"I don't care what your machines recorded." She set the mug down. She was dressed in a black turtle-neck sweater and black corduroy jeans. Her brown glossy hair was pushed back off her forehead by a plastic headband. Her right check bone was purple pink, her chin red and brown with dried blood forming a scrape pattern. Above her left brow was a lump.

McLoughlin sighed. "I've put in a call to Hawaii, and the FBI, but they won't arrive until tomorrow. Help us, here, Nancy...."

"Sam, Lonnie, Louisa, they were my team. My friends. Don't you think I'd tell you, if I could remember?"

"Where's your equipment?" Pintero asked.

"I don't know."

"What happened to the ice cores and the samples the team was packing?"

Nancy shook her head. It was hard to speak. "I.. want to get back out there. I want to go … look for that crack."

"We didn't find any crack. We even bulldozed off the new snow."

"It ran right under our tent. The bore hole was gorgeous…you could look down and see jewel-like blue going on forever…but then there was a small quake, and a crevasse opened up in the snow-pack, and the hole split wide. We dropped flares; we could see there was a cave deep, deep below us…possibly caused by a thermal vent from the volcano."

"And you decided to explore?" Pintaro asked.

She bit her lower lip. "Yes. I remember that much." She looked down at the dregs of crusted chocolate in the mug. Images flashed so intensely that she brought a hand to her eyes. *Rappelling down—an easy descent. Confident, not scared. Caves so beautiful. Sparkling ice globes, huge translucent, wavy ice curtains, glittering ice needles—thousands of them—all glowing incandscent in the flashlight beams.* "I…think…Louisa stayed above and the rest of us decided to investigate the crevice…." *So many caves, many more than expected. One leads to the other, chamber after chamber. Now we're inside rooms with squared walls, sharp corners, smooth, flat ceilings!* "We saw something," she said, her eyes closed. *This is like the inside of a house.* The disorientation, the fear gripped her once more. *We can't explain it, we don't understand. We keep walking. Now we're in a furnished place with pictures on the walls and carpet on the floors.* She could see the frost-dust twinkling in the torch-beams like infinite stars covering a kitchen table, cabinets, sofas, chairs, an old-fashioned television set from the 1950s. She squinted up at McLoughlin. "We were caught off guard. We had to escape."

"And you got out first, abandoning your team?" he asked, his voice cold.

"No! No, I wouldn't…." She bent over, her chin touching her chest, her face twisted by gut-punching memory. She saw them all over again; the ice-glazed man in a business suit, reclining in a chair, reading a stiff and bleached newspaper; the blue baby frozen in its crib, tiny mouth gaping, little fists balled up as if struck in the middle of a cry; the two glistening, frost-caked children seated cross-legged on a glassy braided rug, their attention focused on the snowy television screen. And then there was the woman standing, stranded with a mixing bowl, caught in mid stir, covered with ice-crystal spikes like druzy quills, her eyes dull and wide under frosty lashes. Nancy Wenger began screaming and couldn't stop.

"Nancy, what is it?" McLoughlin shot up from his folding chair, stretched over the table.

Pintero was at the door of Hut 10, calling for help.

"They moved," Nancy panted. "I can see them; we didn't realize at first…it was inches at a time!"

"Who moved?"

"Little shifts and differences in position. The sound of cracking and splitting. We didn't understand until it was too late they were coming for us. The whole family. All of them. Even the baby! It happened so fast. I don't remember how I got back up to the top of the glacier." She clenched her jaws together as her stomach roiled—she couldn't stop herself; she vomited. She dropped to the floor with a crying moan and curled into fetal position.

A nurse ran in, then a doctor—they knelt over her.

McLoughlin stepped to the side and stared at Pintero.

Pintero stared at Nancy Wenger. "What the hell happened to her? Do you think she?…"

"Killed her team? Buried them in the ice somewhere?" He shook his head, slowly, as if it were obvious. He felt relieved. "Mental breakdown, psychotic break, she's been here too long," he replied, pleased that the mysterious disappearances could be so easily explained.

GOL-GOROTH FANE

Frederick J. Mayer

.I do not believe, I do not believe,
but nothing lets meleave,
besides, corpulents say
this is the place to be

Insanity breeds in Silence's plea
whorls of a dead sea's breeze,
inside, full darkness day
and living decay seethe

Insidious blood, carnal knowledge breathes
Life's spoors birth no release,
insides, bear a soiled lay
is any Body free?

LUCIEN GREYSHIRE AND THE GHOST FROM APPLEBEE'S

L.F. Falconer

The three young girls in the corner booth continued to stare. Not due to rudeness, Lucien determined, merely out of morbid curiosity. Their parents attempted to be more furtive in their sidelong glances and struggled with useless, hushed commands to curtail their daughters' blatant surveillance. Lucien no longer cared. With three-quarters of his body severely scarred from a housefire he'd survived as a child forty years ago, he'd grown hardened to the horrified scrutiny of others, the secretive glimpses, the whispers behind his back. At one time his disfigurements brought him shame. Now he wore these scars with honor, deeming his outer grotesqueness more valuable than his business card. A man no one truly wanted to see, yet one not easily forgotten, if he caused anyone nightmares along his journey through life he lost no sleep over it.

Harried to the point of distraction by their children, the two adults in the corner booth remained oblivious to the fact that half their current troubles were caused by the antics of the youthful poltergeist hovering above their table. A spilled glass of milk, the forks fallen to the floor, the plate of French fries toppled onto the youngest girl's lap had nothing to do with the carelessness of rambunctious children, and at this moment, the ghost was ever-so-slowly unscrewing the cap on the salt shaker.

Lucien savored the final bite of his lemon chicken, then dabbed his napkin over the thin lips below the cartilaginous remnants of his nose. He rose to his feet and placed enough cash on his meal check to cover his lunch as well as a generous tip. In response to his appearance, the server had neither balked nor over-compensated. Shrugging on his wool jacket, he took pity on the beleaguered parents in their challenge to maintain a sense of decorum amid the chaos, especially as the children's father had just ruined his own meal with a full shaker of salt spilled upon it. The poltergeist above the table glowed in rapid pulses of jade green.

Leaving his table, Lucien limped directly to the booth the family occupied. Everyone at the table fell transfixed, as if they'd all just been caught with their hands in the till.

Lucien greeted them with a courteous bow. "Good afternoon." He raised his one good eye to acknowledge the ghost hovering above. Bemusedly, the ghost cocked an eyebrow, then darted to the left side of the table taking refuge behind a potted imitation philodendron. Lucien straightened his gaunt frame and withdrew a business card from his inner jacket pocket. "Allow me to introduce myself. I am Lucien Greyshire, and I have a business proposal if you'd be interested." He handed his card to the father, then glanced over at the ghost who peeked through the Kelly green leaves, giving the young shade a polite nod.

The man at the table seemed hesitant to accept the card, but once he took it into his possession, he scanned it aloud: "*Let the dead bring your party to life! Greyshire Incorporated: Unique Halloween Entertainment Services.*" He looked up at Lucien with knitted brows. "What's this about?"

"I'm in need of an Assistant Events Coordinator." Lucien glanced back over at the ghost. "If you're interested, meet me in the park across the street within the hour." He kept his one-eyed gaze on the ghost.

"I already have a job." The man at the table tried to hand the business card back, but Lucien stepped away from the table and gave another slight bow.

"I'll be waiting should you be interested." His papery lips smiled at the ghost before he turned and departed the restaurant.

A somber sky loomed above, gray with pewter clouds billowing like dust. Lucien breathed deeply of the air, still wet from last night's tempest and laced with faint hints of pine, damp bark, and blight. Dying boughs and limbs ripped from their hosts and tossed haphazardly by the uncaring gale littered the park's greensward. Lucien blessed the previous night's storm—the howling winds had covered every muffled scream.

The man's name had been Daniel. He was sixty-seven years old. And now he was dead.

October leaves in persimmon, amber, and blood crunched beneath Lucien's feet while crisp Lake Erie air nipped at his exposed disfigured flesh. He settled onto a park bench, his muscles aching, strained from last night's activities. Out of his jacket pocket, he removed a well-used paperback copy of Peter Nichols' *A Day in the Death of Joe Egg*. He'd barely read three pages when an adolescent apparition tentatively drifted near.

Lucien looked up from his book. Though little more than a translucent shadow, the ghost featured a clinging wet tee shirt, dark jeans, and high-top athletic shoes. He looked to have been maybe fifteen or sixteen at the time of his death, his dark damp ribbons of hair plastered against his skull. Last night's events flickered through Lucien's mind in high-speed clips—*cold waters whipped to a frenzy by the boisterous wind—Daniel's hands clawing at Lucien's own as he gurgled within the spume.*

The young shade scooted swiftly to the left. With a steady gaze, Lucien's good eye trailed the movement. The shade darted back to the right, still fixed beneath Lucien's magnetic stare.

The ghost took a minor step closer. "You can really see me?"

Lucien closed his book. "Indeed."

"Was this job offer meant for me, or for him?" The ghost jerked his head in the direction of the restaurant across the street.

"For you, of course. I thought I'd made that clear."

"You was a bit fuzzy, mate."

"I believe it would have been awkward to speak to you directly when it's only I who am aware of your presence. I'm not certain why you're trying to pull off a phony accent. I happen to know you're an American."

The ghost took a step back, crossing his arms. "And what makes you so smart, huh?"

Lucien winked his sighted eye. "I know many things. It's what I do."

The ghost jutted his chin forward. "But I guess you don't know my Mum's Canadian."

Lucien flipped his jacket collar up to keep the lake-chilled air off his neck. "Point taken, but that's neither here nor there. The important thing is that you have come. You may call me Lucien. And what may I call you?"

"Anything you like, I suppose. In another life, I believe they called me Patrick, but can't recall the last time I heard the name. Could just be a name I like. I dunno. There's not much about life I can remember." He relaxed, looking Lucien directly in the eye. "It's kind of like a shattered mirror— Life, I mean. My life. And I'm afraid if I try to put the pieces back together, I might not like what I see."

"Other than looking like a drowned rat, you're not a bad looking fellow."

The ghost faded slightly. "It's not about my looks. I'm invisible, unlike you. Meaning you no offense, but dude, really…"

Lucien shook his head. "No offense taken. And there's no need to pick up the pieces. It could do you no good now." He swiftly caught a wayward, breeze-blown newspaper page beneath his foot, anchoring it to the ground. "Patrick it is then. The name suits you. So, tell me Patrick, would you like the job?"

Patrick settled onto the seat beside him. "What's in it for me? I'm free to come and go as I please. Don't have to answer to anyone."

"I'd dare say you're rather bored." And lonely, Lucien thought, a feeling he knew too well, being little more than a living wraith himself. "But what a pitiful way to spend eternity—tormenting children in a restaurant. An Applebee's, no less."

"Ah, but there's where you're wrong, mate. I've no ties to the restaurant, and I wasn't tormenting the children. I was tormenting the parents."

"You hold a grudge against parents, do you?"

"It would seem that way now, wouldn't it? But I can't say for sure. Could just be something I do for kicks, you know. Probably one of those broken pieces." Patrick leaned forward, elbows on his knees. "So how come you can see and hear me when no one else can?"

The crackle of flames and smell of charred wood inundated Lucien's memory. Smoke billowing beneath the locked bedroom door. On the other side, his father's shouts…Heavy footfalls…Leaving. "Help me Daddy!" Lucien's frantic cries. Eyes burning. Throat constricting…Hot smoke wrapping him in a shroud.

"I was dead once myself," he admitted, glancing over at the ghost beside him. "A fireman resuscitated me." He had been brought back to life. His mother and brother had been more fortunate, not having to live the ordeal over and over and over again. The nightmares had long ago disappeared, making way for vivid, waking memories.

Patrick straightened in his seat. "That's how you got all them scars, eh? That's rough, man. But that don't explain much. Other folks've been resuscitated. But no one's ever seen me before. So why you?"

"For nearly a year during my recovery, I remained in a state of flux, or half-life if you will." Forced against his will into a world of forgotten shadows, Lucien continued to keep one foot in reality, the other foot in the grave. "A part of me still dwells in the realm of lost souls. Some people might consider that a curse. I view it as a unique gift, for I am in a position to offer those in limbo some comfort."

"Limbo sucks, especially if you're invisible." Patrick's voice broke upon his words.

It was impossible to give the boy a hug; Lucien had to rely on speech. "That's why you feel compelled to cause chaos. It's the only way you can validate your dismal existence."

Patrick leaned back, clasped his hands and twiddled his thumbs, staring up at the steely, cloud-studded sky. A pair of starlings roosted, chattering quietly in the bare treetops above. Patrick shot up like a rocket and thumped the branch, startling the birds into flight.

As Patrick settled back onto the bench beside him, Lucien stowed his book away in his pocket. "What I am offering you, Patrick, is a chance to do something productive with your existence. I could use a man of your talents."

"I have no talent."

"But you do. Very few spirits have the ability to move objects."

"I can only do it if they're not too heavy. I can't budge anything over a couple of pounds. And I don't know why you'd want a limbo ghost anyway. We're a pathetic bunch. Nowhere to go. Nothing to do. Bored, like you said. And boring to boot."

"I can do nothing about whatever is holding you here. But I can offer you a sense of purpose. After tomorrow, I'll be moving on. This is an opportunity you may never come across again."

Patrick kicked at the leaves below his feet, swirling them into a colorful dance upon the sidewalk. "Doing what, exactly?"

"Helping me in my endeavors. That's all."

"What kind of endeavors? What do you do, besides 'know many things'?"

"Well, for one, I throw parties. Huge Halloween parties for the filthy rich. Excruciating extravaganzas really, but I always deliver on my clients' contracts and they're willing to pay me quite well."

"Parties, huh? I think there's more to it than that. You said, 'for one.' So, what's for two?"

Talented *and* attentive. Even better, Lucien thought, allowing his good eye to wander the immediate vicinity for a moment. The threat of more stormy weather kept the park relatively deserted. Ensured there was no one nearby, he quietly confided, "For two—I kill people."

Patrick sprang from the bench. "Hold on a minute!" He raised his hand in a stop action and took a step back. "Tormenting folks is one thing, but I want no part in killing innocents."

Unapologetically, Lucien stared up at him. "Only children are innocent. The rest of us are all guilty of something. Think of me as an extension of justice."

"Are you like some kind of hitman, or do people only pay you for parties?"

Lucien hesitated momentarily. "I do get paid for hosting parties. Quite well, in fact. Yet there are some clients who request an extra dash of pepper on their salad, so to speak."

Patrick paced the concrete, stirring the leaves beneath his feet back into action. "I dunno, mate. I start doing real harm to folks and next thing you know, I'm yanked straight into Hell."

Lucien folded his gnarled hands, his sightless eye gleaming dully in the muted daylight. "I would never ask you to harm anyone. That pleasure is reserved for me, and me alone. I simply need help in orchestrating my events. Hence, the job title of Assistant *Events* Coordinator. Your soul, and conscience, remain unsullied."

A young couple holding hands strolled by, giving Lucien a wide berth. They passed through Patrick, causing him to fade in and out. He stopped pacing and lunged toward Lucien, ripping the newspaper page from beneath his foot. He swatted the couple with it on the back of their heads before setting the page free in the breeze. His bone-colored face distorted by deep thought, he swept back to Lucien's side.

"I'm still not sure this is something I should be taking part in, if you know what I mean," he muttered. "The killing part..."

"I understand your concerns, Patrick. Yet you seem to enjoy tormenting the living, and that's all I would ever expect you to do. During the party. Would you be willing to give it a trial run? I have an event scheduled tomorrow night at the Gates Hotel."

"A party at the Gates?" Patrick snorted and took a step back. "Well that should be a hoot. Those two snobby sisters there don't care much for company, dead or alive, carrying on like the world belongs to only them."

"That's odd," Lucien said. "I found them to be rather charming." It had been those sisters who'd led him to Patrick. Who'd told him of the boy's talent and revealed the details of his untimely death. "And since the hotel is slated to be razed before Christmas, Jasmine and Ruby have graciously agreed to help me host this year's event. One last hoorah for them, so to speak."

"With them two, you've already got the best. What do you need me for?"

Lucien spoke with a smile. "The sisters may be capable of vivid manifestation and bone-chilling audio, but they cannot move things. The party guests will be expecting a magnificent haunted experience. I prefer to give them a night to truly remember."

A green aura glowed from within and Patrick smiled. "Most of these people are parents, right?"

"I would assume so."

"And I don't have to take part in no killing?"

Lucien nodded. "Rest assured, that contract has already been completed." A small white lie. Sometimes a party was simply a party, and a target a deliciously convenient coincidence.

Patrick gusted across the sidewalk, knocking the hat off the woman pushing a baby carriage, then sidled back to Lucien's side. "Can I ask who it was?"

"No, you may not."

"Not even a clue?"

Lucien ran a ragged finger across the thinly-stretched skin of his missing lips as if zipping them shut. There was no need to tell the lad it had been his father. Lucien's own father may have been unsuccessful, but Patrick's had seen the deed through. For thirty years Patrick has wandered in the realm of lost souls and last night the father, like the son, unwillingly surrendered his life within the cold, dark waters of Lake Erie.

He wondered, had Patrick fought as hard to survive as Daniel had?

Lucien rose from the bench. "Stick with me, Patrick and I promise you will never be forced to carry the burdens of my sins. Now, shall we go? There's a pair of fine, 19th century sisters I'd like you to meet."

Lucien limped down the walkway, the leaves beside him swirling in a kaleidoscopic dance.

DOOM OF THE SEASON
Gregg Chamberlain

We are having an Apocalyptic Christmas,
Dodging zombies left and right,
Praying to God
We can make it through one more night.

We are having an Apocalyptic Christmas,
We keep our guns close by.
If our aim is sure
We can hit them in the eye.

Here we are at the end of days,
Faithful friends we stayed somehow.
But if you do get bit. Crud!
Well, I guess that is it, bud,
For now.

With any luck
And we stay the course we follow
If the Fates allow,
We still can hope to live to see a new tomorrow
As we have ourselves an Apocalyptic Christmas now.

www.ingramcontent.com/pod-product-compliance
Lightning Source LLC
Chambersburg PA
CBHW031352170626
46807CB00002B/940